DOVER AND THE UNKINDEST CUT OF ALL

Chief Inspector Dover novels

Dover One

Dover Two

Dover Three

Dover and the Unkindest Cut of All

Dover Goes to Pott

Dover and the Claret Tappers

DOVER AND THE UNKINDEST CUT OF ALL

Joyce Porter

A Foul Play Press Book

The Countryman Press, Inc.
Woodstock, Vermont

This edition first published in 1990 by Foul Play Press,
an imprint of The Countryman Press, Inc.,
Woodstock, Vermont 05091.

ISBN 0-88150-174-3

Printed in the United States of America
10 9 8 7 6 5 4 3 2 1

To Kathleen Wood

Chapter One

CRACK!

Wallop!

''Strewth!' said Chief Inspector Dover.

Gingerly he put up his hand to that side of his forehead which had just been in painful contact with the windscreen. Then he felt his back. Seventeen and a quarter stone hurtling around in the interior of a Mini-Minor can lead to a man being injured for life. When he was satisfied that everything was more or less intact he turned ominously to his wife.

'You bloody fool!' he howled.

Mrs Dover, her hands still gripping the steering wheel, peered white-faced through the rain-soaked windscreen. She had stalled the engine but the wipers were still scraping lazily across the glass.

'Oh, Wilf!' she said in a shaky voice.

'Don't you "oh, Wilf" me!' snarled her husband. 'You damned near killed me! What's the matter now, another bloody puncture?'

It had been one of those days, not infrequent in the Dover menage, when nothing had gone right. It was still barely half past nine in the morning but the Chief Inspector and his wife had already managed to stage three blazing rows and were now apparently heading for their fourth. And they were on holiday, too. What should have been a period of exquisite bliss for Dover – temporarily freed from the strain of looking as though he was working – was already turning into one of those nightmares that we would wish only on our worst enemies.

The cloud of impending disaster had loomed up on an otherwise quite sunny horizon some six months earlier. On the day, in fact, when Mrs Dover had finally made up her mind about how she was going to spend her legacy. Mrs Dover was always inheriting odd sums of money. She had an inordinately large number of comfortably off, elderly relations and, as with the passage of time they departed from this vale of tears, it was usually found that they had remembered Mrs Dover before they went.

Up till now Dover had had no complaints. His wife's little windfalls had been disposed of in accordance with his interested advice and invariably to his greater comfort. But on this occasion, with no less than six hundred and forty-three pounds to play around with, Mrs Dover had gone berserk.

'I'm going to buy a car,' she had announced. 'Don't you think it's a good idea, Wilf?'

Wilf did not, and told her so. When at last he'd come hoarsely to the end of his objections his wife proved unexpectedly adamant.

'I'm still going to buy a car,' she said.

'But you can't even drive! ' protested Dover desperately.

'I shall learn,' she replied proudly.

Dover got nasty. 'You'll never pass the test, not at your age.'

But she did. Whether the fact that before taking her test she had mentioned casually to the examiner that her husband was a high-ranking, influential detective at Scotland Yard helped or not, no one will ever know. She removed her L-plates with an air of smug triumph which made Dover long to belt her one, and announced that they would travel to Filbury-on-Sea for their annual fortnight's holiday by car. Dover, completely snookered, could only fight her decision to the last hopeless ditch.

'And don't say I didn't warn you,' he concluded when all other arguments had failed.

'I won't, dear,' said Mrs Dover with a forgiving smile.

From then on the Chief Inspector had firmly washed his hands of motoring and everything connected with it. The car was resolutely placed in his wife's domain. Hers were the hands that washed it, hers the purse that provided the money for its petrol. She was the one who got out to open the garage doors and worried when bits dropped off the engine. And serve her damned well right, thought Dover.

The holiday had been blighted almost before it had even started. Mrs Dover was still no very great shakes when it came to driving and felt considerably safer when there was no other traffic on the road. They had left the house at five o'clock in the morning. It was pouring with rain and Mrs Dover had hunted for five uncomfortable minutes before she located the switch which worked the windscreen wipers. Thoroughly demoralized and painfully conscious of the sulking bulk of her husband in the seat beside her, she had struggled on through the downpour at an erratic thirty miles an hour.

There had been one break in the monotony. At a quarter to eight they had a puncture. Dover had sheltered under a tree while his wife, now in tears, changed the wheel.

Damp and lowering, he hadn't spoken to her since. Not, that is, until her thoughtless slamming on of the brakes had awoken him so abruptly from his doze.

'Oh, Wilf!' whimpered Mrs Dover again, still staring fixedly in front of her.

'My God!' said her husband, a note of panic creeping into his voice. 'My nose is bleeding!' He groped under his overcoat and produced a grubby handkerchief from the top pocket of his blue serge suit. 'Well, don't just sit there, woman! Do something!'

Mrs Dover turned to look at him. Her eyes were wide with fright. She ignored the handkerchief with its two small spots of blood which her better half was waving reproachfully at her.

'Wilf,' she choked, 'I've just seen a man jump over that cliff.'

'Rubbish!' Dover snorted automatically, and dabbed hopefully at his nose again.

'But I did! He deliberately climbed up over that fence and jumped! I saw him!'

'So what?' said Dover irritably.

'But, that's Cully Point! It's a sheer drop there, right down into the sea. He'll be drowned, Wilf!'

'Not if the tide's out,' said Dover, rarely able to resist scoring a point, however feeble.

'If the tide's out he'll be smashed to pieces on those rocks.' Mrs Dover shivered. She had a vivid imagination. 'Oh, Wilf, I do wish you'd go and look.'

'It's raining cats and dogs,' protested Dover. 'I've got soaked once today.'

'Wilf, there's a man lying down there, dead or dying.'

Dover, having decided that he wasn't going to bleed to death and so taking a more optimistic view, said, 'You've been imagining things. I didn't see anybody.'

'Well, I did,' snapped Mrs Dover tartly. 'And if you look over there by that waste-paper bin you can see his bicycle. That's not my imagination, is it?'

Somewhat disgruntled Dover followed the line of his wife's pointing finger. There was indeed a bicycle propped up against the fence. 'Probably been there for weeks,' he muttered.

'Wilf!' Mrs Dover's voice rose to a near scream. 'Will you go and look?'

With much grumbling and moaning Dover eventually prised himself out of the car. The rain beat relentlessly down on him and the wind tore at his overcoat as he made his way across the road to the small lay-by which had been provided for motorists who wished to stop and enjoy the chilling splendours of Cully Point. He walked over to the bicycle. As he approached a gust of wind caught it and smashed it over on to its side. Dover clutched at his bowler hat and peered glumly at the bicycle. Even he could tell that it hadn't been standing out in that rain for more than a matter of minutes. He glanced back at the car. He could see his wife's white face watching him through the window.

With a curse he lumbered over to the fence itself and, hanging on grimly to a stout post, peered down into the abyss below.

Cully Point from any angle was an impressive sight. A bare, over-hanging cliff, it towered four hundred and thirty-two feet above the swirling churning sea beneath. And Dover was very relieved to see the swirling churning sea. It was high tide and the jagged rocks at the foot of the Point were decently covered with several feet of grey foaming water.

Dover nearly jumped out of his skin as his wife appeared suddenly and grabbed his arm. She looked down too.

'Can you see anything?' she whispered.

'No,' said Dover. 'Thank God!'

'He'll have been swept out to sea for miles by now,' said Mrs Dover in an awe-struck voice. 'They never recover the bodies, not when it's high tide and a rough sea like this.'

'You seem to know a hell of a lot about it,' observed Dover grimly.

'Aunt George used to live in Wallerton – she was Uncle George's wife, you know. We always used to call her Aunt

George; funny really when you come to think about it. I often used to stay with her when I was a girl. I expect it was all over very quickly, don't you, Wilf? He wouldn't last long in a sea like that.'

'If he ever went in it,' said Dover sourly.

'But I saw him! It was as clear as daylight.' Mrs Dover emitted a jubilant squeak, 'Look at that down there! What is it? It looks like a cap to me.'

It looked like a cap to Dover, but he would rather have died than admit it. 'I can't see anything,' he lied.

'Yes, you can! Look there; banging up against the side of the cliff. Yes, look, it is a cap! Dark blue. Or black. I can see the peak. Look, there it is, Wilf! Oh – it's gone.'

Yet another wave surged over the dark sodden object and sucked it down into the whirlpool.

'I can't see anything,' said Dover resolutely and truthfully. 'Anyhow, come on! I'm not standing out here in this gale catching my death any longer. There's nothing we can do.'

He beat his wife back to the shelter of the Mini by a good five yards.

'What shall we do now, Wilf?' asked Mrs Dover when she was once more in the driving seat. All the car windows were steamed up.

'Get a ruddy move on,' rumbled Dover. 'It'll be midnight before we get to Filbury at this rate – what with your driving and punctures and one thing and another. Still,' he sighed with exasperation, 'I suppose it's not far short of a miracle that we've got as far as we have.'

'But we'll have to report this suicide, Wilf,' said Mrs Dover as she pressed the starter. The car was still in gear and Dover took another dive into the windscreen. 'Oh, I'm sorry, Wilf. Seeing that man – it's upset me a bit.'

Through bruised lips Chief Inspector Dover told his wife precisely what he thought of her, her deceased aunt, the inclement weather, the Mini-Minor, her driving and her thoughtless habit of watching complete strangers commit suicide.

'And now,' he concluded, 'we are going to Filbury. Straight to Filbury. I'll be down with pneumonia if I don't get these wet things off.'

His wife looked at him apprehensively. 'We must go to the police, Wilf,' she said, timid but stubborn.

Dover told her what she could do with the police, too. 'And if I've told you once I've told you a hundred times, keep away from 'em! We'll be kept hanging around for hours answering a lot of damned-fool questions and being looked at as though we'd shoved the beggar over the cliff ourselves. They'll find out what's happened soon enough. There's no need for us to get involved. Besides, for God's sake, what have we got to tell 'em, anyhow?'

'But you're always grumbling about members of the public not helping the police,' pointed out Mrs Dover, who knew what she was talking about.

'That's different!' snapped Dover.

'And that man – what's-his-name – he told us to have a go.'

'For crying out loud!' groaned Dover. 'What the hell's that got to do with it?'

Mrs Dover shook her head. 'I'm sorry but I don't care what you say, Wilf. It's our public duty to report that we've seen a man committing suicide and we're going straight to the police station in Wallerton to do just that.' She patted her husband encouragingly on the arm. 'Don't worry, dear, it won't be half so bad as you think.'

After some reflection, Mrs Dover got the car moving again, and a quarter of an hour later they drew up outside the police station in Wallerton.

'You can wait here if you like, Wilf. I shan't be a minute.'

'Not bloody likely!' retorted Dover, still mopping away at his nose which had started bleeding again. 'I'm not letting you go in there alone. And just you keep quiet. I'll do all the talking.'

The station sergeant was listening to Housewives' Choice. He turned the sound down and removed his feet from the desk as Dover and his wife came in. One look at Dover's blood-bespattered face was enough. He took the pencil from behind his ear and reached for the book on the counter. 'Another road accident?' he asked with resignation.

'No.' barked Dover.

The station sergeant looked surprised. He shrugged his shoulders. 'Had a punch-up with the old woman, then?' he inquired pleasantly. 'Bit early in the day for a spot of bother like that but then it wouldn't do for us all to be the same, would it?'

Dover planted two beefy paws on the counter and advanced his face to within a couple of inches of the sergeant's, 'If you would stop bleating like an old sheep with the colic for a couple of minutes, I could tell you what has happened.'

The station sergeant glanced sympathetically at Mrs Dover. 'Been bending the old elbow, has he, love?'

'No, I have not!' bellowed Dover.

The station sergeant took it all in good part. He tapped Dover playfully on his bowler hat with the pencil. 'Now, keep your hair on, Grandpa! There's no need to go raising your voice now, is there?'

Dover gobbled helplessly. He seemed on the point of scrambling over the counter and subjecting the sergeant to grievous bodily harm when the door of the police station was flung open with a bang. Mrs Dover, who had been preparing to restrain her irate husband, relaxed and sat down quietly on a near-by bench.

Two men, both clad in their underpants and nothing else, were pushed forward by a worried-looking young policeman.

'Well, well,' said the station sergeant with evident relish, 'and what, as the bishop said to the strip-tease dancer, have we got here, eh? Here, watch 'em, Darwen!'

The two half-naked men, taking advantage of the momentary lapse in the constable's attention, had started throwing punches at each other. The blows were ill-aimed and lethargic. Neither man was in the first flush of youth and both amply fleshed abdomens were heaving strenuously from their exertions. The police constable had no difficulty in dragging them apart. One man, the bald-headed one, flopped panting across the counter. He had a nasty bruised cut over one eye and the blood had trickled down the side of his face and on to his chest. The other man, wearing underpants with a pale-blue stripe, was muttering under his breath and glaring fiercely at his companion.

'Well, well,' said the station sergeant again when peace and order had been restored, 'this is a bit of a turn-up for the book and no mistake.' He looked at the man with the cut head. 'Why, it's Mr Collingwood, isn't it? Well, well!' He turned to the other man. 'And Mr Davenport?' He seemed over-awed by his identifications. 'All right, Constable,' he said sharply, 'let's be having it.'

The constable put his cap straight and made his report. 'It was Bert McTurk, Sarge, the boatman at the Sailing Club – he called me in. He said these two gentlemen were fighting like a couple of wild cats in the changing room and he couldn't stop 'em. He was afraid they'd be doing each other a mischief. Well, I went in, Sarge, and I couldn't stop 'em either; going at it hammer and tongs, they were, so I brought 'em in here. They've calmed down a bit now, but you should have seen 'em!'

The sergeant jerked his head to one side and obediently the constable moved down to the bottom end of the counter.

'Been drinking, had they?' asked the sergeant softly.

'Not so far as I know, Sarge. It's a bit early in the morning even for that lot, isn't it?'

The station sergeant raised his eyebrows. Then another thought struck him. 'You haven't been laying about you with your truncheon, I hope?'

The constable shook his head.

'Good lad! These are local residents, you know, not blooming trippers. These two won't stand for being pushed around.'

With an air of considerable importance he moved back to the two half-naked and now shivering men.

'Well, now, Mr Davenport, would you like to tell me what happened?'

'I'll tell you what happened,' the man with the bleeding head broke in. 'This raving maniac here picked up a damned great lump of wood and hit me with it.'

'Is that true, Mr Davenport, sir?'

Mr Davenport stared fixedly in front of him. 'I was provoked,' he said stiffly.

'Provoked, my eye! The trouble with you, Chauncey, is that you just can't take a joke. No bloody sense of humour, that's your trouble.' The wounded man hugged himself resentfully. 'Look, Sergeant, I'll tell you exactly what happened. We were in the changing room together, just the two of us. We were going to go out in my boat and Chauncey – Mr Davenport, here – was going to crew for me. And it's the last time I shall ask him to do that, I don't mind telling you. Well, I was just sitting there changing my socks when Chauncey comes out of the john, in his underpants, just like he is now. Well, it happened to strike me that he was beginning to put a bit of weight on so, just jokingly, I said, "My God, Chauncey," I said, "with a bust on you like that you'll have to start wearing a bra before long!" You see? A harmless, innocent remark like that! The sort of thing men are saying to each other in every bloody changing room in the country. Well, you'd have thought I'd suggested seducing his grandmother! He let out a howl, grabbed up this chunk of wood and clouted me across the boko with it before I'd time to get to my feet. Naturally, I had to protect myself. I managed to get the piece of wood away from him but then I found him coming at me all fists and nails. I don't mind telling you, I thought I'd got a raving lunatic on my hands. He just went clean off his rocker.'

The station sergeant was impressed. 'Is this true, Mr Davenport?' he asked.

Chauncey Davenport, now shivering uncontrollably, stared straight ahead. 'I am making no statement without my solicitor

Oh, for God's sake!' exploded Mr Collingwood in disgust. He began rubbing the goose-pimples on his arms vigorously.

'Are you prepared to prefer charges, Mr Collingwood?' asked the station sergeant, searching for his pencil.

'Of course I'm not! Chauncey's an old friend of mine – or was. No, look here, Sergeant, this is a purely personal matter between Mr Davenport and me. There's no call to have the police poking their noses in. In fact, I shall have a few well chosen words to say to old McTurk for fetching your constable in in the first place. Just let's forget about it, shall we? Personally, all I want to do is get back and get some clothes on. I'm absolutely frozen.'

'Just as you like, sir,' said the station sergeant indulgently. 'It's up to you. If you don't want to prefer charges, that's your affair. But I do think you ought to see a doctor about that cut, sir. Looks very nasty to me. The police surgeon's in with the Inspector, I think. I'll fetch him and get him to look at it for you. You, too, Mr Davenport. You've got a few ugly-looking bruises there that could do with a bit of attention, eh? We'll just get the doctor to run the rule over you. I won't be a minute.'

The effect on Chauncey Davenport of this mild, even kindly suggestion was startling. All the colour drained from his face. He clutched the edge of the counter and stared at the station sergeant with horror-struck eyes.

'Doctor?' he screamed hoarsely. 'Doctor? I don't want a doctor! No doctor's going to touch me! I don't want a doctor, I tell you. No doctor! No doctor!'

Before anybody even got around to thinking of stopping him, Davenport dived for the door. As it swung back behind him they could hear his bare feet pattering on the pavement outside.

'Well,' said Mr Collingwood, breaking the shocked silence, 'if you ask me, it's a psychiatrist he wants, not a doctor.'

The station sergeant nodded his head in bemused agreement. 'Has he always been like this, sir? You know, flying off the handle at the least bit of a thing?'

'Good God, no! He'd have never got in the Sailing Club if we hadn't thought he was a pretty sound chap all round. Up to five or six months ago he was the backbone of the place. Bit of a lad where the ladies were concerned – but that's a weakness we've all got, eh, Sergeant?'

'Didn't he go missing from home, sir? I seem to remember his wife coming in here and reporting it. He turned up again, right as rain, after about a week if my memory serves me. Amnesia, wasn't it?'

'That's right.' Mr Collingwood was moving uncomfortably from one bare foot to the other. 'Couldn't remember where he'd been or what he'd been doing. Or so he said. Me, I've got my own theories. I reckon our Chauncey had been indulging in an extended prowl on the tiles. Anyhow, he's never been the same since. He's gone all brooding and quiet, except when he suddenly blows his top like he did this morning.' Mr Collingwood sneezed. 'Oh, dear! And I haven't even got a handkerchief. Look, Sergeant, I think I'd better be getting back to the Club before the Ladies' League spot me and have me run in for indecent exposure. Do you think you could be a good chap and phone for a taxi for me? Tell him to come round the back, eh?'

The station sergeant was only too willing to oblige and chatted pleasantly about this and that with Mr Collingwood until the taxi arrived. Dover fumed apoplectically. All his attempts to break into the conversation floundered on the rock-like refusal of the station sergeant to acknowledge his presence. Dover was reduced to telling his wife that it was all her fault.

At least Mr Collingwood departed, the young constable returned to his beat and the station sergeant had time to spare.

He eyed Dover sourly. 'Oh, you're still here, are you? Now then, what was it? A road traffic accident?'

'No,' snarled Dover, 'it wasn't! We saw a man committing suicide on Cully Point and we thought, mistakenly no doubt, that you would like to know about it.'

The station sergeant scratched his head dubiously. 'You sure you've not been drinking?'

Mrs Dover intervened with diplomatic speed. 'Oh, no, Sergeant, it's quite true. We were driving up along the top of Cully Point and I saw this man climbing up over the rails. Before I could stop the car or anything I saw him jump off, down into the sea. Oh dear, it was horrible!'

The station sergeant scratched his head again. 'Well, what did he look like? Can you give me a description?'

'No, I'm afraid I can't. I'm almost certain it was a man – a young man, I think – but it was pouring with rain at the time and I only caught a glimpse of him.'

'You've no idea how he was dressed? I'm sorry to keep pressing you, madam, but if he went over Cully Point at high tide, well, there's not much likelihood that we'll ever recover the body. They get carried right out to sea, you know.'

'Oh, I know,' said Mrs Dover comfortably. 'I used to stay with my Aunt George here in Wallerton when I was a girl. It's years ago now, of course, but I haven't forgotten the stories they used to tell about Cully Point. We always used to call her Aunt George. She was married to my Uncle George, you see, and ...'

'Right!' Dover broke in rudely. 'That's that, then! We've reported the suicide to you and there's nothing more we can tell you. Come on!' He jerked his head at his wife.

'But just a minute, Wilf,' she protested. 'We haven't told him about the bicycle or about the hat.'

'It doesn't matter,' said Dover, grabbing his wife by the arm and pulling her in the direction of the door. 'Come on, for God's sake!'

'Here, just a minute, Grandpa!' The station sergeant caught hold of Mrs Dover's other arm and started tugging her back. 'Round here I'm the one who decides what's important and what isn't, thank you very much. Now then, what's all this about a bicycle?'

'There was a bicycle propped up against the fence.'

'Belonging to the chap who committed suicide?'

'How the hell do I know? It certainly hadn't been standing there long because the saddle was barely wet.'

'That was very observant of you,' said the station sergeant with unflattering surprise.

'Oh, well,' chirped Mrs Dover happily, 'my husband is a Detective Chief Inspector at New Scotland Yard, you... ouch!' Mrs Dover clutched her ankle. 'Ooh, Wilfred, that hurt!'

Not half as much as it would have done, though, if her husband hadn't fractionally misjudged his kick.

Chapter Two

THE station sergeant's demeanour underwent a rapid change. This great, fat, untidy yobbo didn't look like a detective chief inspector from New Scotland Yard but recruiting had been bad for donkey's years and you never knew. A smarmy and oft repeated 'sir' discreetly replaced the jocular 'Grandpa'. The Chief Inspector and his lady wife, who was now hobbling slightly, were ushered into the Interview Room and offered chairs. Cups of strong nourishing tea were brought from the canteen. Everybody bowed and scraped and touched their forelocks.

'Though, mind you,' hissed the station sergeant to the Inspector who had been summoned to do his share of the boot licking, 'if that old bounder is having us on, I'll throw the book at him. You can get I don't know how many years for impersonating a police officer and I dare swear he's got a bit of form behind him, too.'

They were standing outside the Interview Room, smoothing their hair down, checking that all their tunic buttons were fastened and polishing up their boot toes on the back of their trousers.

'If you think he's an imposter, what the devil did you send for me for?' whispered the Inspector crossly.

'Well, either way, sir, it's a bit too big for me to handle, me being only a sergeant and you being an inspector.'

This obscure reference to an old and festering sore over promotion made the Inspector sigh. Sometimes it made you wonder if the extra money was worth it.

Inside the Interview Room the Dovers were sorting out their differences.

'Now see what you've done!' thundered Dover while his wife elaborately rubbed her ankle. 'We'll be lucky if we get to Filbury by the middle of next week.'

'You'd no call to kick me like that, Wilf.'

'It's nothing to what I'll do to you when I get you out of

here,' threatened her husband. He meant it, too. 'Now, this time, just leave the talking to me, will you?'

Mrs Dover contented herself with hugging her injured leg and nursing her resentment. She had a shrewd idea about how to get her revenge and five minutes later, when all the introductions and pleasantries were over, she got it.

'You know, Inspector,' she began with a smile, 'I've been thinking.' She ignored the warning snort from her husband. 'When Wilf and I were looking over Cully Point, we thought we saw something in the water.'

'You speak for yourself,' snarled Dover.

'I think it was a cap, Inspector, a peaked cap.'

'Oh, really, Mrs Dover? How extremely interesting.'

'Yes, and then that bicycle. Do you know, Inspector, I think that bicycle looked somehow familiar.'

'Oh God!' groaned Dover.

The Inspector raised his eyebrows politely.

'It was just like the one my husband used to ride when we were first married,' simpered Mrs Dover.

'Do you mean . . . ?'

Mrs Dover nodded. 'A policeman's bicycle! One of those old fashioned, sit-up-and-beg ones. No chromium plating, you know, and rather heavy. And that peaked cap we saw in the water – it could have been a policeman's uniformed cap. In fact, I'm sure it was.'

''Strewth!' murmured Dover.

'And,' continued Mrs Dover, smirking triumphantly at her husband, 'the man I saw climbing over the fence – he could have been wearing a blue uniform, now I come to think of it.'

'You don't want to take any notice of her,' blustered Dover. 'She's as blind as a bat. Suffers from hallucinations, too,' he added frantically.

But the Inspector and the station sergeant weren't listening to him. They were exchanging rather puzzled glances.

'Ridiculous!' said Dover, his heart sinking. 'I've never heard such poppycock in my life.'

'Cochran,' said the station sergeant unwillingly.

'Oh God!' said the Inspector. 'Surely not?'

'I told you how queer he was behaving this morning, sir.

And he did go off on his bicycle, because I saw him. Lord, there'll be the very devil to pay if he's gone and croaked himself.'

'Well, hell's teeth,' objected the Inspector, 'it's not our fault!'

'You try telling the Chief Constable that, sir. Apple of his eye, that's what young Cochran was,' the station sergeant pointed out with gloomy relish. 'Thought the sun shone out of that boy, he did. I can't say I envy you, sir, having to tell him what's happened. He'll play blue murder. His own nephew committing suicide.'

The Inspector thought quickly. 'Oh, no,' he said firmly. 'You phone up the Chief Constable and tell him what's happened, or what we're afraid might have happened. And be diplomatic about it. I'm going up to Cully Point to have a look at that bicycle.'

'Good,' said Dover, lumbering to his feet. 'Well, that's settled that. We'll leave you to get on with it.'

'Oh, no, you won't!' retorted the Inspector and the station sergeant in unison.

'I'm on holiday,' whined Dover.

'I don't care what you're on,' snapped the Inspector, tossing respect for rank and seniority to the winds. 'You're not budging an inch until the Chief Constable gets here which, if I know anything about him, will be in under twenty minutes. Sergeant, put a constable outside this door and give him instructions that neither of them is to leave. Now, come on!'

The two local men hurriedly left the room, turning a deaf and callous ear to Dover's objections. For the next half hour Mrs Dover patiently endured the endless stream of abuse which her husband, beside himself at the indignity of being incarcerated in a common police station, poured on her head. In the end even Dover himself began to get bored.

Not that the violent erruption of the Chief Constable into the Interview Room provided much relief. He was in a filthy temper and didn't mind who knew it. Things began to happen with bewildering speed. Mrs Dover, who by now was nearly as sick of the whole affair as her husband, retired unobtrusively into a corner and began thinking about how she would redecorate the lounge should Uncle Percy not succeed in throwing off that nasty chill he'd caught playing bowls last week.

Meanwhile the stronger sex was getting down to it. The bicycle had been recovered from the top of Cully Point and definitely identified as the one on which young Cochran had left Wallerton Police Station that morning. Maps were produced. Times and distances were worked out, due allowance being made for the fact that nobody, not even a world champion, could cycle up to Cully Point in under thirty-five minutes.

'Of course,' observed the station sergeant fatuously, 'it's much quicker coming down.'

The Chief Constable flung him a withering glance before barking a stream of questions at Dover. What time was it – to the split second – that the suicide was observed climbing over the fence? Why didn't he know? Surely a trained and experienced detective would note that sort of thing automatically, wouldn't he? Why hadn't Dover thought to look at his watch? Wouldn't the wettest of wet Police Cadets have thought at least of doing that?

'Aw, get knotted!' muttered Dover under his breath.

'What did you say, man?' roared the Chief Constable who was slightly deaf and very sensitive about it. 'If you've anything to say, say it out loud. I can't stomach people who mumble.'

The Inspector completed his calculations. 'I'm afraid there doesn't seem to be much doubt about it, sir,' he reported miserably. 'The times seem to fit as near as I can judge. Of course, Cochran may have lent the bike to somebody else, but that doesn't seem very probable, does it, sir?'

'Nothing about the entire affair seems very probable to me, Inspector,' growled the Chief Constable nastily.

'What about fingerprints on the bicycle?' asked Dover, feeling he ought to make some contribution.

'We're checking them now,' said the Inspector, 'but with all this rain ... '

'I don't know how I'm going to break the news to his aunt,' said the Chief Constable grimly. 'It'll take some explaining, won't it? A smart young lad with every promise of a brilliant future ahead of him, with everything in the world to live for, suddenly taking his own life? It'll take some explaining, that will.'

'We'll make a full investigation, sir. I can promise you that,' the Inspector assured him earnestly. 'We'll ... '

'I'm not overlooking the fact that my nephew killed himself after a mere six weeks under your command,' observed the Chief Constable with heavy significance. 'Any investigation you carry out is likely to be a bit biased, isn't it? You never liked the lad. I've known that all along. He'd twice your education and three times your brains – not that that's saying much. You were jealous of him, any fool could see that. Because he was a better policeman after twelve months on the force than you'll ever be if you last till you're ninety. Which is highly unlikely. Oh yes, there's going to be an investigation all right, but I'm damned if you or any of your lousy subordinates are going to do it! Sergeant, get me Scotland Yard on the phone and be damned quick about it!'

The station sergeant scurried out of the room and the Chief Constable stalked purposefully after him.

Dover and the Inspector stared at each other.

'He isn't?' moaned Dover.

'He is, you know, sir,' said the Inspector.

'But I'm on leave!'

'You try telling him that, sir. The mood he's in, I reckon he'd get James Bond himself if he wanted him. I knew something like this would happen when he sent his blasted nephew here in the first place. Rotten, sneaking little devil, he was! Trust him to drop us all in it!'

Dover spared a furious glance for his wife. 'Do you hear that?' he bellowed. 'It's all your blasted fault, you and that damned car! If we'd gone to Filbury by train like we've always done, none of this would ever have happened!'

Within a few minutes the Chief Constable was back again. It had all been settled. Nobody at Scotland Yard, where Dover had few friends, had raised a finger to save him. His leave was cancelled and he was placed, body and soul, at the disposal of the Chief Constable.

'They're sending your sergeant down by the next train,' he informed Dover curtly. 'MacDonald, is it? Some damned foreign name like that. Can't see why they don't stop in their own blasted country.'

'But they can't,' said Dover, grasping at what few straws were left to him. 'He's off touring on the Continent.'

'Managed to catch him at the airport just before he left. It's only about seventy miles from here. He'll be along by lunchtime. I've told the sergeant to book the pair of you into a local hotel. Now, I've got to phone my wife and break the tragic news to her. I'll see you in the Inspector's office in fifteen minutes and we'll get down to planning what lines your investigation should take.'

'And what would you like me to do, sir?'

The Chief Constable regarded his Inspector coldly. 'I should like you, Tasker, to drop down dead, but I suppose that's asking too much even from a benign Providence. You can carry on with your normal duties, if any, and just keep out of my way for the next couple of years.'

Mrs Dover's offer to stay in Wallerton and succour her husband in his hour of need was rejected with the contempt it deserved.

'You can go on to Filbury or you can go home or you can stuff yourself!' stormed Dover. 'I don't give a damn!'

'But you'll get your leave later, Wilf. They've only postponed it.'

Dover's answering snort all but dislocated his dentures.

Mrs Dover departed in tears for a solitary holiday at Filbury. The Chief Constable blew his top as his wife went off into hysterics at the other end of the telephone line. The station sergeant occupied himself with trying to look busy and the Inspector hovered around uncertainly and trembled as he thought of the wrath to come.

Dover, an old and experienced hand in these matters, undid the top button of his trousers, removed his boots, propped his feet up on the radiator and went to sleep.

He was aroused some considerable time later by the arrival of Charles Edward MacGregor, detective sergeant and Dover's long standing accomplice in crime. MacGregor, whose holiday had been ruined too, was sulking, but one more miserable face in Wallerton Police Station was hardly noticeable.

Dover greeted him with his usual warmth. 'Got here at last, have you? What did you do – walk?'

MacGregor gritted his teeth.

The Chief Constable had been forced to nip back home to calm his wife down so he was not in the best of moods when Dover and MacGregor eventually trooped in for their briefing. It was short and to the point. From what Dover could gather, and he wasn't straining himself to concentrate, the Chief Constable wanted two things done and done quickly. First, he wanted to know why his nephew, the late Constable Cochran, had committed suicide and, second, he wanted the responsibility for this tragic act to be pinned fairly and squarely where it belonged – on the shoulders of the Inspector in charge of Wallerton Police Station.

'That fool Tasker's at the back of all this,' he asserted, thumping his fist on the desk, 'and, by God, he's going to pay for it! He's had it in for young Peter ever since I sent the lad down here. Had the infernal nerve to accuse me of showing favouritism to my own nephew. How do you like that, eh? I gave it to him straight from the shoulder. "I'm posting Constable Cochran to your division," I said, "because your division is the one that needs a bright, go-ahead chap most. It's the sloppiest division in the whole ruddy force, but we're going to alter that, with or without your co-operation." Tasker being Tasker, of course, he's been nursing a grudge ever since. Can't take criticism, you know, a bad fault that. Well, he's got his revenge. He couldn't get at me but he could get at Peter. And he has! All right, he's going to pay for it, and pay dearly. You'll report direct to me, Chief Inspector, in person. I don't want anything over the telephone. Those damned operators at Headquarters listen in to every word and before you know where you are it's all round the county. Now then, any questions? No? Right! Well, I'm off now. I shall expect to be hearing from you, and soon.'

In spite of the need for urgency and the oft reiterated exhortations to get a move on, Dover proceeded imperturbably at his own pace. He and MacGregor repaired to their hotel, one of the two in Wallerton which were licensed, and had a leisurely and ample lunch. During coffee Dover thought up a number of useless and time-consuming errands which were designed to keep MacGregor on the trot until dinner time and so leave the Chief Inspector free to retire to bed for the afternoon. The investigation proper would, he announced to his unimpressed sergeant, begin on the morrow, when he had had time to work out their plan of action.

'Think,' he said, already yawning, 'that's what you've got to do in our job, MacGregor. Think. Use the old brain. Why, I've solved more problems just by thinking 'em out in the peace and quiet of my own room than you've had hot dinners.'

MacGregor composed his handsome features into a polite if slightly incredulous smile, gave the Chief Inspector his packet of cigarettes and took his leave.

The next morning Dover came downstairs to breakfast almost prepared to knuckle down to some work. Since the previous afternoon he had had fifteen hours sleep broken only by dinner and a pleasant session afterwards in the hotel bar. He was in quite a good humour, all things considered. MacGregor, the blameless instrument, soon put a stop to all that.

'The Chief Constable's just been on the phone, sir. He wanted to know if we'd made any progress.'

Dover's scowl came back. 'At this time in the morning?'

'It is half past nine, sir.'

'I'll have porridge, bacon, egg, sausages and tomato,' Dover informed the waitress, 'and a large pot of tea.' Having dealt with the essentials he turned back to MacGregor. 'And what did you say?'

'Well, I said we were just sort of filling in the background, sir. There wasn't much else I could say, was there?'

Dover snorted unpleasantly. 'What did you find out about this Cochran fellow?' he asked. 'Was he married?'

'No, sir,' replied MacGregor who was quite efficient if given half a chance. 'He was a bachelor. He doesn't appear to have had any family, apart from the Chief Constable, of course. He was living in digs here in Wallerton. They haven't got a station house.'

'What about his friends?'

'Well, he doesn't seem to have had many, sir, not amongst the other policemen at any rate. He's only been here a few weeks, of course, and the other men are naturally a bit wary of him, his uncle being the Chief Constable. Nobody's saying much at the moment but I did gather he'd got half a dozen girls kicking around. I suppose it could be something like that that drove him to suicide.'

'What, a broken heart?' sneered Dover.

'Well, it might be, sir.'

'If you believe that, laddie, you'll believe anything. It's only in books a man kills himself because some chit of a girl said no to him.'

'At least it's as credible a motive as believing that Inspector Tasker drove him to it just to spite the Chief Constable, sir,' MacGregor pointed out.

'Have you finished with that toast? Well, shove it over then. And the butter.'

'Where were you, er, thinking of starting, sir?'

Dover hadn't the faintest idea but there was no point in admitting it to MacGregor. 'We'll go to his digs,' he said. 'Search his room. Have a word with his landlady.'

'But, wouldn't it be better, sir ... ?'

'No,' said Dover shortly, through a mouthful of toast, 'it wouldn't.'

Chapter Three

WALLERTON was a small seaside resort of limited renown and attraction. In this age of the common man it remained select because few people could be found who would put up with the place for five minutes, never mind spend their annual fortnight's holiday there. In the sunshine stakes Wallerton was three from the bottom, but for chilling winds and driving rain it stood second to none in the entire country. The beach was stony and the natives indifferent where they weren't actively hostile. Apart from one cinema and the Winter Gardens (which traditionally closed down for the whole of August) there was little on which the unfortunate visitor could fritter away his long bleak hours of leisure. There was the Sailing Club, of course, but the locals wouldn't admit temporary members unless they had blue blood on both sides going back to the Conquest or a couple of million pounds in their current account – and such people were few and far between in Wallerton.

Still, some hardy annuals and chronic masochists went there year after year for their summer holidays. Quiet and bracing, they called it. It certainly had the virtue of making them markedly less disgruntled with the ennuis of their ordinary, everyday life.

Mrs Jolliott, the erstwhile landlady of Peter Cochran, lived in a part of the town which was even more select than the rest of it. Or, which had been more select. Things change, even in places like Wallerton. Fifty years ago if you lived in Kilmorie Road you really were somebody. Nowadays, however, here and there in the windows of the rather pleasant Late Victorian houses little notices proclaiming 'Apartments' or 'Vacancies' peeped coyly from behind lace curtains. Nobody took in visitors for money, of course. They obliged only because they had so much spare room going to waste and it seemed uncharitable to turn away people who would otherwise be unable to enjoy Wallerton's unique amenities.

There were no little signs in the windows of number 48, though perhaps there soon would be.

The door was opened by a woman who admitted, with visible reluctance, that she was Mrs Jolliott. She had one of those faces which look as though they've been carved, with difficulty, out of granite. Her hands were rough and uncared for. She wore no make-up. Over her strong, well-built figure was an enveloping white apron, starched within an inch of its life.

She had Dover and MacGregor off the front door step and inside the hall in a flash. Not even her nosiest neighbours got time to have a proper look at them. The thin strip of coconut matting in the hall was covered with clean sheets of newspaper.

'Watch where you put your feet,' said Mrs Jolliott. 'I've just done this hall.' She seemed to hesitate for a moment. 'Oh well, I suppose you'd better come into the front room. You won't be staying long.'

The front room was dank and stuffy and reeked of furniture polish. With a martyred sigh Mrs Jolliott removed the sheets of newspaper from three chairs and revealed the yellowing anti-macassars underneath.

'I hope you wiped your boots as you came in,' she said as she motioned them to sit down. 'I've only just done this carpet.'

Dover got straight to the point. 'We've come about Constable Cochran.'

'It had crossed my mind that you weren't here to read the gas meter,' replied Mrs Jolliott tartly. 'You'll be taking his things away with you, I hope? I've got them all packed up. I can't give that room a good clean out till they're gone.'

Dover blew fretfully down his nose. 'Were you surprised to hear he'd committed suicide?'

'I've long got long past the stage of being surprised at what any man does,' sniffed Mrs Jolliott, 'especially these days. There doesn't seem to be any decency or morality left anywhere in the world. Young hooligans! A taste of the birch, that's what they need. It's the only thing they understand.'

'Was Constable Cochran a young hooligan?'

'I thought they liked to be called police officers nowadays? A bit more of this modern tom-foolery! Constable was good enough in my father's day and it ought to be good enough now. Well, Master Cochran didn't try any of his monkey business under my roof, that I can tell you. I gave him no room for doubt on that score. "Guests," I told him, "are not allowed to entertain visitors of the opposite sex in their rooms, fiancées or not." '

'Oh, he was engaged, was he?' asked Dover, thus demonstrating that he didn't call himself a detective for nothing.

'So he informed me,' said Mrs Jolliott darkly. 'Unofficially, he said, whatever that may mean. Though if I were that young flibberty-gibbet Sandra Jackson, I shouldn't count on him making a decent woman out of me.'

Solemnly MacGregor made a note in his notebook. 'Sandra Jackson. Fiancée?'

'Had he had a dust up with her or anything?' asked Dover.

Mrs Jolliott laughed without mirth. 'Over what? The only thing that would upset young Cochran where a girl was concerned would be if she said no. And from what I know of Sandra Jackson that particular word wasn't even in her limited vocabulary.'

'So it wasn't unrequited love?' said Dover with an I-told-you-so look at MacGregor.

'Lust,' said Mrs Jolliott flatly, 'is the word I should use, and unrequited it certainly wasn't. If it had been the other way round, of course, there might, possibly, have been some reason. But he was the one who called the whole thing off, wasn't he?'

Dover blinked. 'Was he?'

'Well, of course. It was me who had to phone her up and tell her, wasn't it? Not that I minded doing that at all. It may be what young people do these days, but that doesn't make it right, does it? Not but what it hadn't already happened as far as those two were concerned right here in Wallerton, and not just the once either. Still, that's no excuse to go flaunting it round the countryside, is it? You'd think a girl would have more self-respect, wouldn't you?'

Dover looked hopelessly at Mrs Jolliott and scratched his head as he wondered what the blazes she was yattering about.

'You say he broke off his engagement to this girl?'

'I didn't say anything of the kind. Don't you start putting words into my mouth.'

'Then what did you say, for God's sake?'

'I don't permit swearing in my house,' said Mrs Jolliott, nodding at one of the many embroidered texts which decorated the walls. ' "Take not the Lord's name in vain," ' she read aloud.

Dover took a deep breath.

'What I said,' Mrs Jolliott continued imperturbably, 'was that he cancelled his holiday.'

'His holiday? What holiday?'

'He had a week's leave starting last Monday week. Didn't you know that? It was all fixed up that he should go away with this girl – this Sandra Jackson. They were hiring a car and going touring or something. Well, at the last minute he just called the whole thing off. He came back here on Sunday evening to supper – I only do a cold supper on Sundays – after he'd been down to the police station to tidy a few things up before he went on holiday. He came in, said he didn't want any supper and would I phone up this Jackson girl and tell her the holiday was off. Well, I'd no objection to doing that, none at all.' Mrs Jolliott's mouth twisted into a faint smile and she flicked an invisible speak of dust off her apron.

Dover regarded her unhappily. 'What happened then?'

'He went to bed.'

'He went to bed?' repeated Dover desperately.

Mrs Jolliott nodded. 'For a week.'

'For a week?' squeaked Dover.

'That's what I said.'

'But, what did he do?'

'Nothing. He just went to bed on the Sunday night and stayed there for the whole week until he got up to go on duty yesterday morning.'

'Was he ill?'

Mrs Jolliott shook her head. 'He said he wasn't. And he didn't look ill to me, not physically that is. I can't answer for his mental state.'

'Didn't you send for a doctor or anything?'

'He told me not to. Not that I would have paid any heed to that if I'd thought he was really sick. I did ask Nurse Smithies to have a look at him, though. She's my other regular lodger. I only have just the two. Two's all I can manage on my own and what with the type of girl you get these days you're better off without them. Especially when you've got a young unmarried man in the house. Better to work your own fingers to the bone than have any truck with young trollops like them. Most of them are foreigners, too, and they're worse than the English when it comes to that sort of thing. Talk about service! The word's got quite a different meaning these days!'

Dover fidgetted uncomfortably in his chair. At this rate they'd be here for a fortnight. Why couldn't they just tell you what they knew, if anything, in a few well-chosen words and then wrap up? He looked with dislike at Mrs Jolliott. 'What did this nurse woman think?'

'Sulking, that was her diagnosis. And she was a District Nurse for forty years so if she doesn't know what she's talking about I'd like to know who does.'

'It all sounds very peculiar,' grumbled Dover.

'It was very peculiar,' agreed Mrs Jolliott. 'Perhaps he just had a brain storm or something.'

'And he didn't tell you what was up with him?'

'No, he didn't. And it wasn't for want of asking either. He said there was nothing the matter with him and he just wanted to be left alone. He wouldn't see anybody. That girl came clamouring round, of course, wanting to know why he'd cancelled the holiday, but he wouldn't see her either.'

'You didn't think of telling anybody at the police station, or letting his uncle know?'

'Why should I? If he wanted to spend his week's leave in bed, that was his affair. Besides, I didn't know he was going to kill himself, did I? He seemed all right when he went off to work on Monday morning.'

Mrs Jolliott didn't encourage her visitors to linger. They heard the vacuum cleaner being switched on before they had reached the bottom of the front steps.

'This blooming business is going to be a real swine, that's for sure,' said Dover. 'Just my ruddy luck to get lumbered with it!'

'And mine,' MacGregor pointed out gloomily.

'Well, you can't blame me for that, laddie. I didn't ask for you!'

MacGregor could well believe it.

'What are we going to do now, sir?'

Dover regarded his sergeant with dislike but answered unhesitatingly. 'Go back to the nick.'

'But oughtn't we to go and see Cochran's girl-friend, sir?'

'We're not likely to get a cup of tea off her, are we, laddie?' asked Dover sarcastically. 'You can go and see her this afternoon. Now then, which way do we go? I don't want to spend all morning trailing around this blasted town.'

Before they could move off the door of Mrs Jolliott's house opened and the good lady herself appeared on the threshold. She gazed disapprovingly at the dirty marks left by the detectives' feet on her clean steps.

'You've forgotten his things,' she hissed in a loud whisper, neighbours having ears as well as eyes. 'They're all up in his room, waiting for you.'

But Dover was not easily swayed from his purpose. A cup of tea he wanted and a cup of tea he was going to have. 'We'll pick 'em up this afternoon!' he bawled. 'After lunch!' Before Mrs Jolliott could get her protest out he had started off down the street at a smart amble. 'Job for you there, laddie,' he said happily as MacGregor caught up with him. Pushing work off on to the shoulders of others was one of his few remaining pleasures.

Dover's decision to repair to Wallerton police station was not entirely frivolous. The visit was productive of information as well as of refreshment. The station sergeant provided both.

He greeted Dover like a long lost friend. As he had already told his wife, he liked the look of the Chief Inspector. 'He's a good, solid chap,' he had observed. 'Down to earth, you know. No side about him, that's what I like. Sort of chap you could have a cosy pint with down at the local.' It was not the soundest of judgements, but it was a charitable one.

'Come into the Inspector's office, Mr Dover, sir! It's more comfortable in there. Here, let me take your overcoat. My goodness me, you have had a soaking, haven't you?'

'Doesn't it ever stop raining in this bloody town?' asked Dover with his usual charm.

'You don't call this rain, do you, sir? You ought to be here in August and see it then. Never stops in August, day or night.

Harry! Take the Chief Inspector's coat and hang it over the radiator and then nip down to the canteen and bring up a jug of tea and three cups. Hot tea, mind you, and look lively about it!'

Beaming resolutely, the sergeant found the box of cigarettes which the Inspector reserved for himself and visiting V.I.P.s, and handed them round. When the tea arrived he produced a bottle of brandy from the filing cabinet and laced Dover's cup liberally.

'It'll take the chill out of your bones, sir.'

'Humph,' said Dover without either enthusiasm or thanks, 'it's a bit late for that. I reckon I caught a cold on my stomach yesterday, all that messing about. I've got a very sensitive stomach, you know. The least bit of a thing and it gets me straight in the gut. I shouldn't be surprised,' he added with gloomy relish, 'if I don't have to lay up with it again before long.'

The sergeant tut-tutted with smarmy sympathy. 'I thought you weren't looking any too chirpy, sir. Tucked up in a nice warm bed, that's where you ought to be.'

Dover sighed and helped himself to another shot of brandy with the air of a Christian martyr already feeling the flames licking round his feet. The station sergeant had gone up markedly in his estimation and Dover rewarded him with a detailed account of his more lurid symptoms.

MacGregor, with a suppressed sigh of his own, took his brandyless tea over to a chair by the window and sat down. At one time Dover's gastronomic revelations had made him sick but long familiarity had produced its own immunity.

Eventually the conversation took a less clinical turn.

'Well,' said the station sergeant, rather unfairly leaping in as Dover paused for breath, 'looks as though we've seen the last of young Cochran. He'll be well out to sea by now, what's left of him. I reckon the fishes are having a good feed.' He chuckled comfortably. 'Poor fellow.'

'Poor fellow, be blowed!' snorted Dover. 'Damned nuisance, that's what he is!'

'And was when he was alive,' said the station sergeant feelingly. 'There's more than one'll be glad to see the back of him round here.'

Dover cocked a quizzical, if bloodshot eye at the station sergeant. 'The Chief Constable thinks he was hounded to death by his copper colleagues.'

The station sergeant grunted. 'He would! Sounds likely, doesn't it? Hounding the Chief Constable's favourite nephew and leading blue-eyed boy to death? We may be a lot of country bumpkins down here but we're not that barmy!'

'What sort of a copper was he?' asked Dover.

The station sergeant looked at him shrewdly. 'Off the record and in the strictest confidence – lousy.'

'Thick?'

'Bent!'

'Bent?'

'Crooked as a corkscrew, in my humble opinion. If he hadn't been the old man's protègé I'd have had him out of here so fast his feet wouldn't have touched the ground. As things were, I kept my mouth shut and looked the other way. What else could I do?' he demanded defensively. 'If I hadn't made it stick I'd have been finished. And if I had, well the Chief Constable would have been gunning for me just the same. More so, probably.'

'What was wrong with him?'

The station sergeant sighed. 'You name it, he was up to it. It shook me, I can tell you. He was up to some tricks a chap with five times his experience wouldn't have thought of in a hundred years. Girls – that was the first thing that started me scratching my head. We don't get much trouble of that kind down here, but we get the odd bit. Every now and then young Cochran would bring one in – shop-lifting or some such charge. He'd take 'em in the Interviewing Room. No chaperone or witness or anything. Half an hour later the girl would come out, looking a bit hot and bothered and pulling her frock straight. All charges dropped. It happened two or three times. I knew what I'd find all right if I went and opened the door. But I didn't. And neither did anybody else.

'And then there was his off-duty hours. He was ear-marked for C.I.D., you know. He'd have been transferred already but even the Chief Constable couldn't move him with less than a year on the beat. Well, I suppose young Cochran thought he'd better start getting his hand in. Started keeping some very queer company and hanging around in some very queer places.'

'In Wallerton?' asked Dover sceptically.

'Oh, we've got our seamy side, sir, never you fear. Even the Ladies' League can't keep a whole town on the straight and narrow, though I must admit they have a damned good try. No, we've one or two characters knocking around that could do with an eye keeping on them.'

'And that's what young Cochran was supposed to be doing?'

'So he said, Mr Dover, sir, so he said. There's two ways of looking at it, isn't there, though? Even so, I've got to admit, he got some results. I heard on the grape vine that the C.I.D. were quite impressed with him. You know what they're like, sir. They think very highly of a young chap who goes out and finds his own villains and brings 'em in without waiting for somebody to tell him. They keep their eye on a young copper who shows a bit of initiative.'

'Oh, very true,' said Dover sententiously. 'That's the hallmark of a good detective, that is. Initiative, drive, thinking for yourself. I'm always telling MacGregor, here, that. Not,' said Dover with a sniff, 'that it seems to have much effect. Why, when I was a detective constable, never mind a sergeant, I ... '

Dover's entirely fictitious reminiscences continued unabated for some considerable time.

MacGregor waited with growing impatience until the eyes of even the station sergeant bulged with boredom and then plunged nobly into the breach. 'A cigarette, sir?'

Dover, who'd never been known to refuse a free fag from anybody, even a dyed-in-the-wool criminal, grabbed for the case. While the Chief Inspector was temporarily speechless lighting his cigarette, MacGregor firmly turned the conversation back into more productive channels. He didn't intend to spend the rest of his life rotting away in Wallerton, even if Dover did.

'You were talking about Cochran's underworld associates, Sergeant,' he said smoothly.

'Yes, that's right.' The station sergeant was grateful to find himself once more in the centre of interest. 'Like I was saying, Cochran started going out into the highways and byways, as they say, and began bringing in the odd tiddler. Nothing spectacular. He didn't nick a Train Robber or anything, but he collared quite a nice selection of small fry.'

'Very commendable,' observed Dover. His stomach rumbled – a sure sign that he'd done enough work for one morning.

'Ah, so you might think, sir, but, I dunno, it all stank a bit to me.'

Dover raised a languid eyebrow. His interest in the late Constable Cochran, Wallerton and crime in general was waning rapidly.

'Too pat, sir,' explained the station sergeant, who had not yet learned the butterfly nature of Dover's powers of concentration when lunch was in the offing. 'I don't know about you, sir, but I'm always suspicious of these cases where everything's cut and dried and every loose end neatly tied up in a bow. Life, in my experience, isn't like that, sir. There's always a few discrepancies, a few things that don't fit in. But when Cochran nabbed somebody it was different. Take Charlie Hutchinson, for example, nicking radio sets from cars. We've been after him for months without being able to lay a finger on him. But one dark night Cochran just happens to be lurking out of sight not fifty yards from the very car that Charlie's got his eye on. Not only that, but when Cochran runs Charlie in he had no less than five other radio sets on him – all stolen. And to cap everything, Cochran even runs the fence in as well. And then there was ... '

'I get the point,' said Dover wearily. He yawned and made little smacking noises with his lips.

MacGregor glanced surreptitiously at his watch. Hell's ringing bells, it was only just after twelve! He was blowed if he was going to let the old fool pack it in as early as this. 'You think he was getting tipped off, do you, Sergeant?'

'That's it. You just keep off me and my friends and I'll give you the nod when one of my enemies is up to a bit of villainy. Something along those lines.'

'But you've no proof?'

'No, it's just a feeling. When you've been in the police as long as I have, you learn to respect your intuition.'

'Was there anybody in particular that you thought Cochran was hob-nobbing with?'

'Well, now, it's funny you should mention that,' said the

station sergeant comfortably, and quite oblivious of Dover's black looks. 'Cochran was on first-name terms with half the town, of course, before he'd been here five minutes. He was that type. But, soon after he got here, he chummed up with a chap called Bill Hamilton. Now we've never been able to pin anything on Hamilton but we've had our suspicions for years. He started off in the second hand car business when he first came here a year or two after the end of the war and, naturally, he flourished like a green bay tree. Then he branched out' – the Sergeant chuckled – 'if you'll pardon the expression, into several other lines. Nothing absolutely bent, you understand, but everything he touched seemed to be just on the edge, if you see what I mean. Now, young Cochran was thirty years younger than Hamilton so it was an odd sort of friendship, even though they did have certain interests in common.' The sergeant paused expectantly. Dover had now got his eyes shut – he always claimed he thought better that way – so MacGregor kindheartedly obliged.

'Really?' he said.

'Skirts!' said the station sergeant with a knowing wink.

'Oh, yes?' said MacGregor, turning to a fresh page in his notebook. 'Well, we'll follow that up. It won't do any harm to have a word with Mr ... what did you say his name was?'

'Hamilton,' said the station sergeant, his face breaking into a delighted grin of anticipation. 'William Hamilton.'

'And where can we find him?'

'Well now, that's not a question I'm really qualified to answer.' The station sergeant was rocking with barely suppressed mirth.

MacGregor smiled politely and waited.

'He's dead!' chortled the station sergeant. 'Not four weeks ago!' His laughter turned into a cough and he went dangerously red in the face. 'Murdered!' he spluttered as he leaned, choking and wheezing, over the Inspector's desk.

Chapter Four

THEY had to wake Dover up to tell him the joke. It was some time before they could make him grasp the point.

'Who was murdered?' he demanded ferociously. 'Here, what time is it? I want my lunch.'

'William Hamilton,' said MacGregor, enunciating the syllables loudly and clearly.

Dover glared at him. 'And who's William Hamilton when he's at home?'

'William Hamilton was a close friend of Cochran.'

'Cochran?' said Dover frowning. 'All right!' he roared as MacGregor opened his mouth to explain that, too. 'I remember. Well, so what?'

'William Hamilton was murdered only a few weeks ago.'

'By Cochran?'

'Oh, no!' put in the station sergeant hastily.

'Well, who did murder him then?'

'We don't know, sir.'

Dover's mouth assumed its most petulant pout. His last shreds of patience were already exhausted. He was fed up, bored and hungry. 'Then what the hell,' he growled, 'has he got to do with it?'

The station sergeant looked puzzled. 'Do with what, sir?'

'Anything!' bellowed Dover. 'What the blazes is going on here? Don't you understand the Queen's English, man?'

It was MacGregor who, as usual, stepped in where an angel would, with some justification, have feared to tread. 'We were just discussing Cochran's friends, sir, and the sergeant here happened to mention that one of his close associates, William Hamilton, had been murdered recently. I thought it might possibly be significant.'

Dover stared at him with unconcealed disgust. 'If you've started thinking we'd all better look out, hadn't we?'

The station sergeant was looking uncomfortable. 'There is

just one thing, sir,' he said tentatively. 'This chap, Hamilton, well – he wasn't exactly what you might call, well, murdered exactly, if you see what I mean.'

Dover just contemplated the now gently sweating station sergeant. Then he turned slowly and just contemplated MacGregor. MacGregor industriously practised his signature in his notebook and waited for the storm to break.

Dover sucked in his breath. MacGregor and the station sergeant cringed instinctively. Dover rose in all his majesty to his feet and settled his bowler hat into the furrows on his forehead.

'We'll continue this when I've had my lunch,' he announced with dignity and stalked out.

Unhappily the station sergeant hurried after him. 'I'm off duty at two o'clock, sir.'

'Indeed?' said Dover with the sweet smile of a tiger faced by a particularly succulent lamb. 'In that case we will all foregather in my room at the hotel at five p.m. this afternoon. We don't want to keep you hanging around here in your free time, do we, Sergeant? Ah!' A constable came up with Dover's overcoat and helped him into it. 'Thank you, laddie!'

Surreptitiously the constable wiped his hands on the seat of his uniform trousers.

'I promised to take the wife to see her auntie this afternoon,' the station sergeant whispered in an aggrieved tone to MacGregor. 'She fixed it all up weeks ago. What am I going to do?'

'You're going to be in his hotel room at five o'clock, if you know what's good for you,' MacGregor told him with little sympathy. 'What on earth did you say Hamilton was murdered for when he wasn't?'

The station sergeant didn't get time to answer. There was a muffled howl from the street outside as of a bullock being slaughtered. MacGregor took to his heels and ran.

Dover had fully intended to be up and dressed by the time the station sergeant arrived at five o'clock. Unfortunately that blithering idiot MacGregor didn't return from his afternoon's expeditions until ten minutes before zero hour. Dover decided to remain where he was – in bed. It was warm and comfortable, which was more than could be said of the rest of the hotel bedroom. Outside, the July rain streamed down out of a bleak July sky.

The station sergeant arrived promptly, if resentfully, upon his hour. MacGregor opened the door and hoped that the ill-tempered slating he had just received from Dover had not penetrated the solid woodwork. The station sergeant staggered into the room carrying a heavy suitcase.

'I don't remember inviting you to stay for a week,' said Dover with heavy-handed irony.

'Oh, no, sir!' The station sergeant was about to take all in good part (it being one of the pleasanter traditions in the police that junior officers always laugh heartily at their superiors' jokes) when he suddenly caught sight of Dover reclining on his couch. It was a sight to make strong men tremble. The Chief Inspector's pasty, flabby face was surmounted by an untidy thatch of thin black hair. His two button-like, malicious little eyes were still screwed up with sleep. Above his pouting rose-bud mouth twitched a tiny black smudge of a moustache and a short stumpy nose. More, regrettably, than the Chief Inspector's face was visible. Fleshy shoulders, clothed in a yellowing long-sleeved vest, rose from admidst the bed-clothes. Two buttons on the neck of the vest were missing, affording tantalizing glimpses of Dover's hairy chest.

The station sergeant gaped, mouth open.

'Where's that dratted tea?' demanded Dover, scraping the palm of his hand over his five o'clock shadow.

'It's just coming, sir.' MacGregor, hearing the tea cups rattling outside, got up and opened the door again. 'Shall I be mother, sir?'

'I shouldn't be surprised,' said Dover unpleasantly. 'And four lumps for me, remember.' He glared at the station sergeant who was still standing awkwardly in the middle of the room. 'You paralysed or something? Sit down over there. I'll come to you in a minute.'

There was a pause while MacGregor poured the tea out.

'I came over a bit queasy after lunch,' Dover informed the room in general. 'A bit bilious, you know. I had to get into bed to keep warm.'

'Nasty cold sort of day, sir,' agreed the station sergeant.

'I'd no small change for the gas fire, either,' explained Dover, bringing a note of pathos into his voice. 'Either of you lads got a shilling on you?'

Both lads fished obligingly in their pockets and produced five separate shillings.

'Oh,' said Dover with an innocent smile, 'that's very kind of you. Stick one in the meter, MacGregor, and light the fire. You can leave the others on the mantelpiece.'

MacGregor, inwardly cursing himself for presenting his lord and master with a couple of barely solicited bob, did as he was told and then started handing the tea round.

'Now,' said Dover, dropping a lump of strawberry jam down the front of his vest, 'what have you been up to, MacGregor?' Delicately he scraped the jam off with his knife and replaced it on his bread and butter.

'I went to see Miss Sandra Jackson. She was Cochran's girl-friend, you remember, sir.'

'Of course I remember!' snapped Dover. 'I'm not senile yet, laddie. And if you have a memory half as good when you get to my age you won't be doing so badly.' He blew on his tea.

'Well, she didn't seem to know anything, sir. Just that Cochran had called their holiday off at the last minute and that she hadn't seen him since a week last Saturday and he seemed normal enough then.' MacGregor solemnly consulted his notebook. '"As cheeky as a boxful of monkeys and sexy with it" – to quote her own words, sir. She went round to his lodgings to see what the dickens was going on but she couldn't get past Mrs Jolliott. After that she decided he could stick it and that two could play that sort of game, and she's made no attempt to get in touch with him since.'

'Humph,' said Dover. 'Any cake? Well, get on with it, laddie! You haven't spent all afternoon interviewing one twit of a girl, have you?'

'No, sir, though she isn't the easiest person to talk to. I don't think she's quite normal, really – not in the head that is.' MacGregor smirked. 'Though there was nothing wrong with the rest of her, I will say that. She seemed to think she ought to figure in Cochran's will; the pair of them being as good as man and wife, she claimed. It took me a long time to convince her that Cochran's heirs were no concern of mine.'

Dover grunted, and stretched out to pass the plate of cakes to the station sergeant.

'Well, sir,' continued MacGregor, 'after that I went round to Mrs Jolliott's again to collect Cochran's things. I carted them all round to the police station and examined them there, but I'm afraid I drew a complete blank. There was nothing there to give us any lead on why he killed himself. He seems to have had a reasonable amount of money in the Post Office Savings Bank, nothing excessive, of course, which might have been suspicious. Just a reasonable balance. There were very few private papers and none of them helpful. Of course Mrs Jolliott had already cleared his room out before we got there. She says she hasn't removed or destroyed anything, but we can't be sure. We've only got her word for it.'

'Oh, you can trust Mrs Jolliott,' said the station sergeant who was restlessly counting his off-duty hours slipping by. 'She's on the Committee of the Ladies' League.' He made it sound like a pronouncement of canonization.

'The Ladies' League?' asked MacGregor.

'Yes, you've heard of them, surely? They're very powerful here in Wallerton. Practically run the town, you might say. They started up orignally just after the war – the First World War, of course – to stop Wallerton from getting spoiled. Since then they've gone from strength to strength. I reckon we've got the most unspoiled sea-side resort in the whole blessed country. They just oppose absolutely everything. That's why we've only two licensed hotels, no fun fair, no bowling alley, no bingo and practically no anything else you are to name. They do most of it through their husbands, of course. Talk about petticoat government! And it's getting worse, not better. They've started branching out now.' The station sergeant lowered his voice. 'Do you know what they did a couple of years ago? There's a fair-sized ladies' shop on Sea Parade, Morrison's, been there for donkey's years. Well, young Morrison thought he'd liven things up a bit – just as a gimmick, you know. Of course, he'd never have done it if his father had been alive. His father had more sense. Well, young Morrison, he gets one of those topless dresses and sticks it in his main window. Just as a joke, really. Well, you'd have thought he was organizing sexual orgies on the front line from the row that blew up. Mind you, the Ladies' League were quite fair about it. They gave him ten minutes to get the whole bang shoot removed from the window. Miss Billson, she's a retired gym mistress from the High School, she stood outside on the pavement with a stop-watch. Young Morrison, the fool, tried to bluff it out. Said it was a free country and he wasn't breaking the law and all that sort of rot. And a fat lot of good it did him, too.'

'What did they do?' asked MacGregor kindly. 'Burn the shop down?'

'Worse, because that way young Morrison would have got the insurance at any rate. No, they just boycotted him. The word was sent round and not a single woman living in this town so much as put one foot over the threshold. They all closed their accounts and that was the end of young Morrison. Three quarters of his staff handed their notice in and in just over a month he sold out. Dropped a packet on the deal, too, from what I've heard. Cleared out of the town, too. Went into a monastery, so they say, but I reckon that's a bit of an exaggeration. Oh, you've got to watch your P's and Q's in Wallerton if you want to survive. There was that fellow ... '

'Quite,' said Dover. He turned to MacGregor. 'So what it all boils down to is that you've buggered around all afternoon for nothing?'

'Well, I wouldn't quite put it like that, sir.'

'No,' said Dover moodily, 'I don't suppose you would. You'd wrap it up in a lot of flowery language, but it wouldn't change the facts, would it?'

'Perhaps the sergeant here might be able to give us a lead, sir.'

'Wadderyermean?' growled Dover.

'I was going to tell you about the Hamilton business, sir,' said the station sergeant eagerly. 'I've taken the liberty of bringing the file along with me in case you'd like to have a look at it.'

'What,' said Dover, 'that?'

The station sergeant looked at the heavy suitcase with considerable pride. 'It was a very complicated case, sir.'

'It must have been!' was Dover's morose comment. 'That's the trouble with you lot these days. Too much damned paper.'

'Oh well,' – he sank deeper into the bed and lay almost flat on his back, gazing up at the ceiling – 'I suppose you'd better tell us all about it. But, for God's sake, keep it short! We don't want to be here all night.'

It was a sentiment to which the station sergeant subscribed, but, on the other hand, the Hamilton affair was the most lurid thing that had ever happened in the whole of Wallerton's history and it seemed a pity not to make the most of it.

He looked anxiously at Dover and sought for the right note of breath-taking drama which would force the Chief Inspector to open his new closed eyes. Inspiration dallied. What might have been a grunt or what might have been a snore came from Dover's lips.

'This chap, Hamilton,' gabbled the station sergeant, uncomfortably aware that he wasn't doing himself justice, he was found dead in his own front garden.'

''Strewth!' murmured Dover and rolled over to face the wall.

'With no clothes on,' added the station sergeant.

'Very saucy,' mumbled Dover.

'And horribly mutilated.'

Dover yawned.

'I should have thought you'd have heard about it, sir,' said the station sergeant resentfully. 'It was in all the papers. We'd hundreds of reporters milling around. And the television.'

Dover grunted and pulled the bed-clothes up to his chin.

The station sergeant looked as though he was going to burst into tears. Once more MacGregor took pity on him. 'Perhaps you could give us the details?' he suggested encouragingly and even went so far as to get his notebook out.

The station sergeant turned to him gratefully. 'Well, this chap, Hamilton – he was a middle-aged, married man – went out one evening to our local Country Club. That's what it's called though actually it's on top of a warehouse near the railway station. He spent the evening there until he left about half past twelve. He'd had a fair amount to drink so they phoned up for a taxi for him. Nothing unusual about that. It had happened once or twice before. Well, the taxi took him home and dropped him off at his front door. And that's the last time he was seen alive.'

'By the taxi-driver?' asked MacGregor.

'That's right. He says Hamilton got out and paid his fare. He wasn't paralytic, you see, just had a few too many, that's all. Then the taxi drove back off to the garage. The following morning the milkman found the body just inside the front garden. Hamilton's house has got a bit of a garden in front, you know, and a low stone wall. All his clothes were in a neat pile beside the body.'

'Had he been robbed?'

'No, I don't think so. He'd over fifty quid in one pound notes in his wallet.'

'Hm,' said MacGregor thoughtfully.

Deep and steady breathing came from the bed.

'You said Hamilton was married? Where was his wife?'

'She was at home, in bed asleep. They slept in separate rooms, apparently, so she'd no idea that Hamilton hadn't come home or that anything had happened to him. We don't even know if he went into the house. The front door was locked but, of course, he'd got a key.'

'Didn't any of the neighbours see or hear anything?'

'Well, it's a bit of a funny sort of street, you see. They did used to be posh town houses in the old days, but now they're mostly offices. There's six houses right opposite Hamilton's place all belonging to the Town Council – the Borough Surveyor and the Rating Office and things like that. They're completely empty at night. The people in the house next but one to Hamilton were away. The house next to him is offices but the one on the other side is occupied. They have their bedrooms at the back, though, and they say they didn't hear anything.'

'So you drew a blank?'

'Well, not quite. There's an elderly lady who lives in a top flat down at the end of the street. She says she saw a green van drive along at about half past four that morning and stop outside Hamilton's house. According to her, she saw two men get out of the van, which was facing towards her by the way, and go round the back. She couldn't see what they were doing and after a couple of minutes they got back in the van and drove off. It wasn't much help. She couldn't give us much detail. We followed it up but we didn't get anywhere.'

'But it wasn't murder?'

'No. Everybody thought it was at first, of course. Headquarters descended on us like a pack of ravaging wolves. We haven't had what you might call a real juicy murder case in the county for years and the Chief Constable went after it like a terrier after a rat. We had everybody in on it. He called men in from the other end of the county, everybody was on overtime and all leave was cancelled. You'd have thought the Third World War had broken out. Well, then we got the path. report and that deflated things a bit. Seems he'd got a clot on the brain or something and it had burst or whatever they do. Could have happened any old time, the doctor said. Well, the C.I.D. poked around for a few days but their heart wasn't in it and gradually everything quietened down. It wasn't even a nine days' wonder in the end.'

MacGregor closed his notebook. 'Well, it certainly does seem a bit of a mystery, doesn't it? He died from natural causes, you say, but the body was stripped and mutilated. Very odd.'

There was a great heaving and puffing from the bed. Dover's face, rather pink from his exertions, emerged. 'What the blazes,' he demanded bleakly, 'has all this to do with young what's-his-name chucking himself into the ruddy sea?'

'Well, sir,' explained the station sergeant, none too confidently, 'when all the hoo-hah died down over Hamilton and everybody went off on to other jobs like they always do, the Chief Constable sort of turned young Cochran loose on it. He was a sort of friend of Hamilton, you see, and the Chief Constable thought he might be able to get a fresh lead on the business. He didn't reckon it would do Cochran any harm, either, him being ear-marked for C.I.D., as you might say. It'd give him some practical experience and, of course, it'd be a real feather in his cap if he solved it.'

'My God!' snarled Dover, sitting up in bed and showing every sign of actually getting out of it. 'Do you mean that an ordinary uniformed copper who's hardly broken his bloody boots in gets handed a murder case like this on a bloody plate?'

'Well, it wasn't exactly a murder case, sir,' the station sergeant pointed out.

'Don't quibble!' roared Dover, swinging his legs out of bed and revealing long woolly underpants. 'And shove my trousers over! No wonder we never solve any crimes these days. You country bumpkins, you want to get your fingers out! I've never heard anything like it. I'm not surprised you've got policemen jumping off cliffs every five minutes.'

While he delivered himself of this tirade Dover proceeded to get himself dressed. There was the usual tussle to fasten the top trouser button and the usual effort to reach his shoe laces. When all his clothes were finally tossed on he peered at his face in the dressing-table mirror and dabbed at his hair a couple of times with a disgusting-looking hair brush.

'Action!' said Dover. 'That's what you want down here. Action! And drive! And a bit of common sense,' he added scathingly. 'Chief Constables' nephews, my Aunt Fanny! It's a good thing the public doesn't know how their money's being spent, by God it is! Well, come on, MacGregor, you great fool! Don't just sit there!'

MacGregor scrambled to his feet. 'Where are we going, sir?'

'Where are we going, sir?' mocked Dover, adding a lisp for good measure. 'In your case, laddie, I often wonder.'

'Will you want me, sir?' asked the station sergeant, completely taken aback by this sudden flurry of activity.

'Not unless you're going to pay for your own dinner,' growled Dover.

Chapter Five

MACGREGOR and the station sergeant looked at each other. The station sergeant mopped his brow.

'I thought he was up and off to clear the whole business up here and now,' he said shakily.

'Not him.'

'More of what you might call a thinker, is he?' asked the station sergeant, still gazing in stupefaction at the open door through which Dover had departed.

With commendable loyalty MacGregor refrained from making any comment.

'Oh, well,' sighed the station sergeant, 'it takes all sorts, doesn't it?' He looked glumly at his suitcase. 'What shall I do with that lot?'

'You'd better leave it here. He'll want to have a look at it, when he's had his dinner.'

MacGregor had some difficulty with his Chief Inspector when he finally joined him in the dining-room. Dover was in an evil temper. For the most part his spleen was directed against the unfortunate station sergeant whom he now referred to as that 'fat sponger'.

'Me buying a dinner for a sergeant!' he grumbled. 'That'll be the day!'

'I don't think, sir, ...'

'Well, I do, laddie! I've had enough experience of hangers-on like him to spot 'em when I see them. Touch you for any damned thing, they will – cigarettes, beer, the lot. You want to watch him, laddie, or he'll take a softy like you for a real ride.'

When he had exhausted the iniquities of the station sergeant Dover turned to women. He was not likely to forget who was the source of all his present troubles.

'Lolling on the beach in a deck chair at Filbury,' he complained sullenly, 'that's what she'll be doing. Drops you straight in the flaming dirt and then clears off without so much as an apology. Let it be a warning to you, laddie. You feed 'em and clothe 'em and work your fingers to the bone for 'em, and what happens? They shop you. Never get married, laddie, it's a mug's game.'

'Oh, come now, sir!' MacGregor tried to laugh him out of it. 'Mrs Dover couldn't have helped seeing what she saw.'

'She could have kept her trap shut,' said Dover truculently. 'I told her: "Drive on," I said, "it's nothing to do with us." Women! You might as well talk to a brick wall.'

'Things might be worse, sir.'

'I don't know how,' snorted Dover.

'I was thinking, sir, if we could – well – get cracking and, you know, find out what drove Cochran to commit suicide, we might still be able to get away on leave. We'd have only lost a couple of days, say, and we might be able to tack them on to the other end.'

It was delicately put, but Dover bridled instinctively at the implications.

'It shouldn't be too difficult, sir,' persisted MacGregor, 'not if we put our backs into it.'

Dover regarded him with undisguised disgust. 'And what,' he asked sarcastically, 'do you propose we do? Forge a farewell note? Hey! That's an idea! If we could get a sample of his handwriting ... '

'I think,' said MacGregor firmly, 'that we should reinvestigate this Hamilton business.'

Dover's bottom lip pouted out. 'There's no flaming evidence that it's got anything to do with Cochran's suicide,' he protested.

'Well, what do you suggest we do, sir?' MacGregor controlled his impatience and tried to speak reasonably.

Dover thought. 'Re-investigate the Hamilton business,' he said after a long pause, and sighed.

MacGregor jumped in happily. 'You see, sir, it's my theory that Hamilton's killing may have been one of these ritualistic murders – because of the mutilation. Wallerton is a sea port, sir. There are probably all kinds of odd characters hanging around.'

'Like one-eyed Lascars and sinister Chinamen, I suppose? I should have thought there were more boarding houses than opium dens in this dump.'

'But the mutilations, sir, how do you explain them?'

'I don't,' said Dover flatly.

'If it was some sort of foreign gang that got Hamilton, Cochran may have got on to them and ...'

'And they put the voodoo on him and he jumped off Cully Point?'

'Stranger things have happened, sir.'

'Not in Wallerton they haven't, laddie!'

With considerable reluctance Dover permitted himself to be bribed into some further study of the Hamilton case. MacGregor installed him in a small musty writing-room, fetched a couple of rounds of drinks and went upstairs to get the papers from the suitcase.

While Dover sat and moodily drank his beer MacGregor hunted happily through the contents of the suitcase. The investigation had been handled thoroughly if with, in MacGregor's opinion, little imagination. There had been no less than 1,752 house-to-house inquiries which had produced no relevant information of any kind. MacGregor tut-tutted in a thrifty Scottish way over such lavish expenditure of public money.

'There's one thing, sir,' he remarked to Dover in an effort to revive the Chief Inspector's rapidly flagging interest, 'Hamilton wasn't mutilated in order to hinder identification.'

'I never thought he was,' said Dover scathingly. 'He'd have hardly been dumped in his own front garden with all his belongings piled up beside him if that was what they were after, would he?'

'Er, no, sir. I suppose not. They must have done it for revenge, I should think. Look, sir, his face hasn't been touched at all.' MacGregor passed a large shiny photograph over.

'Ugh!' said Dover, passing it rapidly back again. 'Do you mind? I've only just had my dinner.'

'It is rather nasty, sir, isn't it?'

'Nasty? From the waist down he looks like a pile of butcher's mince!'

'All done after death, according to the path. report, sir,' said MacGregor examining dozens of other photographs with, in Dover's opinion, an unhealthy relish.

'What with? A bacon slicer?'

'A small sharp instrument, sir. Maybe a scalpel!'

'Oh God, don't tell me we're looking for a mad doctor now! Didn't they find any bloody clues?'

'Apparently not, sir. There was the report by the lady who saw the green van with the two men in it and that's about all.'

Dover sighed. 'Was he married?'

'Hamilton? Oh, yes, sir.'

'Right. We'll go and see the wife.'

'The wife, sir? I don't think she'll be much help. Her evidence doesn't add up to anything. You see, sir, she ... '

'First rule of detection, laddie,' said Dover ponderously as he rose to his feet. 'When a husband's murdered, it's the wife who's done it.'

'Oh, not invariably, sir,' said MacGregor with a nervous laugh. He was distressed to find that the celebrated Dover method of investigation was once again raising its head. As a system its sole merit was its simplicity.

'Nine times out of ten, near as dammit,' said Dover.

'Ah, but the tenth time, sir!'

'If you get through your career in C.I.D. solving nine murder cases out of ten, laddie, you'll be Commissioner before you're thirty,' said Dover hitching up his trousers and yawning.

'Well, yes, I know, sir, but you just can't go around arresting the wife whenever a husband's killed.' MacGregor was uncomfortably aware that this was more or less precisely what Dover did do. 'What about the exceptions, sir?'

'You can't win 'em all,' said Dover philosophically. 'We'll go and see Mrs Hamilton in the morning. Meantime, you can go through that lot with a fine tooth comb. Who knows, you might spot something the local boys have missed.'

At ten o'clock the following morning it was still raining, though not so heavy. Dover and MacGregor made their way down Minton Parade.

'This is the house, sir.'

'And about time, too. When are they going to let us have a car?'

'Tomorrow, sir. Or the day after.'

'Or next Preston Guild! If I've got all this walking to do you'll have to get a taxi.'

'Well, I thought this morning, sir, since it was only just round the corner ... '

Dover sniffed unpleasantly. With a sigh he leaned over the garden wall and looked at the entirely undistinguished patch of grass which lay on the other side. 'Where was the blooming body?'

'Er, right here, sir, tucked up under the wall. Hiding it from the road as much as they could, I suppose.' MacGregor fished importantly in his briefcase and produced one of the official photographs.

'Never mind!' growled Dover. 'I can imagine. And don't keep waving those dratted photographs at me. They fair turn my stomach.'

'Are we going to interview Mrs Hamilton, sir?'

'Might as well,' said Dover sourly. 'At least we'll be out of the rain.'

He pushed himself off the wall and gazed morosely round. A flicker of life came into his mean little eyes. 'I thought that fat sponger said that there were some council offices on the other side of the road,' he said accusingly.

MacGregor followed the direction of the Chief Inspector's eyes. No council offices. He looked back at the house.

'Oh, I'm sorry, sir. This is number 15. It's number 25 we want. It's the numbers, you see, sir, they're practically illegible. I'm terribly sorry, sir. Number 25 must be a bit higher up.'

'And he calls himself a blooming detective!' murmured Dover. Not entirely displeased at having caught his subordinate out, he stumped off after MacGregor who was peering intently at the house numbers.

'I think this is it, sir.' MacGregor advanced halfway up the front steps and looked closely at the number on the door. It was obscured by several layers of old and blistered paint but MacGregor was satisfied that he had now found the right house.

Having surveyed one front garden Dover wasn't going to waste his time examining another, scene of the crime or not. 'Ring the blooming bell,' he ordered, 'and let's get on with it.'

Dutifully MacGregor rang and rang and rang. By the time Dover had lumbered up the steps precisely nothing had happened. The house remained as apparently lifeless as it had been when MacGregor's finger first made contact with the bell push.

'She must be out, sir.'

The rain trickled off the brim of Dover's bowler hat. He reflected, not for the first time, that it was a dog's life and lashed out with a malicious kick at the door. Still nothing happened. Again Dover applied boot to wood.

MacGregor's alert young ears picked up a muffled sound from the depths of the house. 'I think somebody's coming, sir.'

From behind the door came a sustained rattling and clinking as bolts were withdrawn and keys turned in the locks. With a weary creak the door scraped open by at least six inches. Above a stout taut chain a shadowy face appeared.

'Wat yer want?'

MacGregor, after a moment's hesitation, raised his hat politely. 'Mrs Hamilton? I wonder if we could have a few words with you. This is Detective Chief Inspector Dover. We're from Scotland Yard.'

One suspicious eye regarded MacGregor warily.

'Wat yer want?'

MacGregor looked at Dover as if expecting him to assume the initiative. Dover glowered back. 'For God's sake, get on with it!' he hissed.

'We would like to ask you a few questions about your husband's, er, death, Mrs Hamilton.'

'Oh yerse?' said the eye.

Dover dug his elbow into MacGregor's ribs as an encouragement to speed things up.

'Perhaps,' ventured MacGregor, 'we could come inside?'

'Why?' demanded the eye.

MacGregor looked despairingly at his Chief Inspector. 'Well, you don't want all the neighbours watching us, do you?' he smiled persuasively.

'Don't bother me.'

MacGregor tried an appeal to her sympathy. 'It is raining rather heavily,' he pointed out. 'We're getting soaked.'

'Yer'd better come back when the sun's shining in that case.'

Dover got his boot in the narrow opening a split second after the door had started to close.

''Ere!' protested the eye. 'Wat yer think yer doing?'

'Open this door, you old hag!' snarled Dover, never very strong on public relations.

The eye assumed a cunning look. 'Yer'll have to take yer foot out first. I can't unfasten the chain 'cept with the door closed.'

Dover, in spite of much evidence to the contrary, wasn't a complete fool. He had, moreover, cut his professional teeth on some pretty fly characters in the old days. 'I'm not that daft,' he sneered.

'Looks like stalemate then, dunnit?'

'You can get into serious trouble for obstructing the police in the execution of their duty,' blustered Dover.

'I know me rights. Yer can't come in 'ere without I lets yer.'

'We can get a warrant, you know,' thundered Dover.

'Well, you hop off and get one, mister.'

There was a pause while both sides considered the situation.

'We just want to ask you a few simple questions,' said Dover plaintively.

'It's no good arsking me. I don't know nothing. I just went to bed that night after 'e'd gorn out and I didn't know nothing till they told me next morning.'

'Had your husband any enemies?'

There was a sardonic laugh from behind the door. 'Just about every husband and father in Wallerton, I shouldn't wonder. Not to mention a few sons.'

'Oh, it was like that, was it?'

'So I've been told. I reckon I was the only woman in the whole town he didn't have those sort of ideas about. Dirty pig! He tried to get rid of me, you know. Wanted a divorce. Got his eye on some young bit of fluff down by the harbour end. I told him what he could do with his divorce. "You can take yer divorce," I told him, "and stuff it!" I haven't put up with his goings on all these years just to let some young tart get her thieving hands on everything.'

'Was he a wealthy man?' asked Dover in some surprise.

'Pretty warm. I'll be all right, don't chew worry. Ten thousand quid in insurance alone.'

'Ten thousand?' said Dover, and looked significantly at MacGregor.

'I kept the payments up meself,' said Mrs Hamilton proudly.

Dover regarded what little he could see of her with approval. Just like a woman! Yack, yack, yack. Putting the noose round her neck with her own tongue, as you might say. Only, to Dover's great regret, there was no noose in these benighted days.

'He must have led you a terrible life,' he said, trowelling on the sympathy.

'I've had more than me fair share,' agreed Mrs Hamilton.

'I expect your friends felt pretty bad about it, too,' suggested Dover, not quite seeing Mrs Hamilton disposing of her husband in such a bizarre fashion single-handed.

''Ere, what chew hinting at?'

'Oh, nothing,' said Dover soothingly.

'He died natural. That's what they said at the inquest. He died natural.'

'Well, now, I'd hardly call it that.'

'It were nothing to do with me. I was in bed.'

'Of course,' said Dover. 'Now, look, why don't you just let us come inside so we can have a nice cosy little chat about it?'

Perhaps his tone was too treacly. Perhaps Mrs Hamilton just got bored. At all events she retreated quietly and with a certain amount of dignity down the hall to where she kept a coal hammer for just such an occasion. She returned to the door with the coal hammer concealed behind her back and, sportingly, gave Dover a last chance. 'Are yew going?'

'Your husband was a friend of Cochran, the policeman, wasn't he?'

Mrs Hamilton swung the coal hammer. Dover saw it coming but was unable to get his foot out of the way in time. The coal hammer struck fair and square on the toe of his boot.

Dover screamed.

Mrs Hamilton, having successfully achieved the withdrawal of the offending foot, slammed her front door shut and began shooting the bolts back into place.

Meanwhile the Chief Inspector, bellowing with pain and fury, hopped around on one leg. MacGregor stared at him with more embarrassment than concern as heads began poking out of windows and doors opened from one end of the street to the other.

'Er, are you all right, sir?'

'You bloody fool!' howled Dover. 'Don't just stand there. Do something!'

Luckily for MacGregor the delicate decision of what to do for his injured Chief Inspector was taken by other and more capable hands. Two middle-aged ladies, fairly bristling with self importance and the urge to succour their fellow-man, were already coming up the steps at a near gallop. They had been walking past the house when Mrs Hamilton had delivered her blow against the forces of law and order. At the first scream these two Good Samaritans had exchanged delighted glances.

'Come on, Bella!' cried the fatter one and, touching the bow of blue ribbon on her bosom as though it were some form of talisman, resolutely led the way. Bella, panting a little and with eyes sparkling, was close behind.

No words were wasted. When they reached the top of the steps the pair of them snapped into action like a well-drilled team. MacGregor was shouldered ruthlessly aside. Bella kicked away Dover's uninjured leg and, since it was the sole support of his not inconsiderable bulk, brought him crashing to the ground. Then she flung herself smartly on top of him with a technique derived from what she had seen of the wrestlers on the telly. As she landed on his chest Dover's mouth involuntarily opened. Whether to utter some words of greeting or merely because the air in his lungs had got to go somewhere will never be known for, at the precise moment that his jaws opened, Bella's friend, the fatter one, rammed the handle of her shopping basket between his teeth.

'Move over a bit, Bella,' she commanded, still forcing the basket handle down Dover's throat.

Obediently Bella moved down on to Dover's stomach while her friend replaced her on his chest.

Comparative quiet reigned. Dover, now turning a very funny colour, could manage no more than a few gasping grunts. The two ladies rested on his prostrate form and concentrated on getting their own breath back.

When she had recovered her composure the fatter one smiled reassuringly at a horrified MacGregor.

'Good thing we happened to be passing,' she remarked.

MacGregor nodded, speechless.

'We've both got our First Aid certificates,' said Bella

with the air of one making polite conversation over the tea cups.

'I'm chairman of the First Aid Sub-committee of the Ladies' League,' put in the fatter one. She touched her blue ribbon again. 'You see, I've got a little red cross on mine.'

Dover began to struggle feebly. His face was getting black.

The fatter one regarded him complacently and shoved the basket handle in a bit further. 'He's quietening down now,' she observed. She glanced up rather patronizingly at MacGregor. 'I'll bet he had you worried there for a moment, didn't he? Still, it says in the handbook that epilepsy always looks much worse than it really is, and it's usually right, isn't it, Bella?'

Bella nodded. 'It's very good, that handbook,' she agreed. 'It's never let us down yet, has it, dear?'

'Epilepsy?' asked MacGregor weakly.

'The important thing,' said Bella, closing her eyes the better to recall the handbook's pearls of wisdom, 'is to ensure that the patient doesn't bite his tongue. Hence' – she opened her eyes and beamed at MacGregor – 'the basket handle. You should never use your finger. He might bite it off.' She giggled.

MacGregor gulped. He felt extremely diffident about contradicting two such capable women, but Dover's condition was clearly deteriorating.

'It's not epilepsy,' said MacGregor unhappily. 'I'm most frightfully sorry, but the lady who lives here she – well – she hit him on the foot with a hammer, I think.'

The ladies looked disappointed but they took it very well. Chuckling ruefully they hoisted themselves to their feet.

'More haste, less speed, Bella,' said the fatter one good-humouredly as she pulled her basket handle out of Dover's mouth.

'Impacted fracture, dear?' suggested Bella hopefully as Dover lay panting at their feet.

'Could be,' said the fatter one, pursing her lips judicially. 'Could be. We'll tackle it on that assumption, anyhow. Have you got your penknife handy, dear?'

Chief Inspector Dover was certainly down, but he was not out. Making a supreme effort he raised himself up on one elbow and, managing to munch his teeth back into position, flung a touching and desperate appeal to MacGregor.

'Keep 'em off me!' he wheezed and fell back exhausted.

MacGregor smiled awkwardly at the two ladies who were now rummaging in their handbags.

The fatter one was unperturbed. 'Nothing to worry about, young man,' she assured MacGregor breezily. 'It's a common reaction with patients. We're quite used to it, aren't we, Bella? Being unappreciated doesn't worry us. It's a good sign, really. Shows the victim has got over the shock. Ready, Bella?'

The two ladies sank on their knees by Dover's feet and yanked his trouser legs up. Dover kicked out feebly.

'Who the hell are they?' he demanded in a voice hoarse with panic. 'Burke and Hare?'

The fatter one shook her head when she saw Dover's stout black boots. 'It's no good, Bella,' she told her friend, 'we'll never be able to cut those off with your penknife.'

'Maybe this young man has got a stronger one, dear?'

Obligingly MacGregor began fishing in his pockets.

Dover stopped him. 'Sergeant!' he roared. 'I'm warning you! If you let these two harpies lay another finger on me, I'll fix you good and proper, by God, I will! Tell 'em to shove off and mind their own blasted business!'

But it was the fatter one who resolved the situation. 'We need an expert on this,' she announced firmly as she got to her feet. 'Good thing Hazel's just next door. She'll be able to fix him up.'

'Will she be in now, dear?' asked Bella, gratefully accepting MacGregor's's assistance as she too stood up.

'Oh, yes, she has a surgery every morning. Well,' – the fatter one slung her handbag cheerfully on her arm – 'brace yourself, Bella! Chair lift!'

It was no easy task but once Bella and her friend had made up their minds to aid and assist suffering humanity, aid and assist they did. There were protests and groans and squeals of pain from Dover as he was hoisted to his feet and his arms draped round the plump shoulders of the two ladies. There were grunts from the ladies as, their hands clasped under the Chief Inspector's posterior, they took the strain.

MacGregor, feebly hovering around and making half-hearted offers of assistance, picked up Dover's bowler hat and followed behind as the unwieldy trio lurched and staggered down the steps. Dover clutched his two supporters tightly round the neck and only stopped groaning to scream whenever danger appeared to approach his injured foot.

Perspiring profusely the two ladies manoeuvred their burden out of the front gate and carried it a short distance along the pavement. Interested spectators were still watching from their windows and doorways.

'Right wheel, Bella!' gasped the fatter one.

They turned into the next gateway and boggled slightly at the new flight of steps which loomed before them like another Everest.

Dover turned his head and addressed his sergeant. 'What the blazes are they up to now? My God, you're going to pay for this laddie!'

MacGregor, who was after all a detective, had been putting two and two together and had moreover spotted the brass plate on the door. 'It's all right, sir,' he said. 'They're taking you to a doctor.'

Bella, groping blindly for the bottom step, missed it.

'Oh, help!' moaned Dover, tightening his stranglehold on the necks. He turned again to MacGregor. 'For God's sake, tell 'em to get a move on! My foot's killing me!'

The ladies were flagging but they were made of stern stuff. They reached the top of the steps and almost fell in through the open doorway.

MacGregor, stepping over the threshold in their wake, glanced at the brass plate. He stopped horrified, refused to believe his eyes and read it again. A cold sweat broke out on his forehead. He hurried into the hallway in a vain attempt to ward off the disaster which was sure to come, but he was too late.

Dover was already being carried through two ranks of interested spectators towards a door marked surgery. There were two men, six women, three children, five cats, one boxer dog, two budgerigars and a snake in a box with holes in it.

Chapter Six

'ARE you sure it's this foot?' asked Miss Hazel ffiske sceptically.

'Of course I'm sure!' snapped Dover with a great deal of irritation. 'Look at that bruise!'

Miss ffiske, sniffing contemptuously, dabbed at the indicated spot with a piece of damp cotton wool. 'Dirt,' she said, and held up the cotton wool in eloquent silence as proof.

Dover scowled sullenly at her. 'Are you sure it's not broken?' he demanded.

'Of course I'm sure. There's no damage at all. She'd have needed a steam hammer to get through those boots.'

Miss ffiske shoved Dover's foot into a bowl of warm water, yanked it out again, wiped it and had another look. Sighing deeply she got to her feet and went over to a cupboard. She took out a large bottle, uncorked it and poured a sour green liquid over Dover's toes.

'What's that?' asked Dover, anxious and suspicious.

'Horse liniment,' said Miss ffiske.

The uproar which had been caused by Dover's dramatic entry into the surgery had long since died down. His stormy outrage at finding he had been brought to a female veterinary surgeon for treatment had been comparatively short-lived. In his state of health any expert attention was, he conceded grudgingly, better than nothing. He had had, he said unkindly, his belly full of amateurs.

After this remark there was little difficulty in persuading Bella and her friend to take their departure.

While Dover died a thousand noisy deaths MacGregor had made the introductions and explanations and Miss ffiske had got down, with more than a hint of unwillingness, to the business of ministering to the sick.

'I don't know what you wanted to go bothering poor Mrs Hamilton for in the first place,' observed Miss ffiske, as they waited for the horse liniment to dry. 'She's been as mad as a hatter for years and she's gone clean round the bend since that business about her husband.'

'But that's what we wanted to see her about,' said MacGregor. 'We're sort of re-opening the case.'

'I can't think why,' was Miss ffiske's tart rejoinder. 'Good riddance to bad rubbish, if you ask me. He should have dropped down dead years ago.'

'Oh, you knew him, did you?'

'I could hardly live next door to him for ten years without knowing him, could I? He was a dreadful man. He had the morals of a tom cat and when he'd been drinking – ugh!' She shuddered.

'But, surely he didn't try to force his attentions on you, did he?' asked Dover spitefully. Miss ffiske was in her early fifties and looked more like a retired bantam-weight boxer than anything else. She was small and wiry with a scrubbed pugnacious face and short stiff hair chopped into an uncompromising bob. She was not the type that any man, however lecherous and however drunk, would have accosted light-heartedly.

Miss ffiske seized Dover's toes and bent them vigorously up and down. She ignored the howls this brief sample of manipulation produced. 'There, I told you there was nothing broken.'

'If there wasn't before, I should damned well think there is now,' growled Dover. 'Where did they train you? In the elephant house?'

'No, unfortunately,' Miss ffiske snapped back at him, 'otherwise I should have been better qualified to handle you!'

MacGregor stepped in quickly before the situation could degenerate any further. 'You were telling us about Mr Hamilton, Miss ffiske?'

'Oh, was I? Oh well, I haven't really had much trouble with him personally for some years now. He was a nuisance at one time, always making suggestive remarks – you know the sort of thing – but I soon put a stop to that. He didn't get any encouragement from me! But then he started going to this disgusting club they have and coming back blind to the world at all hours of the night. A couple of times he's come hammering on my door at well past midnight and shouting that he couldn't get in. I warned him if it happened again I'd send for the police, and I would have done, too. A man like that ought to be kept behind bars permanently. Of course, he said he'd mistaken the house. They do all look alike, I know, and you can't see these dratted numbers in the day time, never mind late at night but, knowing him, I wasn't prepared to accept any excuses.'

'I said,' said MacGregor. 'But on the night of the murder, or rather – well – the night he died, you didn't hear anything at all, I understand?'

'Not a squeak,' said Miss ffiske. 'When I go to bed, I go there to sleep – unlike some people. And, anyhow, our rooms are at the back of the house.'

'Our rooms?'

'My receptionist, Miss Gourlay, lives here, too,' explained Miss ffiske curtly. 'Well, if you've no more questions I'd like to be getting on with my work. You can put your sock on now, Mr Dover.'

'You couldn't just have a look at that corn on my little toe while you're about it, could you?' asked Dover.

'No.' said Miss ffiske, 'I couldn't. And now, if you don't mind, I've a room full of patients waiting out there and, not being part of the National Health, my time is money. That'll be seven and sixpence and you can pay my receptionist on the way out.'

'Perhaps I'd better ring for a taxi, sir?' asked MacGregor.

'Nonsense!' said Miss ffiske sharply. 'Plenty of exercise, that's what he needs. The worst thing he can do is let that foot stiffen up. Keep him on the move, sergeant. A good brisk walk four times a day will do him a world of good. He's grossly overweight, anyhow.'

Before Dover had time to think up some appropriate and cutting rejoinder, the surgery door opened and a young woman with a weak but pretty face came in. Like Miss ffiske she wore a white overall with the blue bow of the Ladies' League pinned on the left breast. She seemed confused to find the two detectives still there and blushed deeply.

'Oh, do excuse me,' she stammered. 'I didn't realize … I'm so sorry … '

'What is it, Janie?' demanded Miss ffiske.

'Oh, er, nothing. It doesn't matter.'

'You must have come in here to tell me something. What is it?'

'It's just Mrs Widgery-Smith, dear, but I can come back.'

'What about Mrs Widgery-Smith?' Miss ffiske sounded a trifle impatient.

Miss Gourlay blushed deeper and flung a reproachful glance at her employer. 'It's about her little pussy cat, dear.'

'Well?'

'She wants to know when she can bring it in for its operation.' Miss Gourlay's voice sank to an embarrassed whisper.

'What operation?'

Miss Gourlay's eyes flicked nervously at Dover and MacGregor. 'Oh, *you* know, dear.'

'No, I don't know!' retorted Miss ffiske stubbornly. 'And I do wish you'd stop being so blasted namby-pamby, Janie! If she wants the damned cat neutered, why don't you say so instead of beating about the bush like something out of a Victorian novel?'

'I'm sorry, dear,' murmured Miss Gourlay.

'When does she want to bring it?'

'Friday morning, if that's all right with you, dear.'

'It'll do. Tell her ten o'clock. And just see you don't forget to get the operating theatre ready this time.'

'No, dear,' said Miss Gourlay and thankfully withdrew.

'Women!' snorted Miss ffiske. She slammed a few drawers in her desk to relieve her feelings. 'I sometimes wonder why I bother!'

MacGregor, on his knees fastening Dover's bootlace, looked up politely.

'You spend thousands of pounds on the best equipped operating theatre for a hundred miles and what happens?' Miss ffiske addressed her question to the room at large and stayed not for an answer. 'Some fool of a girl doesn't even remember to take the blasted dust sheets off!'

'It must be very annoying,' sympathized MacGregor, rather forcefully assisting Dover to his feet. The Chief Inspector looked like sitting there all day.

Miss ffiske looked at the pair of them in some surprise, as though she had forgotten they were there. 'Eh? Oh, well, yes,' she said gruffly. 'Still, she's got some very good qualities. Devotion. Loyalty. And she doesn't usually forget things. Well, you're off, are you? Good. And, remember, plenty of walking. Just tell that kid with the over-fed pekinese to come in, will you?'

'Quite an exciting morning, sir,' observed MacGregor with a merry laugh as he helped Dover down the steps.

'That's one way of putting it,' said Dover grimly. 'I noticed you were playing your usual role of interested spectator. It's coming to something when a Chief Inspector gets beaten up while his blooming sergeant stands by watching.'

'It's getting on for twelve o'clock, sir. I expect you'll be feeling like some lunch. It'll only take us a couple of minutes to get back to the hotel.'

The same thought had already crossed Dover's mind but the Chief Inspector was nothing if not pig-headed. 'I couldn't eat a thing,' he grumbled. 'Not after what I've been through. Fair turned me over, it has.'

'Oh,' said MacGregor, rather at a loss. 'Well, perhaps you'd like to go and have a lie-down in your room, sir?'

Dover eyed his sergeant suspiciously. 'You seem damned keen on getting back to the hotel, don't you? What's the matter? Developed an allergy to work now – on top of everything else?'

MacGregor gritted his teeth. With Dover in this mood whatever you said was wrong.

Meanwhile Dover made a genuine effort to be as awkward as possible. 'Wasn't there some woman witness or other in this street?'

'Well, yes, sir. There was a Miss Doughty, I think the name was. She was the one who is supposed to have seen the green van and the two men on the night Hamilton died.'

'We'll go and see her,' said Dover. 'Which way is it?'

With considerable difficulty, since Dover was hanging on to his arm like grim death, MacGregor hunted through his pockets for his notebook. He had taken the precaution of making a few notes in case Dover tried to stump him. He found Miss Doughty's address and carefully orientated himself. This was not the occasion to walk the Chief Inspector in the wrong direction.

At last he made up his mind and announced his decision to

the impatiently waiting Dover. 'This way, sir. But I think I should warn you that Miss Doughty apparently lives in a flat on the top floor.' He looked up pointedly at the tall houses lining the street. 'I don't suppose there'll be a lift, sir.'

Dover snorted contemptuously and started off with a gallant limp. 'I can manage it all right, laddie,' he said with withering sarcasm. 'More to the point is, can you?'

This remark effectively stopped MacGregor making any complaint as he laboured up to Miss Doughty's flat bearing the greater part of Dover's weight in addition to his own. When they reached the top MacGregor was panting and sweating. Dover, cool as a cucumber, regarded him with a malicious grin.

'Ring the bell, laddie! If you've got the strength left, that is.'

MacGregor jabbed viciously at the bell push. While he waited for the door to be opened he occupied his time by composing yet another letter to the Assistant Commissioner requesting a transfer to some other – any other – senior detective at Scotland Yard. He was fully absorbed in steering a course between a brutal exposé of the truth and rank insubordination when the door in front of him opened noiselessly.

'Ho, ho!' throbbed a rich fruity voice, quivering with timbre. 'Ho, ho! Will you come into my parlour, said the spider to the fly!'

MacGregor blinked. In front of him loomed a tall matronly figure bundled up in a faded kimono.

'Miss Doughty?'

'The same, darling boy, the same. Come in, come in, whoever you are!' Large dark eyes, liberally bedaubed with mascara, eye shadow and false eyelashes, rolled invitingly.

MacGregor nervously took a step backwards.

'Don't be shy, darling boy!' A hand, beautifully manicured but none too clean, shot out from the folds of the kimono and fastened on MacGregor's arm. With surprising strength Miss Doughty began to draw him into her flat.

'Chief Inspector!' MacGregor's voice was panicky.

There was a non-committal grunt from Dover. He had found a chair on the landing and had thankfully sat down on it. Now his eyes were closed and his mouth was beginning to sag open.

'Chief Inspector Dover, sir!' The second call was more penetrating.

Dover opened his eyes reluctantly.

Miss Doughty released her hold on MacGregor's arm. 'Oh, there are two of you, are there?' She leered roguishly. 'Is he as pretty as you, darling boy?' She stepped out on to the landing and had a look. 'Oh, no, he's not! Where on earth did you find him, darling boy? In a dustbin?'

Miss Doughty wouldn't see sixty again. It is just possible that she wouldn't see seventy either. However, she was fighting off old age with all the weapons at her command. She swayed her hips provocatively as she led the way into her sitting-room and sat down with conscious elegance, her back to the window.

'Scotland Yard?' she questioned in vibrant tones. 'How divinely thrilling! And what can I do for you?'

MacGregor looked at Dover. Dover was staring absent-mindedly at a mantelpiece packed with photographs, mostly framed and all signed.

'Aha!' Miss Doughty waggled a playfully reproving finger. 'You're looking at my photographs, you naughty man! I know what the next move is – you'll be asking for my autograph! Well, if you're a good boy I might just give you one!'

Dover scowled and retreated deeper in to his chair.

'You were an actress, were you, Miss Doughty?' asked MacGregor politely. It was a reasonable deduction as most of the photographs were of people in theatrical costumes and poses.

Miss Doughty looked annoyed. 'Of course, darling boy! And still am! Ah, well,' she forgave him with a gracious smile, 'you're probably too young to remember me in my hey-day.' She swept a hand in Dover's direction. 'But *you're* not, darling! *You* haven't forgotten Doris Doughty and her Troupe of Four. My public were always wonderfully loyal to me.' Dover's eyes had acquired a blank, vacant look so, very sensibly, Miss Doughty switched back to MacGregor. 'Of course, I never gave them any rubbish, darling boy. Nothing but the best from Doris Doughty. And none of your West End commercial muck, either. The Bard, that's what I gave them. And I took him to the people. Schools, village halls, army camps during the war. Oh, how those dear soldier boys loved me! That's where the real people are, darling, not sitting in five guinea boxes and covered with diamonds. This,' she selected a photograph from a small table by her elbow, 'this is me in Lear. What a triumph that was! We played to packed houses from one end of the country to the other.'

'You played Cordelia, I suppose?' said MacGregor, doing a bit of showing off as he reached for the photograph.

'Cordelia!' trilled Miss Doughty, drawing herself up in full majesty. 'Damn it, darling boy, I played Lear!'

Awe-struck MacGregor looked at the photograph. Beneath the Father Christmas beard and woolly eyebrows, the face was undoubtedly Miss Doughty's. 'How very, er, interesting,' he gulped.

'There are no star parts for women in Shakespeare, darling boy. Sarah Bernhardt knew that – you've heard of *her*, I suppose? No, if a real actress wants to do Shakespeare she's got to do it in tights.' She chose another photograph. 'That's me as Macbeth. Tartan trews, you see. Very fetching. And this is me as Richard the Third. Not my part, really. I've far too good a figure to play a hunchback. And this is me as' – she laughed archly – 'Othello. What you might call a black-face part, eh? And this is me as Hamlet. How's that for a calf? James Agate called my performance as the Dane the most astonishing thing he'd ever seen in forty years of theatre going. How's that for a compliment?'

'You concentrated on the tragedies, did you?' asked MacGregor, clutching frantically at the photographs which were being showered upon him.

'Had to, darling boy,' said Miss Doughty ruefully. 'That's me as Antony in Antony and Cleopatra. There were only five of us, you see. You can't possibly do a Shakespearian comedy with only five actors. Be reasonable, darling boy!'

'I should have thought it was pretty difficult to do a Shakespearian tragedy,' said MacGregor.

'Practically impossible, darling boy! Couldn't be done in these days, not with these so-called actors you see preening themselves in the soap advertisements. Catch them playing eleven parts in one evening, but that's what dear Ethel did, night after night. That's her playing Juliet to my Romeo.' MacGregor accepted yet another photograph. 'Oh, it took some doing, I can tell you. We had to cut the play down to its bare essentials but we were true to the spirit. I always insisted on that. That's me as Coriolanus. We did that for ENSA in 1942. Do you know, a soldier boy came up to me after the performance with tears in his eyes. He could hardly speak, the poor child. He said that for the first time since the war began he really knew what he was fighting for. Wasn't that sweet? A corporal in the Pay Corps, I think he was.'

Dover's stomach rumbled. He yawned widely, scratched his head and took over. 'Hamilton,' he said. 'What's all this about a green van on the night he was chopped up?'

'Oh, you've come about Hamilton, have you?' Miss Doughty's deep voice sank into black tragedy. 'Such a tedious business.'

'What exactly did you see?' asked Dover. 'There's no need to go into detail. Just give us the essential facts.'

Miss Doughty assumed a doleful expression. Then she smiled. 'How about a little snifter, darlings, just to keep our peckers up? You fetch the glasses and the tonic from the kitchen, darling boy. I've got the gin here.' She gave the little table by her elbow a coy tap.

MacGregor dutifully played the part of a waiter. 'Tonic for you, Miss Doughty?'

'No, thank you, darling boy, I'm slimming.' Miss Doughty dispensed a generous quantity of gin for herself and considerably less for her guests. 'Bottoms up, darlings!'

'The green van,' prompted Dover wearily.

'Ah, yes.' Miss Doughty fortified herself with another draught from the tumblerful of gin, sat up straighter in her chair and gazed into the middle distance. 'Usually I sleep like a log, darlings, but on this particular night my slumbers were somewhat disturbed,' she declaimed. 'About four o'clock I arose to make myself a warm drink. Instead of returning to bed I took my drink and sat in a chair by the window, thinking to refresh my soul with the sight of the dawn breaking over the roof tops. Imagine my surprise when, glancing down into the street below, I saw a small green van coming towards me down the street. Usually at night we have virtually no traffic in this quiet backwater.'

Dover caught MacGregor's eye and nodded.

Unobtrusively the sergeant got up and went to the window. 'You were sitting here, Miss Doughty?'

Miss Doughty flapped his question aside. 'Don't interrupt me, darling boy, not when I'm in full spate. Now, where was I? ... coming towards me down the street. Usually at night we have virtually no traffic in this quiet backwater. Naturally, there being nothing else to watch, I watched the van. It stopped just about by the Hamiltons' house. All the lights were put out on the van and then I saw both doors open and two men got out. They went round to the back of the van and opened the rear doors. I couldn't see clearly what happened then but I had the impression that they carried something heavy out of the back of the van and put it over one of the garden walls. I couldn't tell which one. Then the men got back in the van and it drove off. I did not make a note of the number. The van was small and green and I did not see any writing on the side of the van. When the van had gone I went back to bed. There.' Miss Doughty blinked triumphantly. 'How's that for a statement?'

'Very good,' said Dover sourly. 'Sounds almost as though you'd learned it off by heart.'

'Read a thing twice and I've got it off pat. Up here,' replied Miss Doughty, tapping her head with one hand and treating herself to a stiff gin with the other. 'Mark of an old pro. Besides,' she looked solemnly at Dover, 'it's about the sixth time I've gone through it. I did it four or five times right at the beginning and then that young man came round again a week or so ago, and now you two.'

'Young man? Was his name Cochran?'

'I think so,' said Miss Doughty, not enunciating quite so clearly. 'Don't really remember. Handsome boy, though. Bit of a devil if you ask me, but very handsome. If I'd been fifty years younger ... Well, gentlemen,' she gathered her kimono round her and reached yet again for the bottle of gin, 'if you have no further questions, it's time for my luncheon.'

It suited Dover, who'd had more than enough of the silly old coot.

'There are one or two questions,' began MacGregor.

Dover scowled malevolently at him. 'Later, laddie, later!' he said. 'Miss Doughty wants her lunch and I want mine.'

'I'll see you out,' announced Miss Doughty with blurred dignity. Her eyes acquired a slight squint and she stood bolt upright. MacGregor grabbed her as she swayed. 'Whoops! Steady, ye Buffs!' she giggled and sat down abruptly.

'Oh, leave the old soak alone,' snapped Dover, already half way to the door. 'She's over three parts sozzled.'

'But we can't leave her like this, can we, sir?' MacGregor looked anxiously at Miss Doughty who was now sleeping peacefully, a faint smile on her lips.

There was no answer. Dover had gone.

Chapter Seven

'WHAT a dump!' grumbled Dover.

They were sitting in the hotel lounge having their after-dinner coffee. Dover, his injured foot resting on a stool, had some justification for his comment. The room was bleak, shabby and cold. The other guests had either already retired to bed so as to build up their strength for the ozone-impregnated rigours of the morrow, or were in the television room watching whatever the B.B.C. chose to provide them with. Only the very lowest people in Wallerton watched commercial telly.

The leaves of a plastic palm tree quivered in the draught which blew continually through the entire hotel.

'What a day!' said Dover gloomily.

MacGregor was inclined to agree with him. The morning had been bad enough but at least something had been happening then. The afternoon had been unbearably dreary. Dover, of course, had retired to his room to think about the case and rest his toe. MacGregor had been left to kick his heels around as best he might, and Wallerton on a wet July afternoon was not a place overburdened with amusements. The cinema didn't open until six o'clock and MacGregor considered it beneath his dignity to patronize Wallerton's sole Amusement Arcade.

'We're wasting our bloody time,' observed Dover.

'Perhaps you could convince the Chief Constable of that, sir?' said MacGregor, always an optimist.

'I've tried,' said Dover, his jowls wobbling miserably. 'I rang him up just before dinner. I told him we were stuck up a gum tree.' He sighed self-pitying. 'It was no good. He told me he'd promised his wife he'd leave no stone unturned to find what had driven his nephew to suicide. Stupid devil.'

MacGregor nodded and thought longingly of his ruined holiday.

'It's me that's got to turn the stones up, you notice,' Dover pointed out truculently. 'Not him. Oh, dear me, no – not him.'

'If only we knew which stones, sir.'

'Quite,' said Dover vaguely.

'Do you think we're getting anywhere at all, sir?' asked MacGregor.

'Do you?'

'Not really, sir.'

'Let's begin at the beginning. You never know, we might have overlooked something. Now then, young Constable Cochran – blast him – commits suicide ...'

'We think he did, at any rate, sir.'

Dover's face fell. 'Don't start that! If that young blighter turns up out of the blue all bright and smiling, I'll boot him off Cully Point myself, so help me! No, he's a gonner. He must be.'

'Now all we've got to do is find out why, sir,' said MacGregor with a merry laugh. It was meant as a joke.

Dover scowled blackly and continued as though MacGregor's interruption had never taken place. 'Motive for suicide. His private life?'

MacGregor shook his head. 'Not that girl anyhow, sir. Somebody might swing for her but nobody'd commit suicide over her – not unless they were completely crackers.'

'Which Cochran, as far as we can judge, wasn't. Well, what about his fellow coppers? He wasn't popular at the station, you know. The Chief Constable might be right. They might have all ganged up on him and given him hell till they drove him to it.'

MacGregor shook his head even more firmly. Not without justification he considered himself an expert on what would or would not drive a young policeman to take his own life. 'He could have told his uncle, sir, or,' MacGregor grew starry-eyed, 'asked for a transfer. The Chief Constable's nephew; why he could have pulled every string in the book.'

'Well, that just leaves us with something to do with his work. But even if he'd stumbled on to something that was pure dynamite, I still don't see why he should kill himself. If he'd been bumped off – well, that'd make some sort of sense, wouldn't it?'

'You don't think there's any tie-up with this Hamilton business then, sir?'

Dover pursed his tiny rosebud mouth and wrinkled his little black moustache. 'Well, it's odd, and so's Cochran's suicide. I'm buggered if I can see any other connection. Damn it, Hamilton wasn't even killed.'

'Suppose it was a gang of some sort, sir,' – MacGregor had not wasted the entire afternoon – 'and they meant to kill him for revenge or something. Well, before they can, he has this attack and dies, so they just go on and mutilate the body and dump it in his front garden as an awful warning.'

'To who?' asked Dover sceptically. 'That stupid old cow, Mrs Hamilton?'

'Maybe to Cochran, sir. They were friends, you know.'

'Garn! Who says so? Only that old sponger of a station sergeant and he's probably talking through the back of his fat head. Still,' – Dover scratched his jaw – 'you may be right about somebody intending to croak Hamilton and he thwarted 'em by dropping down dead. Not that that gets us much further.'

'The two men in the green van, sir?'

'You don't think that sodden old biddy could see a barn door across the room, do you?'

'She told a very coherent story, sir, and she's stuck to it. I checked her original statement in the file. As far as I can tell it's word for word exactly the same as the one she told us.'

Dover blinked. 'Is it really?'

'Yes, sir.'

Dover moved his bulk uneasily in his chair. 'By the way,' he asked with elaborate casualness, 'do you know if that Doughty woman is a member of this blooming Ladies League or whatever it is?'

'Oh yes, definitely, sir. She'd got one of those blue bows pinned on her kimono.' MacGregor regarded Dover suspiciously. 'Why did you ask, sir?'

'Oh, just wondering.' Dover gazed with interest at the ceiling. 'Just that they seem thicker on the ground in this godforsaken town than leaves in autumn. That animal doctor woman is one. So's her girlfriend assistant. Those two women who damned near killed me with their first aid are. So's Miss Doughty, and Cochran's landlady. There can't be much that goes on in this town that they don't know about.'

MacGregor yawned. 'That's what the station sergeant said, sir. He said they practically run the place. No wonder it's not exactly jumping with life.'

'There must be *something* to do somewhere,' complained Dover, scratching his stomach this time. 'Here, didn't Hamilton spend his last evening in some night-club or other?'

'Yes, sir, the Wallerton, er, Country Club, I think, though it doesn't sound very likely, does it?'

'It sounds a damned sight better than here,' said Dover, hauling himself to his feet. 'Come on!'

'Where are we going, sir?'

'To this Club, you damned fool! Where else?'

'Now, sir?'

'Well, not if you're too worn out with your exertions, of course,' said Dover caustically. 'We don't want to overtire you.'

'Oh no, sir, I'm all for it,' said MacGregor, not considering it politic to point out that if anybody dragged their feet in the partnership it wasn't him.

'Good,' said Dover, sitting down again. 'Well, you go and phone for a taxi and then nip upstairs for my hat and coat.' He settled back in his chair and closed his eyes. 'Tell me when you're ready.'

When the taxi dropped the two detectives outside the Wallerton Country Club their hopes for a gay evening took a severe battering.

'Where the hell is it?' demanded Dover crossly.

MacGregor peered round. The taxi had abandoned them in an insalubrious part of Wallerton. They seemed to be surrounded by decrepit garages, untidy builders' yards and mouldering warehouses. The street lights were few and far between, and a cat ran squawking out from under MacGregor's feet as he picked his way through old cabbage leaves and broken bricks towards a partially open doorway. The yellow light which oozed through the crack was just sufficient to allow him to read the shoddy, handwritten board hanging on the door.

'I think this is it, sir!' he called to Dover.

Dover, limping markedly to emphasize the inconvenience he was patiently suffering, groped across the street to join his sergeant. 'You're joking, of course,' he observed in his surliest tone.

'Oh no, sir. This is it, I'm afraid.'

'Wallerton *Country* Club,' said Dover firmly. 'Wallerton *Country* Club, that's what you said.' He surveyed the masses of brick and concrete which hemmed them in. 'This isn't what I call a country club.'

'It isn't what I call a country club, either, sir,' MacGregor pointed out with commendable patience. 'But I'm afraid this is it. Are we going in?'

'Might as well,' said Dover gloomily. 'Oh no, laddie,' – as MacGregor pushed the door open and stood back politely – 'after *you*.'

MacGregor imperceptibly shrugged his shoulders and stepped across the threshold. Somewhat to Dover's disappointment nobody smacked him across the head with a pick-axe handle or inserted a flick-knife between his ribs.

MacGregor found himself in a small square entrance hall. The floor was not only uncarpeted but unswept as well and the walls were blank slabs of concrete relieved only by some illegible graffitti. In the right hand wall was a minute lift, its ornate bronze gates blackened with dirt and dust. MacGregor, urged to proceed further by the toe of Dover's boot scraping down his heel, took another step.

'And what do you want?'

The hoarse, unfriendly voice had come from the dim recess on the right, an area of Stygian shades partially concealed by the opening door. Hesitantly MacGregor moved forward and peered into the gloom.

An enormously fat man, sitting on a kitchen chair in the corner, sullenly returned his gaze. Apart from the fact that the fat man was completely bald, was tieless and collarless and had a pair of old white tennis shoes on his feet, there was nothing especially remarkable about his appearance.

'Er, good evening,' said MacGregor, uncomfortably aware that the smile that had the old ladies swooning was going to get him nowhere here.

'What do you want?' repeated the fat man with an asthmatic wheeze.

'The Wallerton Country Club?'

'You a member?' said the fat man, hardly moving his lips as he spoke. He appeared to be conserving his energy for more strenuous exertions, like breathing.

'Well, not exactly,' began MacGregor. Dover, having judged that there was going to be no violence, elbowed him aside.

The fat man registered the new arrival with the faintest jerk of his head. 'Cops,' he remarked and for a moment seemed as though he was going to follow this condemnation with the traditional expectoration. However, he refrained, apparently thinking that it wasn't worth the effort. Instead he turned ponderously to his right, raised a heavy hand and, before either MacGregor or Dover had realized what he was doing, slowly pressed a bell push in the wall three times.

With a glint of satisfaction in his eyes, he waited for the detectives to make the next move.

Dover scowled furiously at him. 'Where the hell is this club?' he asked. It always put him in a bad temper to see other people sitting when he had to stand.

'Upstairs,' said the fat man. 'Fifth floor.'

Dover stared suspiciously around the entrance hall. 'And I suppose that lift is the only way of getting there?'

' 'Sright.' The fat man seemed quite pleased that Dover was appreciating the situation. 'And the lift stays up on the top floor until I rings for it to come down. Very slow it is, that lift. Takes three minutes to come down and four to go up. You'd hardly credit it, would you?' He paused. 'That is, if it doesn't break down.'

'There must be some other way up,' put in MacGregor officiously. 'What about the fire regulations?'

The fat man turned a bored eye on him. 'Staircase. Round the back. Always kept locked. Well, you've got to in this neighbourhood, haven't you? You open it by pushing one of them bar things down, from the inside of course. The fire officer was quite satisfied with it.'

'Well, nobody's going to raid you in a hurry, are they?' said Dover truculently.

'No,' agreed the fat man easily, glad to have things on a clear footing, 'they're not.'

'Look,' said Dover, who'd had more than enough of standing

there like a proper lemon, 'do we look like a flaming police raid?'

'No,' said the fat man with the merest hint of a smile, 'who says you was?'

'You rung that warning bell, didn't you?'

'Just to let the manager know we'd got a couple of new arrivals, so's he send the lift down.'

'Oh,' scoffed Dover, 'I suppose you ring in just the same way for a couple of ordinary customers? I wasn't born yesterday, you know.'

'Neither,' said the fat man amiably, 'was I.'

A remark did nothing to improve Dover's temper during the lengthy wait which followed until, accompanied by strange clankings, the lift finally came trundling down.

'Go ahead,' said the fat man. 'It's all yours.'

Dover and MacGregor, with some difficulty, inserted themselves into the lift and stood stomach to stomach as it slowly and uncertainly laboured upwards.

'Quite a clever set-up,' observed MacGregor, feeling obliged to help pass the time with a bit of idle chatter.

Dover blew disgustedly down his nose. MacGregor turned his head to one side.

'Well, there's one consolation, sir,' – MacGregor resumed with a policeman's optimism – 'they must have got something to hide. They've had time to sweep all the vice in Soho under the carpet by now.'

Dover regarded his sergeant as best he could in the dim light. 'Why don't you belt up?' he asked wearily.

The manager himself was waiting to greet them when they emerged on the top floor. His wizened little face glowed with pleasure as Dover forced his way, at MacGregor's expense, out of the cage.

'Well, if it isn't Chief Inspector Dover! That's a bit of a turn-up for the books, I must say! And here was me expecting some of those crummy flatties they've got the nerve to call coppers round here. Come along in, sir! Drinks are on the house.'

He led the way down a shabby corridor with Dover lumbering behind him. Half way down he spoke to the Chief Inspector over his shoulder in a low voice. 'That your side-kick, is it, sir? Cor, strike a light. We'd have eaten two of him before breakfast in the old days.'

These were precisely Dover's sentiments but he was too busy trying to place the little manager to waste his time running down modern-day policemen. He still hadn't succeeded when he found himself ensconced at a corner table with a double whisky in front of him.

'Drop of the real stuff,' the little manager assured him as he slid on to the bench next to Dover. 'Out of my own bottle. Well, here's to crime!' He chuckled uproariously and dug Dover in the ribs.

With a glum face Dover took a tentative sip of his whisky. It was all right. With a sigh he examined the room in which he now found himself. It was dimly lit, that goes without saying. Each table had its own small table lamp with a thick imitation parchment shade. There was no other lighting except for a couple of milkily glowing signs reading, respectively, Cocks and Hens. There were, perhaps, a dozen people scattered around. Ten of them were girls and two were waiters, dressed vaguely as farmer's boys, and they all had their eyes fixed in an unwinking stare on Dover and his two companions. No doubt the clientele proper had diplomatically withdrawn by the back stairs some time ago.

'It's a bit early yet,' explained the manager helpfully. 'Things liven up later on.'

'So I should hope,' said Dover. 'Looks like a vicarage tea-party at the moment.'

The little manager laughed and laughed until the tears rolled down his cheeks. 'Oh, you're a one, you are, Mr Dover!' he guffawed, smacking the table with the palm of his hand. 'He doesn't change much, does he?' he asked MacGregor. 'Still the same old ba ... ' He interrupted himself just in time with a fit of coughing.

'You've met the Chief Inspector before then?' asked MacGregor.

'Met him?' The little manager roared with laughter again. 'I'll say I've met him, the old ... bogie! Why, if I'd a quid for every time he'd run me in I'd be sitting on my backside in the South of France by now, straight I would. Here, Mr Dover, sir, how about introducing us?'

Dover, conscious that his image was going to take severe hammering if he didn't look smart, thought quickly. 'I would,' he said, 'if I knew what name you were using these days.'

They nearly had to retrieve the little manager from under the table after this witticism. Still spluttering with flattering mirth and mopping his eyes, he performed the introductions himself.

'Joey the Jock,' he said, extending a tiny brown paw across the table. 'Otherwise Joseph Aloysius O'Daley, but you can call me Joey.'

'Sergeant MacGregor,' said MacGregor in his turn, shaking Joey's hand.

Joey the Jock? Dover sighed. Could be Evans the Post for all he knew, or cared. He finished his whisky.

'You've not changed much, Mr Dover, sir,' said Joey, smiling to show that the observation was meant to be complimentary.

Dover sniffed.

'I was wondering if you'd still recognize me,' said Joey, 'after all these years.'

'Never forget a face,' said Dover solemnly. 'You can't afford to in my job.'

'I heard you was in town,' said Joey, signalling for more drinks.

'Did you?' said Dover.

'Come about Hamilton, have you?' said Joey idly, handing round his cigarette case.

'Hamilton?' said Dover, wondering what the dickens they were talking about now.

His reply sent Joey off again. Sobbing with laughter, he even rested his head on the table to relieve his aching sides. Dover regarded the heaving shoulders with distaste while MacGregor smiled wisely as though he knew what it was all about. The ten girls and the two waiters just looked.

'Well,' said Joey when he had at last recovered his powers of speech, 'that's what he was known as when he come to live up here. After all, even in Wallerton, you can't go around calling yourself Sunny Malone and not expect the neighbours to look at you sideways, can you?'

'Sunny Malone?' MacGregor looked at Dover for guidance and explanation.

'Bit before your time, Sergeant,' said Joey kindly. 'Though I don't doubt you'll have heard of him. He was one of the first of the big boys, just after the war. He'd got Barking and Dagenham and Ilford tied up so tight you couldn't change your mind without paying him his percentage.'

'Oh, yes.' MacGregor nodded his head. 'I think I've heard of him. Protection racket.'

'That's the boyo!' said Joey with approval. 'You're not as thickheaded as I thought you was. Damn sight brighter than the local flatties, at any rate. They still don't know who Hamilton really was – not unless you've told 'em, Mr Dover.'

Very portentously Dover shook his head. If there was one sure thing amongst all these shifting sands it was that he had not revealed to the local police the true and notorious identity of the late Mr Hamilton.

'How *did* you spot him, Mr Dover?' asked Joey, not a man who could leave well alone.

Dover scowled at him reproachfully. 'Professional secret,' he said lamely.

'Garn!' laughed Joey. 'Now pull the other one! It'd be a photograph, wouldn't it? Ah, I thought so. They showed you a photograph of the corpus derelictus and you recognized it. That's what comes from having a trained mind.'

'I pride myself,' said Dover, putting a bold front on it, 'on never forgetting a face. Or a name.'

MacGregor choked over his whisky.

'Don't I know it!' chuckled Joey with rueful appreciation. 'What do you think made me tuck myself away in Wallerton?' he asked MacGregor. 'Because your Chief Inspector made things too flaming hot for me in the Smoke, that's why! Eyes like a hawk, he had, and him hardly dry behind the ears in those days. Taking the bread out of my mouth, that's what he was doing.'

MacGregor, now thoroughly bemused, looked somewhat incredulously at Dover and then, receiving no enlightenment there, directed his gaze back to Joey. Joey beamed at him. There was some justification for MacGregor's scepticism. Joey the Jock may have been motivated by fulsome flattery or it may have been that he just had a bad memory; whichever way it was his rosy picture of Dover as a keen young cop was totally erroneous.

MacGregor, in any case, had no stomach for sitting there patiently while Dover's praises were being sung, and he redirected the conversation rapidly. 'Why did Hamilton leave London in the first place?' he asked.

Joey shrugged his shoulders. 'He got like a lot of us, old and fat and lazy.' It was a pure coincidence that he was looking at Dover when he made this remark. 'The Tallahassee Brothers moved in. You remember that mob, Mr Dover? Nasty lot, they were. Sunny Malone could see the writing on the wall same as anybody else. If he'd hung around and argued the toss he'd have been lucky to get away with a chiving. And they'd have carved up his missus, too, soon as look at her.'

'Chiving?' said MacGregor, suddenly becoming very alert and watchful. He glanced at Dover to see if that master mind had got the point. The Chief Inspector, however, was fully occupied in gazing fixedly at his glass, which happened to be empty again.

'Not half,' said Joey. 'There were terrors with a razor, those Tallahassee lads. Some of the things they did was horrible, proper horrible.'

'Where are they now?' demanded MacGregor, leaning steely-eyed across the table.

'Search me, mate! Laying flat on their backs with a tombstone on their chests, I hope!'

'Hamilton,' said MacGregor, 'this Sunny Malone, what was he doing in Wallerton?'

Joey looked uneasy. 'I told you. He retired. Come up here to live quiet on his ill-gotten gains.' He managed an unconvincing laugh.

'Come on,' snorted MacGregor, 'don't give me that! He was back on the old game, wasn't he? Back on the protection racket?'

Joey shifted about in his seat and looked appealingly at Dover. Dover pushed his still empty whisky glass idly round the table.

'Aw, come off it,' said Joey, eyeing MacGregor warily. 'Give a fellow a chance.'

'Perhaps you'd like to tell me about it, Joey,' said Dover, coming at last to the rescue. 'Just the two of us.'

'That's right, Mr Dover,' said Joey eagerly, and mopped his brow. 'I don't mind doing a bit of singing, for old time's sake as you might say, but I don't want to give a blooming recital.'

'Quite,' agreed Dover smugly.

'Here, Alicia!' Joey bawled across the room to a bored-looking girl sitting by herself at one of the tables. 'There's a gentleman here I want you to look after, a special friend.'

Alicia's jaws were moving slowly up and down. She broke the rhythm momentarily and swivelled her eyes questioningly in the direction of a small door in the wall behind her.

'No, you stupid cow!' hissed Joey. 'In here.' He smiled invitingly at MacGregor. 'Why don't you go and have a nice, cosy little chat with Alicia, eh? You'll like her. She's a nice girl. Been in the nick a couple of times, too, so you'll have something in common. And, just a word of warning, Sergeant,' he added as a very reluctant MacGregor got to his feet, 'keep your hands on your wallet, eh?'

Chapter Eight

WITH MacGregor out of the way being entertained by the fair Alicia, Joey the Jock looked happier. He ordered Dover another drink and slid up closer to him on the bench.

'They're not the same, these young 'uns, are they?' he remarked sorrowfully. 'You want a bit of give and take in your job, don't you, Mr Dover? Helps to make the wheels go round, if you see what I mean.' He shook his head. 'But these young 'uns, they don't have no idea of what I call compromise. You scratch my back and I'll scratch yours. Why, in the old days, back in London, I could have named you a score of coppers who were – well – accommodating. Not bent, mark you, but what you might call short-sighted. And it paid off for them, too. We didn't forget 'em, oh dear me, no! There's a good few of you high and mighty bogies up at the Yard who wouldn't be where you were today if it hadn't been for a bit of a helping hand from the likes of me. Not that I've ever been one to grass, but – well – if somebody scratches my back I don't mind, once in a while, scratching his.'

'Quite,' said Dover, mildly irritated to find that he had Joey the Jock practically sitting on his lap. Confidential conversations were all very well but there was a limit. He shoved Joey off a couple of inches and got down to business. 'What about Hamilton?'

'You won't forget it was me what told you?' asked Joey anxiously.

'I won't forget.'

'Well, Hamilton – I soon got used to calling him that, especially seeing as how he told me what he'd do to me if I ever so much as breathed his real name – he come up here to retire, really. He'd made his packet and things had got too rough even for him up in the Smoke, so he thought he'd call it a day. He opened up this garage place because, of course, he'd got to account for his money somehow and – well – second-hand cars, who's to know? A kid of two could fiddle it. But he was a right bent bastard, Hamilton was. He couldn't have kept off it even if he'd had a million quid a week coming in. First he tries a bit of dealing in stolen cars, but that's a dicey business, especially in a town like Wallerton where they've nothing else to do except poke their noses into other people's business. Then, oh, it'll be a year or more ago now, he finds the perfect answer. He starts going in for the money-lending business. Not in a regular way, of course. He didn't deal with what you might call the suckers. No, he was smart. He lent money to crooks.'

Joey took a quick glance at Dover's face to see if all this was sinking in. It was hard to tell. The Chief Inspector's eyes were half open and every now and again he raised his glass to his lips. These were the only signs of life or interest. Joey frowned. He felt, reasonably enough, that he was entitled to more appreciation than this.

'He lent money to crooks,' he repeated and edged a bit closer. 'Dead clever, that was. He'd got plenty of spare cash kicking around, more than he knew what to do with, really. And the risks was negligent. Some bright boy comes along with a nice little plan for doing a pay roll job or robbing a bank or something. He'd explain it all to Hamilton, and get the benefit of his expert advice for free, by the way, and if Hamilton liked the look of it, he'd stake him. Lend him up to a couple of thou' or so for incidental expenses. When the job's done, back comes the wide boy and pays back the loan, with interest. And that wasn't peanuts. Never less than a hundred per cent and sometimes a hell of a lot more. Always in cash, too.' Joey appealed somewhat desperately to Dover. 'It was a damned good racket, wasn't it? Clever?'

Dover sighed. 'Suppose somebody gypped him? Cleared off without paying the loan back, or the interest?'

Joey looked at Dover with surprise. 'We're not all crooked, Mr Dover,' he declared with dignity. 'Besides, Hamilton was dead careful. He wouldn't have no truck with all these long-haired young tearaways that bash old ladies up for a handful of small change and a pension book. He stuck to the professionals. People who'd got a bit of a reputation to keep up and who you could trust. And, anyhow, Hamilton had the whip hand, didn't he? He knew all about the job, see? Right down to the last detail. If anybody crossed him up he could tip the rozzers off and get the whole lot nicked as easy as pie. And he was as safe as houses, wasn't he? It's no bleeding crime to lend a few quid to a pal who's down on his uppers, is it? You don't know he's going to buy a couple of yards of jelly with it, now do you?'

Dover grunted. He was getting fed up. The seat was hard and the atmosphere, in spite of the lack of customers, smokey. He yawned widely. If this was Wallerton's idea of a wicked and dissolute evening out, you could keep it! He, Dover, was ready for bed. He yawned again. Joey the Jock looked at him in awe. Dover's yawns were enough to strike terror into the hearts of bolder men.

'Ahduyecominit?' said Dover, as his dentures came together with a resounding click.

'Eh?'

Dover regarded Joey wearily. Why was it that he always had to deal with the fools and morons of this world? 'I said,' he repeated slowly, 'how do you come in it?'

'How do I come in what?' asked Joey, retreating smartly into thickheadedness.

Dover glowered at him. 'Well, you weren't Hamilton's probation officer or father confessor, were you?'

'No,' admitted Joey cautiously, 'I wasn't.'

'For God's sake!' snarled Dover with mounting irritation. 'I don't have to spell it out for you, do I?'

'Well,' said Joey, trying to play it nonchalantly, 'me, I was just a bystander, see? An innocent bystander. I retired up here about the time Hamilton was starting up this new racket. Arthritis it was, in my hands. Well, in my line of business it was the kiss of death, wasn't it? Well, I decided to open this club, see? And that was an up-and-a-downer, if you like, but in the end I got my licence. Well, who turns up as one of my first bleeding customers but Sunny bleeding Malone. You could have knocked me down with a sledge-hammer. I knew him all right, and he knew me. I told him I was strictly on the level these days and he says so was he. All he wanted was somewhere quiet to meet his friends. Well, you know who his friends was. Before long, when Hamilton's reputation had got around, I'd every villain worthy of the name for a couple of hundred miles around dropping in for a double Scotch and a quiet chit-chat with Hamilton. There was nothing I could do about it even if I wanted to. And why should I? They was all fully paid-up members, they weren't breaking the law and they were good for trade. Most of my local customers come along in the afternoons, see, during office hours. They don't have to make up any cock and bull stories for their wives, see, like what they would have to do if they come in the evenings. Hamilton's cronies used to come at night. Well,' – Joey waved a disgruntled hand – 'you can see what it's like now they don't come. Like a bleeding cemetery!'

'Oh?' said Dover, inspecting the club morosely in his turn. The girls and the waiters stared reproachfully back at him through the gloom. Even MacGregor broke off the animated conversation he was having with Alicia to look questioningly at his lord and master. 'I thought I was responsible for the falling off in trade.'

Sorrowfully Joey shook his head. 'No, not really. There wasn't more than a couple here when you turned up. We let 'em out the back way, same as usual. And I'll dare bet Fred downstairs hasn't turned away more than three of them since you've been here.'

'Why turn 'em away?' asked Dover. 'It all looks harmless enough to me.'

Joey winked and grinned broadly. 'Ah well, there's maybe a bit more than meets the eye, Mr Dover. I don't keep a dozen of Fluffy Chicks sitting around just to look pretty, you know.'

'Fluffy Chicks?'

'I couldn't have Rabbits,' explained Joey bitterly. 'Something about fringing some bleeding copyright. So I made 'em Fluffy Chicks. Hadn't you noticed? They're all dressed up in chicken costumes and bleeding expensive they were, too.'

Dover peered round. 'Oh, yes,' he said doubtfully, 'I see.'

'Of course,' Joey rested his chin on his hands, 'those Bunny girls, they have all sorts of funny rules about them. Treat 'em more like they was Vestry Virgins than flipping tarts what's there to take your mind off the bill. I don't have any of that sort of nonsense here. Besides, if you ask me, I think it's nasty – all those girls with fishnet tights and cleavage just for looking at. What sort of bleeding degenerates do they get there anyhow? It wouldn't do for my customers, I can tell you. Whatever else they are, they have got red blood in their veins.'

Dover sighed. Neither Bunnies nor Fluffy Chicks sparked off a flicker of interest in him. The bench on which he was sitting was beginning to make its presence felt, even through the ample layers of flesh which protected the relevent part of Dover's anatomy. It is highly possible that he would have chucked it in there and then if yet another dully glowing glass of whisky had not appeared before him. With the air of one sacrificing himself for the cause he picked up the glass. 'What about Cochran?' he asked. It was as good a way of passing the time as any.

Joey the Jock was showing signs of restlessness, too. It's one thing to give the cops a warm welcome when they call, but quite another to go pouring drink down their fat throats for hours on end. And this podgy old slob wasn't the world's brightest conversationalist by a long chalk.

'Cochran?' said Joey. 'That young flatfoot? Here, there's a story going round that he jumped off Cully Point. That's a turn up for the book, eh? Last person in the world I'd have thought would have done anything like that. What did he do it for? Suffering from some incurable disease, was he? Mind you, I can think of a couple that young fellow-me-lad could have picked up, but you can get treatment for 'em these days and it's quite confidential.'

Dover eyed Joey the Jock with some amazement. Out of the mouth of fools, he thought, ... still, it was an idea and one, as it happened, that had not occurred either to himself or to Clever Boots MacGregor. An incurable disease? Yes, that would be a nice tidy solution which should satisfy everybody. He must get MacGregor to follow it up. No, on second thoughts, since it looked like being the most productive line so far, he'd follow it up himself and let the credit fall where it was due – on his worthy shoulders.

'Did Cochran look as though he was ill?' he asked Joey.

Joey shook his head. 'No, fit as a fiddle and twice as lively as a cricket the last time I saw him.'

'And when was that?'

Joey wrinkled his brow in thought. 'Oh, I suppose about ten days or a fortnight ago. I forget now. He was in here one night, semi-official like, asking about Hamilton. Same as you're doing, Mr Dover,' added Joey with a chuckle. 'You'd better look out! Or keep away from Cully Point!'

'And what did you tell him about Hamilton?'

'Nothing that he didn't already know. Hamilton was in here most nights, used to have a few drinks, do a bit of business, you know, have a chat, as you might say, with one of the girls.' Joey winked and dug Dover slyly in the ribs. 'I've got a couple of private rooms round the back if you ... No? Oh well, suit yourself. Well, this last night before he died Hamilton was in here about the same time. I think he was expecting to meet somebody but they didn't turn up. Not that there was anything unusual in that. It often happened. Anyhow, Hamilton sat around drinking until about half past midnight. Then he decided to call it a day and asked me to get a taxi for him. He'd done it once or twice before. He'd pick up his own car again in the morning. I rang up for a cab and off he went and that was the last I saw of him.'

'Was Cochran in the Club that night?'

'Well, I don't really remember ... no, I don't think he was. He'd have been sitting with Hamilton if he had been and I'd have remembered that.'

'Were they in this money-lending business together?'

Joey opened his eyes very wide and made a comical show of being shocked. 'What are you suggesting, Mr Dover, and him a policeman! No, him and Hamilton were pretty thick but that was social, not business. They were both bits of devils where the girls were concerned, but that's as far as it went. Besides, Hamilton wouldn't have shared a crust of bread with a starving kid, never mind split a lucrative little racket like the one he'd worked up with somebody like Cochran, who'd no capital to put up. Mind you, I was beginning to wonder if perhaps Cochran was going to try and muscle in. He'd have been a tough proposition to hold off if he had. He must have known quite a lot about Hamilton and his little games.'

'Did Cochran come here often?'

'To the Club? A fair amount. He was a member, of course. I wasn't too keen at first on having a bleeding flattie hanging around the place, but after a bit I realized he was keeping his mouth shut even if his eyes was open. Besides, what with one thing and another I reckoned I'd got as much on him as he had on me.' Joey's eyes twinkled. 'There are limits, you know, about how far a policeman's supposed to go in the line of duty and young Cochran went way, way beyond 'em. You ask any of my girls.'

At this point in the conversation one of the waiters came up to Joey and whispered confidentially in his ear.

Joey listened and looked annoyed. 'Hell's bells!' he complained. 'Not that old fool again! I told him last time he was getting past it.'

'Shall I get a doctor?' murmured the waiter.

'Christ, no!' said Joey. 'I'll come and sort it out. I'm sorry, Mr Dover, there's a bit of trouble in the kitchen. Still, I don't think there's anything more I can tell you, so if you'll excuse me ... You can find your own way out, can't you?'

Joey hurried off. MacGregor, who had been watching impatiently, abandoned his Fluffy Chick to come and join Dover.

'Any luck, sir?'

'Hamilton was financing bank robbers and the like in return for a share in the loot. He used to meet his clients here. It looks as though young Cochran had a pretty shrewd idea about what was going on, but what's-his-name doesn't think he was in on it. Not yet, anyhow.'

MacGregor whistled silently. 'Gosh, sir, that looks promising, doesn't it?'

'Does it?' said Dover unenthusiastically.

'Well, yes, sir! It all ties up with what we thought before. Suppose Hamilton got mixed up with a bunch of really tough crooks and they had it in for him over something. Maybe he shopped them or cheated them. They decide to beat him up, perhaps, or even kill him, but he dies first. So they dump his body as a sort of awful warning. Then Cochran starts nosing around, his motive doesn't matter, finds out who's responsible for the Hamilton business so they fix him, too ... '

'Look,' said Dover, 'for the umpteenth time – nobody *fixed* Cochran. He committed suicide. Damn it, I was there! Do you think I wouldn't have noticed a gang of murderers up on Cully Point? I'm not blind, laddie. Besides, my wife – blast her – actually saw Cochran with her own eyes climb over the railings and jump. There was nobody else around for miles.'

'But, sir,' began MacGregor, eager to propound all three of the theories he had dreamed up to explain this little difficulty, 'suppose ...'

He missed his chance. Two of the dumber Fluffy Chicks came swaying over to the table and sat down. It was a purely reflex action, triggered off by the sight of a couple of unaccompanied men. Both Chicks had been told that these men were detectives but the information had either not sunk in or had long ago seeped out. As Joey himself would have been the first to claim, he didn't choose his girls for their brains.

'Are you going to buy us a drink, dearie?' asked the blonde Chick, slipping a befeathered arm round Dover's neck and ruining what could have been a beautiful friendship by her thoughtless question.

'Hop it!' said Dover bluntly.

MacGregor unwound his Chick, a brunette with greedy eyes and clutching hands, and tried to push her away.

But the Chicks had their living to earn and knew only too well that maidenly modesty got you nowhere. They settled themselves down resolutely, smoothed their feathers and reiterated their demands for liquid refreshment. The blonde Chick even took a sip out of Dover's glass to show that she was serious.

'Ooh!' she chirped. 'That's a drop of the real stuff! We'll have four more just like that, Ernie!'

The waiter, who had materialized out of the darkness said, 'Very good, sir!' and scuttled away before Dover could stop him.

MacGregor, sensing that he was going to get the blame for all this, tried to reassure his pouting superior. 'We shan't get rid of them without buying them a drink, sir.'

'We shan't get rid of them by buying them one, either,' retorted Dover sourly as the waiter appeared flourishing a tray with four glasses on it.

'Thirty-seven and six, sir,' he said calmly as he put the drinks down on the table.

Dover came within an inch of breaking a blood vessel. 'What is it?' he spluttered. 'Molten gold?'

'We call 'em the Kiss of Death, sir. One of our specialities.'

MacGregor reached resignedly for his wallet, but the Chief Inspector stopped him.
'They're on the house,' he said. 'We're guests of the manager.'
'First I've heard of it,' said the waiter, beginning to get nasty. 'Thirty-seven and six, service not included.'
'We can't buy drinks,' Dover pointedly out triumphantly. 'We're not members. It's against the law.'
Silently the waiter fished in his pocket and produced two small, plastic-covered cards. He placed them carefully on the table. 'You've been made honorary members, sir. Compliments of the management. Thirty-seven and six.'
Stupefied Dover accepted defeat and permitted MacGregor to settle their account.
The two Fluffy Chicks had watched the proceedings with interest.
'Drink up, Syb,' said the blonde one who now realized she had made a bad mistake in choosing Dover. 'There's no more where this one came from. I don't know where the real gentlemen have got to these days, honest I don't.'
The brunette Chick was not quite so pessimistic. She, after all, had got the dashing MacGregor who was beginning to repulse her advances with diminishing vigour. If only they could get rid of that fat old devil, and the blonde Chick, the whole evening might not yet be lost. 'You've got lovely eyes, dearie,' she said, nearly gouging one out with the artificial beak perched on top of her head as she advanced her face to the sergeant's. 'Did anybody ever tell you you've got lovely eyes?'
MacGregor lowered them bashfully to the table, Dover's presence inhibiting an otherwise rather polished technique.
'An't he got lovely eyes, Peg?' demanded the brunette Chick, feeling that her opening gambit was too good to abandon.
'Smashin',' agreed her companion, busily trying to extract a quill which was piercing painfully through her down-covered brassière.
'D'you know,' said the brunette Chick thoughtfully, 'he's got eyes just like Chauncey, when you come to look at 'em close.'
'Oh, Chauncey!' said the blonde Chick in disparaging tones.
This idle remark evidently re-festered an old sore. The brunette Chick grew quite annoyed. 'Yes, Chauncey!' she re-

peated, sitting very upright and fluffing out her feathers. 'And what's wrong with Chauncey, may I ask?'

'Oh, nothing! 'Cept he seems to have had the good taste to drop you like a hot brick.'

'You mangy old cat! Just because he's not been in for a night or two, there's no call for you to go venting your spite.'

'Just a night or two!' The blonde Chick let fly with a raucous shriek of laughter. 'He's not been in for months and well you know it! That's what comes of trying to keep a fellow all to yourself, dearie. He gets dead bored with you!'

The brunette Chick, predictably, refuted this unkind observation and proceeded to counter-attack with a few barbed criticisms concerning a certain Charlie. Before long both ladies were swopping insults with gusto and imagination.

MacGregor switched off completely and passed the time thinking his own dark thoughts, but in the recesses of Dover's mind a nebulous something had been nudged into wakefulness. In a lesser man, or in a lesser detective, the matter might have been ignored and the hazy memory that the name Chauncey had been heard before would have been allowed to sink back into the morass. But Chief Inspector Dover, for motives which remain obscure but were certainly inspired, decided to pursue the problem.

He interrupted the Chicks. 'Who's Chauncey?' he demanded.

The Chicks, who had left Chauncey a good five minutes altercation behind, gaped at him open-beaked.

'Chauncey?' repeated the brunette Chick, suddenly on her guard. 'Chauncey? Oh, he's a chap I know. One of the members, as a matter of fact.' She exchanged a warning glance with the blonde Chick and, tossing off the remains of their drinks, they both prepared to take their leave.

'Sit down!' growled Dover, his mind rootling away to unearth where he had heard the name Chauncey before. 'Is Chauncey his Christian name?'

The brunette Chick nodded.

'What's his surname?'

The brunette Chick smiled brightly. 'I'm afraid I'm not allowed to tell members the name of other members. You'll have to ask the manager.'

'I'm asking you,' said Dover heavily and menacingly. 'Don't start trying to make things difficult for yourself.'

'Oh, tell him, for gawd's sake!' advised the blonde Chick who had a wide experience of policemen turning nasty on you.

'Why don't you tell him?' her friend asked. 'You know his name as well as I do.'

'Because he wasn't *my* fancy man, that's why!' the blonde Chick retorted haughtily, preening a feather or two on her scanty costume.

'Come on!' said Dover in a voice that indicated his meagre supply of patience was running out.

'It's Davenport,' the brunette chick said, 'Chauncey Theobald Davenport, if you must know.'

'And she can give you a description of his birth marks if you want,' added her sister Chick unkindly.

Dover's eyes crossed slightly as he concentrated. MacGregor, fearful that the old fool was on to something, watched him intently.

'Ah!' said Dover and smiled with an air of great satisfaction. 'Chauncey Davenport.'

It was the name of one of the two men who had been brought into the police station when Dover had been trying to report the suicide which his wife had so inconsiderately witnessed. He was the one in the striped underpants. The one without a sense of humour who had started the fight. The one who had refused, dramatically, to let the police surgeon examine his wounds.

'Ah!' said Dover again, with the express intention of mystifying MacGregor. In fact, if it hadn't been for the expression of frustrated fury on MacGregor's face, Dover might have let the matter drop there and then. Had he done so it is highly unlikely that the mystery of Constable Cochran's death would ever have been solved. From such small acorns great big oak trees grow.

'Hm,' said Dover, jutting his bottom lip out portentously. 'Very interesting,' he murmured and shot a glance at MacGregor to see how this was going down. Apparently it was going down very well. MacGregor was fidgetting impatiently and clearly dying to ask what it was all about. 'Hm,' said Dover again, wondering hard what he could say next.

The two Fluffy Chicks watched him suspiciously.

'This Chauncey what's-his-name,' Dover plunged in rashly, 'you say he's stopped, er, coming to the Club?'

The brunette Chick nodded her head unwillingly.

'When did he stop?'

'Oh, months and months ago,' chipped in the blonde Chick spitefully.

'He had a nervous breakdown.' The brunette Chick leapt to the defence of her lover. 'He went missing, you know, and lost his memory or something. Overwork, they said it was.'

'Ha, ha!' laughed the blonde sardonically. 'Well, that's a new name for it, I must say! The only work he ever did ...'

'Why don't you keep your trap shut?' snarled her friend. 'Just because he never took a fancy to you ...'

'Never took a fancy to me? I like that! He tried it on a good few times, I don't mind telling you, but I happen to have my standards. I can't stick these men who think that they've just got to jerk their heads at you and you'll come running. So, unlike you, dearie, and unlike every other cheap little tart, amateur or professional, in this god-forsaken town, I said no!'

Chapter Nine

MACGREGOR tried every means, subtle and crudely blunt, to find out what Chauncey Davenport and his amorous adventures had got to do with anything. He was so intent on this line of investigation that he completely forgot to ask why Dover hadn't told him about the true identity of Mr Hamilton. Dover, however, stubbornly refused to reveal all. This was partly due to sheer meanness and partly to the fact that the Chief Inspector really didn't know himself. He just had an ill-defined, cloudy sort of impression that there was some connection between Chauncey Davenport and Constable Cochran. They had both been members of the Country Club, of course, but it wasn't only that. What more it was, Dover grandly decided to think about on the morrow. He'd had a hard day and you never got any gratitude for flogging yourself to death.

It had been no later than half past eleven when Dover and MacGregor had left the Country Club, their Fluffy Chicks having fled the roost as soon as Dover had indicated that he had finished with them. The barman rang up for a taxi and barely concealed his astonishment when he received a mere fourpence for his trouble. Dover and MacGregor entered the lift and slowly descended to the ground floor. The doorman watched them leave in silence, contenting himself with making an obscene gesture of farewell to their departing backs.

In the taxi MacGregor took it upon himself to display some initiative in the partnership and asked the driver if he was the one who'd driven Hamilton home on that fatal night.

'No,' said the taxi-driver.

MacGregor asked him if he knew the man who had driven Hamilton.

'Yes,' said the taxi-driver.

'Does he work for the same firm?' asked MacGregor.

The taxi-driver became loquacious. 'He does.'

'What's his name?' MacGregor's usually excellent memory

had let him down and it was too dark in the car to read his notes.

From the darkness of the back seat came a scornful sniff. 'How to be a detective in ten easy lessons,' said Dover; sotto voce.

'Arthur Armstrong,' obliged the driver.

'Mate of yours, is he?'

'No.'

'Oh,' said MacGregor, wishing he'd never started the conversation. 'Is he on duty now?'

'No.'

'Well, what time does he come on then?'

'Midnight till eight in the morning.'

'I suppose we'd better leave it till tomorrow, sir.' MacGregor sank back in his seat.

'Leave what?' grunted Dover.

'Well, questioning the taxi-driver, sir. He's a very important witness. He was one of the last people to see Hamilton alive.'

'And good luck to him!' rumbled Dover.

'Shall we leave it till tomorrow then, sir?'

'Too right we shall,' said Dover sourly.

'You'll have to be early,' said the taxi-driver suddenly. 'He'll be in bed by nine, soon as he's had a meal.'

Dover groaned.

As things turned out it was after half past ten before MacGregor managed to get Dover, who had developed his limp again, to the cottage in which Arthur Armstrong lived.

The cottage looked poor but respectable and Dover sniffed contemptuously. He was more than a bit of a snob and was always resentful that none of the really juicy cases involving the aristocracy ever seemed to come his way. He would dearly have loved to put his feet up in some marble halls for a change. Still, he made an unaccustomed effort to look on the bright side, the down-trodden peasants who inhabited this modest cot might be good for a mid-morning cup of tea.

It was a woman who opened the door. She had a rosy-red face and was wiping her wet hands on her apron. She looked like a woman who had worked hard all her life and who would be completely lost if she hadn't got a duster or a scrubbing brush in her hand.

MacGregor's suave announcement that they were detectives from Scotland Yard threw her into considerable confusion.

'Oh dear, oh dear,' she kept muttering as she showed them into a tiny kitchen. Dover, as was his custom, headed straight for the most comfortable chair and dropped down heavily into it. He found himself a mere six inches away from a cheerful fire which was roaring up the chimney, but since they were enjoying yet another of Wallerton's blustery, bracing days, that was no disadvantage.

MacGregor seated himself at a small table covered with a green, bobble-trimmed, velvet tablecloth. Mrs Armstrong, she had confessed with resignation that she was Arthur's mother, stood and hovered. Worried as she evidently was, she still gave more than half her attention to a large saucepan bubbling dyspeptically on the gas stove.

'I can't understand it,' she said as much to herself as to anybody else, 'I can't understand it.' She darted across to the gas stove and raised the lid of the saucepan. 'They said he was cured. I mean, well, he's been all right for over a twelvemonth now, hasn't he?'

Dover looked at her with acute distaste and hooked a small stool forward to rest his injured foot on. A pile of old newspapers and magazines, which had been stacked on the stool, duly collapsed on to the floor and Mrs Armstrong, apologizing profusely, hurried to pick them up. Dover raised his eyebrows and scowled at a television sat standing in the corner. It was worth the examination. The entire set, with the exception of the tube, was swathed in a hand-knitted coverlet of red and blue wool. It was too much for the Chief Inspector. Composing his face into a sneer, he leaned back in his chair and closed his eyes.

Once again MacGregor shouldered the burden of the interrogation. He spoke loudly and clearly in an effort to wean Mrs Armstrong's attention away from her gas stove.

'We would like to ask your son a few questions about the night he drove Mr Hamilton home from the Country Club.'

Mrs Armstrong shot towards the kitchen table and grabbed a spoon out of the cutlery drawer. 'Oh, he wouldn't do anything like that to a man. I mean, it stands to reason, doesn't it?'

MacGregor took a grip on himself. 'You remember Mr Hamilton, don't you?' he asked slowly and carefully. 'The man whose dead body was found in his front garden about a month ago?'

'Oh yes?' said Mrs Armstrong distractedly.

'Your son drove him home that night.'

'Well, that's his job, him being a taxi-driver.'

MacGregor gave up. 'Is your son at home, Mrs Armstrong?'

Mrs Armstrong was now slicing potatoes at an incredible speed into her saucepan. 'Oh, yes.' She seemed grateful for a straight-forward question. 'He's upstairs in bed. Did you want to see him?'

'That was the idea, rather,' said MacGregor, lapsing into mild irony.

It was wasted on Mrs Armstrong. She concentrated on adding a generous helping of salt to whatever brew she was manufacturing and just didn't answer.

There was a mild grunt from Dover. MacGregor took it as a warning that somebody's patience was becoming exhausted.

'I would like to see your son, Mrs Armstrong.'

'Oh? Well, I should come back about three o'clock this afternoon then, if I was you, sir. He's usually up about then.'

There was a definite snort from Dover. MacGregor fixed Mrs Armstrong with a firm eye and eventually got through to her with the message that two high-ranking detectives from New Scotland Yard were not to be denied. Young Armstrong must be roused from his slumbers forthwith and brought downstairs.

Mrs Armstrong turned down the gas under her pan and, rather surprisingly mumbling something under her breath about the Gestapo, left the room.

There was a moment's silence. Dover opened his eyes and looked round. 'Been carted off in a plain van, has she?' he remarked pleasantly and closed his eyes again.

Five minutes went by. The cosy fire, the comfortable chair and the stuffy room did their work. Dover's mouth dropped open and his head lolled helplessly to one side. Even MacGregor was beginning to find it difficult to keep on the alert.

Suddenly there was the sound of voices from upstairs, then a yelp, then a series of heavy bumps, then a dull crash.

Mrs Armstrong opened the kitchen door. 'He's fallen downstairs again,' she said. 'I keep telling him to take his glasses upstairs to his bedroom with him but oh, no, he knows best. Lose his head, that boy would, if it was loose. Where did you leave 'em then?' she bawled over her shoulder. 'On the mantlepiece? Well, don't you move till I've got 'em for you. I don't want the whole place smashed to smithereens.' Pausing only to peep under the saucepan lid, she scurried across to the fireplace. Dover's propped up leg was barring the way. Mrs Armstrong thought she could reach without disturbing the Chief Inspector. She was wrong.

A detective's life is one of constant danger. To survive a man needs razor-sharp reactions. Chief Inspector Dover had been a detective for over twenty years. Some people, MacGregor for instance, might have thought that the old man's reflexes had got bogged down in the fat which draped his unshapely form. Some people would have been goggle-eyed, as MacGregor was, to see Dover's seventeen and a quarter stone leap dramatically out of the chair and fling itself on Mrs Armstrong before that poor woman could get so much as half a squawk of terror out.

The pair of them came crashing to the ground. In their progress they broke the stool and rocked the television set on its table. Mrs Armstrong put up a brave fight but she was no match for Dover. Bellowing ferociously he soon overcame her. Her struggles, her grievous cries for help, her shouts of rape, became weaker and fainter.

MacGregor managed to get Dover's hands off Mrs Armstrong's throat just in time. Somewhat dazed, the two combatants began to sort themselves out. Both were panting and dishevelled. Mindful of his priorities MacGregor helped his Chief Inspector back into his chair before turning to assist Mrs Armstrong. He was just disentangling her from the wreckage of the footstool and trying to get her on her feet when yet another figure appeared in the already overcrowded kitchen.

It was a young man, in pyjamas and with his hair standing up like a flue brush. He groped his way into the room and bumped into the kitchen table.

'Arthur!' screamed Mrs Armstrong, the prospect of yet more disaster acting on her like a tonic. 'Stay where you are!' She let go of MacGregor's supporting arm and smoothed down her apron. 'His glasses! He can't see a thing without his glasses.' She moved towards the mantlepiece.

'Never mind,' said MacGregor quickly, 'I'll get them.'

Even with his glasses on young Arthur Armstrong had difficulty in distinguishing the various objects in the room, as his attempt to sit on Dover's knees showed. For one heart-stopping moment MacGregor thought the whole thing was going to start up again, but the Chief Inspector was wide-awake now. He contented himself with employing the toe of his boot to propel Arthur Armstrong three quarters of the way across the room. Mrs Armstrong caught her son just before he reached the gas stove.

MacGregor, employing all his organizing ability and tact, finally got everybody sitting down at a safe distance from everybody else.

But Mrs Armstrong had not yet forgotten and forgiven. 'I don't know what come over you, sir,' she complained to Dover. 'I thought you was sitting there sound asleep like a baby.'

'You banged my sore foot,' retorted Dover accusingly. 'You want to be more careful. Well, for God's sake, MacGregor, get on with it! We haven't got all blooming day.'

Arthur Armstrong seemed quite grateful when MacGregor spoke to him by name. He turned eagerly in the direction of the authoritative voice, called MacGregor 'sir' and answered the questions briefly and to the point.

Yes, he had driven Mr Hamilton to his house from the Wallerton Country Club on the night in question. No, Mr Hamilton was not drunk, just a bit merry like, sir. No, he had not seen anything suspicious or in any way out of the ordinary. He had just dropped Mr Hamilton outside his house. Mr Hamilton had paid the fare and given him, Arthur, a ninepenny tip. No, he had not seen Mr Hamilton actually enter his house. When he, Arthur, had driven away Mr Hamilton was still standing on the pavement. No, there was nothing at all unusual about Mr Hamilton's behaviour as far as he had noticed, and Mr Hamilton had said, to the best of his recollection, nothing of any significance at all.

MacGregor sighed and looked disappointed. Dover was less downcast. He'd long ago given up expecting anything from anybody, and really helpful witnesses just didn't, in his rather jaundiced experience, exist at all.

Dover gazed into the depths of the fire. 'Had you driven this Hamilton chap back home at night before, laddie?' he asked suddenly.

Arthur jumped and gawped vaguely in Dover's direction. It seemed doubtful whether he really appreciated that there was a fourth person in the room, in spite of the kick he had received for lèse-majesté. 'Well, yes, I think so, sir, a couple of times, or three maybe, since I've been driving.'

'And how long's that?'

'Six or seven months now, sir.'

'How did you find the house?'

'Find the house, sir?'

'That's what I said, laddie. You got cloth ears or something? How did you find the house?'

'Well,' – Arthur seemed to have trouble in finding the right words – 'Mr Hamilton, he told me the address and I just drove there.'

'When you got to the street, how did you know where to stop the car?'

Arthur sighed. 'Mr Hamilton had told me the number. When I seed it, I stopped. Is that what you mean, sir?'

'It'll do, laddie,' said Dover, nodding his head. 'It'll do.'

MacGregor looked at Dover suspiciously. He was the first to complain that the Chief Inspector's contribution to their professional partnership was virtually nil, but in his heart of hearts he preferred it that way. He had a high opinion of his own ability, not unjustified when it was contrasted with Dover's, and he rather fancied himself in the role of bright young detective solving everything while his senior colleague floundered about completely baffled. This was a somewhat optimistic, even romantic view of their joint exploits, but MacGregor had long ago convinced himself that it was a true one. This made it all the more distressing when Dover, by sheer accident or blatant good luck, occasionally saw the wood while MacGregor was still admiring the trees. And the Chief Inspector was not the man to share his rare inspirations with anyone, never mind a jumped-up, prissy detective sergeant who was getting a damned sight too big for his boots anyhow. Mac-

Gregor was thus forced to keep his weather eye wide open and start thinking furiously whenever Dover roused himself to ask some particular question. What did the old fool mean now, for instance, by asking about how Armstrong found the house. MacGregor cudgelled his brains and the light dawned. Of course! He waited for Dover to pursue the point.

The Chief Inspector switched his questions to Mrs Armstrong. 'How,' he demanded bluntly, 'did this son of yours ever become a taxi driver? He's as blind as a perishing bat.'

'He's not!' Mrs Armstrong rose spiritedly to the defence of her offspring. 'He can see near as good as anybody with his glasses on.'

'It were Mrs Liversedge what fixed it,' said Arthur with a stupid grin.

'Yes, well there's no call to go into all that,' retorted his mother, speeding as she always did in moments of crisis to the gas stove.

'Oh, I don't know,' said Dover easily, having no intention of budging from this warm and comfortable haven till lunch time. 'I'd like to hear about it. And while you're up, missus, how about making a cup of tea, eh?'

Mrs Armstrong had little choice but to acquiesce to this delicate hint. While she banged around with the tea caddy and cups and saucers, she grudgingly related how it was that Arthur had become a taxi-driver. Dover, musing happily by the fire, nodded his head from time to time to show that he was still listening.

'Our Arthur's never had what you might call a proper chance, really,' began Mrs Armstrong, having a quick peep into the saucepan to steady her nerves. 'What with his dad passing over when he did and him never seeming to settle down properly at school. He's a good lad, clever with his hands, really, but not much good at book-work and me not able to help him, of course, like his dad might have done. Well, when he left school he had two or three jobs but he couldn't seem to find anything to suit him, really.'

'Here, Mum!' Arthur broke in to protest. 'I had eighteen jobs in nine months. That woman at the Labour said I was the record-holder for the town. You ought to tell him that.'

'I'll tell you something if you don't keep quiet,' snapped his mother. 'These gentlemen aren't interested in how many jobs you've had and it's nothing to be proud of anyhow.' She warmed the teapot vigorously. 'You just go and see if you can find some biscuits in the cupboard. Oh, no,' – as Arthur jerked enthusiastically to his feet – 'never mind! I'll get 'em. We don't want you knocking this poor gentleman's leg.'

Dover beamed at this touch of real consideration. 'Go on,' he said encouragingly.

'Well, then he started to get into bad company.'

'Ooh! I didn't, Mum. It was all my own idea.'

'I shan't tell you again, Arthur!' warned Mrs Armstrong, pouring out the tea. 'You young ones are all the same these days. If you ask me,' – she turned back to Dover – 'it was that job at the cinema that did it. You know what some of these films are like, and there was the dark, too. Well, that started him off getting interested in things – you know.'

'What sort of things?' asked MacGregor, feeling it was about time that he took some part in the conversation.

Mrs Armstrong's face took on an even rosier hue. 'Oh, you know, *things*,' she said, and began to give the draining board a good scrub.

'Girls!' explained Arthur cheerfully.

'He began bringing home all sorts of those sexy books,' Mrs Armstrong's voice dropped to a whisper. 'And then he took to hanging around outside late at night. He used to go up to the nurses' Home.'

'They never drew their curtains,' said Arthur with a chuckle.

'Well, one night some man – one of their boy-friends, I shouldn't wonder – caught him at it and gave him a right good thrashing. Blooming nerve, I thought, knocking our Arthur about like that.'

'Near bashed the living daylights out of me,' commented Arthur mournfully.

'No more than you deserved, my lad!' said his mother, wielding her scrubbing brush with increased energy. 'Another cup of tea for you, sir? Well, it cured him, I will say that. He gave up his Peeping Tom tricks, but, of course, that wasn't the end of it.' She sighed. 'The next thing I knew about it was a great big policeman coming round and hammering on my door. They'd had complaints, you see, and, of course, it was our

Arthur.' She gave a deeper sigh and wiped her hands on her apron. 'A warning he got, that first time, and they told him to go and see a doctor. That didn't do him much good. Told me he'd grow out of it. He didn't say when, though. Next time they put him on probation and said he'd have to go to one of these physiatrists. Once a week he went, regular as clockwork. I saw to that. It didn't cure him, though. Then our Arthur went and did it in this doctor's waiting room in front of all his other patients, so that was that. Well, I didn't know where to turn. They were beginning to talk about prison and I don't know what. I mean, prison for a lad like our Arthur! It wasn't as though he was really bad or anything. It's just that he would keep on doing it, didn't seem as though he could stop, somehow.'

MacGregor cleared his throat. He had been hoping that Dover would ask the obvious question but the master mind appeared too occupied with swilling tea. 'What was it, exactly, Mrs Armstrong, that your son was doing?'

Mrs Armstrong looked embarrassed. It was not her nature to call a spade a spade, especially when it was such a nasty spade as this one. And, besides, you'd expect an educated young gentleman like this to *know*, wouldn't you? 'Well, he used to sort of – well – show himself,' she said faintly. 'Middle-aged ladies he used to pick. Don't ask me why. This physiatrist had the nerve to say it was something to do with me. Blooming cheek! I've worked my fingers to the bone bringing that lad up decent. Nobody could have done more for him. I've devoted my whole life to him, especially with him being a bit on the simple side. Wherever he got it from he didn't get it from me, that I do know.' Mrs Armstrong folded her arms and glared with exasperation at her son.

The tap of Mrs Armstrong's eloquence seemed to have been turned off. Dover was just enjoying the blessed silence which filled the room when MacGregor, as usual, had to go sticking his oar in.

'What happened then, Mrs Armstrong?'

'Well, it was like a miracle, really. You wouldn't hardly credit it. You see, it was Arthur picking these middle-aged ladies that did it, really. Nearly all of 'em belonged to the Ladies' League and, of course, they were up in arms about it and no mistake. They kept writing to the police and the council and goodness knows what. Well, when it looked like nothing was going to stop him, one of them came to see me. She was very nice about it, really. She said they quite understood that Arthur probably couldn't help himself but, in a respectable town like Wallerton, with visitors and everything, they just couldn't let him go on and do nothing about it. Well, I said I could quite see that because it was a nasty business all round and I shouldn't have liked it myself, but what could we do about it. Well, she said that the Ladies' League was there to help people, whatever some folks might say about it, and they thought they could get him cured if I'd let him go away for a bit. They had to have my consent, you see, because he's not twenty-one yet. Well, to cut a long story short, eventually I said yes and off his lordship went and since then we've had no trouble. Thank God!'

Dover moved his chair back from the fire. One side of him was sizzling. 'How long was he away?' he asked, blinking his eyes and stretching himself.

'Oh, I forget now. A week or ten days.'

'But what has all this got to do with your son being a taxi-driver?' Smugly MacGregor congratulated himself on probably being the only person there who remembered the source of this long-winded rigmarole.

'Well, he had to get a job, didn't he?' queried Mrs Armstrong reasonably. 'I couldn't afford to keep him at home for evermore eating his head off, and his unemployment had run out and we weren't going on the National Assistance, that I can tell you. We never have and, as far as I can help it, we never will. But he couldn't get a job, you see. There's not much work in Wallerton for lads of his age, specially in the winter, and, of course, what there was they wouldn't give him. Everybody knew, you see. So this Mrs Liversedge – she was the lady that came to see me – she said she'd see what she could do. Well, her husband runs this taxi firm so eventually they decided they'd teach him to drive and make a taxi-driver out of him.'

'But how on earth did he ever pass his test?' asked MacGregor, staring in bewilderment at the grinning and myoptic Arthur.

'Oh, Mrs Liversedge was a magistrate,' Mrs Armstrong explained proudly. 'She had a word with the examiner.'

'But he must be an absolute menace on the road,' protested MacGregor, horrified at the mere thought of Arthur behind a steering wheel.

'He certainly isn't!' Mrs Armstrong was offended. 'He only drives between midnight and eight o'clock in the morning and there's no traffic in Wallerton at that time.'

'But even so ...'

'Mrs Liversedge said that anybody that wants a taxi after midnight deserves all they get,' announced Arthur righteously. 'She said they're only drunks and suchlike from the Country Club.'

'But suppose it's an emergency,' said MacGregor. 'Suppose somebody's got to go to the hospital or something?'

'Then,' responded Arthur simply, 'they ring up the other firm. Anybody in Wallerton knows that and the visitors don't matter. I hardly ever get a call when I'm on duty. I spend most of my time washing the cars.'

Chapter Ten

ON that encouraging note the police intrusion of Mrs Armstrong's cottage virtually came to an end.

Dover, somewhat half-heartedly because MacGregor had announced the time in a meaningful voice, had bestirred himself to ask Arthur where he had gone for his miraculous treatment. Arthur took an unbelievable time to indicate that he didn't rightly know. He rambled on about car rides and clean white sheets and the sweets they had given him, all mixed up with memories of a Sunday school outing to Brighton in 1954. Mrs Armstrong, equally vague, was unable to help. She had been so grateful to Mrs Liversedge that she hadn't felt it incumbent on her to inquire where her son was being taken.

'Oh well,' Dover grunted as he rose stiffly to his feet, 'we might have a chat with Mrs Liversedge some time.'

Mrs Armstrong, now slicing carrots at a rate of knots, shook her head. 'She passed away a couple of months ago. Very sudden it was. Pneumonia.'

Dover was not sorry. One less interfering old busybody in the would could only be put on the credit side.

'What do you think, sir?'

'Eh?' Dover looked up from the menu. 'Oh, well, I'm going to have the steak and kidney pud.'

'No, sir.' MacGregor fought to keep his exasperation under control. 'About the case?'

'Oh, *that*,' said Dover, and went back to his menu. 'What's *pot au feu*?'

'Beef stew, sir.'

'Well, why the blazes can't they say so,' grumbled Dover.

But MacGregor was not to be denied. 'I may be wrong, sir,' he went on when the business of ordering lunch had been completed, 'but I've had the impression once or twice that you were on to something.'

'Who, me?' said Dover, trying to look innocent.

'Well, I have had that impression, sir. I thought perhaps you'd seen a chink of light somewhere.'

'As far as I'm concerned, Cochran's dratted suicide is almost as big a blooming mystery as it was when we started.'

'Almost?' MacGregor pounced like a tiger.

Dover leered maliciously. 'I reckon anybody who's forced to live in a dump like this has got motive enough for sticking his head in a gas oven every now and again.'

'Oh,' said MacGregor, thwarted. 'So you haven't got a theory?'

Dover shook his head.

'Nor about the Hamilton business, sir? I thought from the way you were questioning young Arthur Armstrong that, maybe ... ?'

'You heard the questions, laddie,' said Dover with aggravating smugness, 'and you heard the answers. You should know as much about it as I do.'

'But I don't know *anything*, sir,' complained MacGregor.

'Hard luck,' said Dover.

MacGregor glared at him. This sort of thing had happened before. Dover had kept on protesting, right up to the last minute, that he was completely at a loss and then had suddenly produced a rabbit out of his hat. It wasn't always the right rabbit, but that was beside the point.

On the other hand, MacGregor ruminated, as he watched the unedifying spectacle of his Chief Inspector with both feet in the trough, there had been other investigations when Dover had claimed to be equally at a loss. And had been. MacGregor shuddered at the very thought of those cases. They were enough to bring a blush of shame to the cheeks of the most barefaced parasite on the police vote. Dover hadn't lost any sleep over them of course. 'You can't win 'em all,' he used to say as he shrugged off yet another disaster.

The point was, then, was the old guzzler telling the truth this time or not? MacGregor eyed his lord and master dubiously. It was difficult to tell. He was such a blatant liar. On the other hand, his great fat head was usually devoid of ideas of any sort, especially where his detective duties were concerned, so the odds were that he was completely at sea on this particular occasion, too.

'I've got a few tentative ideas of my own, actually, sir.'

Dover didn't even bother to raise his head from his plate. 'Have you? Congratulations.'

'I was wondering if I might – well – sort of follow them up, sir.'

Dover turned a suspicious eye on his subordinate. 'What are they?'

'Well, sir,' said MacGregor, as cagey as the Chief Inspector about sharing any of his bright ideas, 'it's a bit difficult to say.'

'Try,' Dover suggested unhelpfully. 'What's *crème brûlée*?'

'Burnt cream, sir.'

Dover turned to the waiter. 'I'll have plum duff, savvy?'

The waiter looked superciliously down his nose at this podgy peasant with the disgusting table manners. 'Oui, monsieur,' he said with as much of a sneer as he dared, 'je sais. Plum duff!'

'Well, come on, laddie!' said Dover impatiently, as MacGregor was longing for the floor to open under his feet. 'What's on your mind?'

'It's the Hamilton affair, sir.'

'Well, I hope you don't think that stupid nit Armstrong had anything to do with it. More fool you, if you do.'

'He has a police record, sir,' MacGregor pointed out primly.

'It wasn't for grievous bodily harm or carrying a concealed weapon or anything like that, was it, you damned fool?'

'His mother said he'd been keeping bad company, sir,' MacGregor insisted.

'God help us!' groaned Dover and rolled his eyes alarmingly.

Macgregor was beginning to get a bit annoyed at these antics. 'You yourself caught him out in a downright lie, sir.'

'Did I?' said Dover.

'He said that he could see the number of Hamilton's house with no trouble at all. Well, that's ridiculous, sir! You saw those house numbers right down the entire street. I've got perfect vision and I could hardly make them out in broad daylight. How could Armstrong, with his eyesight, possibly see them on a dark night? He was obviously lying.'

'Who says it was a dark night?' asked Dover, showing an unfortunate tendency to quibble over non-essentials.

'It says so in the police file, sir. A fine dark night with no moon.'

Dover, of course, was in no position to argue about what was or was not said in the police file since the pressure of events and his own lethargy had so far prevented him from even looking at it. 'It still doesn't mean Armstrong is lying,' he said.

MacGregor permitted himself a rather superior laugh. 'I'm afraid I can't see any other explanation, sir.'

'No,' said Dover broodily, 'you wouldn't.'

'And if he's lying, sir, that means he's got something to hide.'

'Such as?'

'Well, my theory is this, sir, that Hamilton was bumped off by some of his underworld associates – only, of course, he dropped down dead on them first.'

'So they made mincemeat out of him just for the fun of it?'

'More or less. I don't see anything incongruous in that. You know what some of these gangs are like, sir. They're always carving people up with their knives.'

'And where does Cochran come into all this?'

MacGregor frowned. 'Well, I'm not quite clear about that, sir. I've got one or two ideas, though. For instance, he may have been in some sort of partnership with Hamilton, in spite of what Joey the Jock says. We know they were both hanging around that Country Club and an association like that looks more than suspicious to me. So, when Hamilton cashes in his chips, Cochran takes it as a dreadful warning and realizes that the same fate awaits him. Scared out of his wits, he commits suicide off Cully Point.'

Dover elaborately made no comment. He just gazed up at the ceiling, blew his cheeks out and whistled tunelessly.

'On the other hand,' said MacGregor, uncomfortably aware that his theories seemed much more convincing before they had been put into words, 'it's quite possible that Cochran wasn't hand in glove with Hamilton. Maybe he was hanging around Hamilton because he was suspicious of him. Playing detective, you might call it. Somehow he found out who was responsible for Hamilton's death and they found out that he'd found out and so, once again, Cochran gets the wind up and kills himself. That would explain why he spent his week's leave in bed. He was hiding.'

Dover looked at his sergeant as though he couldn't believe his ears.

'Something along those lines, sir,' added MacGregor lamely.

'And the taxi-driver, Armstrong, is a member of the gang?'

'Well, yes. Or just a helpless tool, perhaps.' MacGregor could feel the sweat breaking out on his forehead.

Dover slowly and wonderingly shook his head from side to side and tut-tutted softly to himself. 'And what line of investigation was it you were thinking of following up?'

Unobtrusively MacGregor got his handkerchief out and, under cover of blowing his nose, dabbed his brow. 'Well, I thought I could dig around a bit, sir,' MacGregor cleared his throat, 'and try and find some of the people Hamilton was dealing with. You remember, sir, the Country Club manager mentioned that the night he died, Hamilton was waiting for somebody who didn't turn up. Now, if we could find out who this interview was with ... '

'A lemon,' said Dover.

'I beg your pardon, sir?'

'A lemon,' repeated Dover. 'That's what the answer'll be. Anyhow, if you want to waste your time on it, that's your funeral.'

MacGregor could hardly conceal either his delight or his surprise. The Chief Inspector was not habitually so sympathetic to youthful aspirations. 'Do you mean I can go ahead, sir?'

'That's what I said, isn't it?'

MacGregor pushed his chair back from the table. 'Now, sir?'

Dover chewed his lip moodily. 'I don't see why not. I shan't want you again this afternoon. I've got a few ideas of my own I want to think out.'

MacGregor treated this shoddy old white lie with the contempt it deserved. 'Well, I'll be off, sir.'

'Here, hang on a minute,' said Dover. 'Leave me that packet of cigarettes. I seem to have run out.

The prospect of being let off the leash to follow his own bent had gone to MacGregor's head. 'They've got plenty in the bar, sir!' he observed cheekily.

Dover scowled. 'Oh, have they, laddie? Well, you can just nip in and get me a couple of packets before you go. And I don't want those damned filter-tips, either.'

MacGregor's mini-revolt thus set him back precisely ten shillings and twopence. Regretfully, because even in these days detective sergeants are not rolling in money, he chalked it up to experience.

When MacGregor had gone Dover ordered himself another coffee and sat brooding over the luncheon table, much to the annoyance of the dining-room staff. Dover was thinking. It was not an occupation he indulged in frequently but, when he did, he was thorough about it. Knives and forks were chucked noisily into drawers, crockery was tossed from one end of the room to the other, table cloths were shaken with a snap like a whip lash. Dover sat on, oblivious. The foreign waiters chatted furiously amongst themselves and, driven to the limit, began piling the chairs on to the tables.

It would be unfair to accuse Dover of putting himself to the trouble of cudgelling his brains over the Cochran–Hamilton affair merely so as to be able, at a later date, to spit in MacGregor's eye. This unworthy motive had its place in the scheme of things, but it was by no means the principal one. Nor was it true that the Chief Inspector was spurred on solely by the desire to resume his holiday. An uninterrupted fortnight of Mrs Dover's company was not the sort of thing likely to inspire her husband to exert himself. No, although no one could accuse him of taking the affair seriously, none the less he was mildly intrigued by it.

Unlike MacGregor, he scornfully pooh-poohed the idea that Arthur Armstrong was a sadistic thug, or had even been used by a gang of sadistic thugs for their own necrophilic purposes. That left the problem of why Arthur Armstrong had said that he had seen the number of Hamilton's house when, obviously, he could have done nothing of the sort. With typical perverseness Dover decided to believe that Arthur Armstrong was speaking the truth. That meant that he *had* seen the number of Hamilton's house. But how?

Suppose – a beatific smile, which reduced the still waiting waiters to paroxysms of rage, spread over Dover's pasty features – yes, that was indeed a possibility. Could be done easily, too.

Bit of sticky paper, say, and the light left on, that's all you'd need. Quickly set up and quickly taken down again without leaving any traces. And it was most unlikely, at that time of night, that any casual passer-by would notice it or bother his head about it if he did.

Ho, ho! Now they were getting somewhere! Dover chuckled to himself. But where, exactly? The Chief Inspector's bottom lip jutted out sulkily. Oh well, he'd have a think about that later. What else was there?

MacGregor thought that Hamilton had died while some gang was in the process of murdering him. That seemed reasonable enough, so Dover duly wracked his brains to think up some other explanation. Suppose they weren't trying to kill Hamilton? Well, if they were just giving him a beating-up, it all came to much the same thing. What else could they, whoever they were, be doing to him, for God's sake? Dover mused for some considerable time over those mutilations. They just didn't fit it. There were plenty of East End gangs of thugs who frequently chived up the opposition, but Dover could not recall a case in which they had exercised their art on an already dead body. Besides, in Dover's experience, the face was the usual target and Hamilton's face, unlike the lower part of his body, hadn't got a scratch on it. Dover sighed. It was all very confusing. However much somebody might have had it in for Hamilton, would they really go to the extent of stripping him – dead or alive? The accepted method was a few artistic waves with a razor and a few swift kicks where it would do the most harm. And could anybody in their right senses, including that insufferable young nitwit MacGregor, really see Wallerton in the height or depth of the tourist season as the scene of gang warfare of this sort? London, Liverpool, Brighton even – but not Wallerton.

The subject of one dead body naturally led Dover on to think about the other; or rather the lack of it. Cochran's. Dover was tired of wondering why Cochran had killed himself, unless he found out he looked like remaining in Wallerton for the rest of his natural. Jumping off Cully Point was a funny way to go, though. Not at all what he, Dover, would have chosen. He wondered why Cochran had. Of course, it did save the cost of a funeral, there being no body. Suicides get some very queer ideas at times. I wonder when, thought Dover, Cochran actually made up his mind to jump? Perhaps he did it on the spur of the moment and that's why he chose Cully Point. If you hadn't got a gas stove or an overdose of sleeping pills handy, it was probably as good a way as any. Dover wrinkled his nose. But, surely, Cochran hadn't made up his mind on the spur of the moment? What about that week's leave he'd spent in bed? Personally, Dover couldn't think of a better place, but he was broadminded enough to realize that it wouldn't be everybody's idea of bliss.

Funny, he thought, how everybody in Wallerton seemed to do things for a week. There was Cochran going to bed for a week. There was that Chauncey whatever-his-name-was having amnesia for a week. There was Arthur Armstrong going away for a week's treatment and coming back cured.

Dover dropped his cigarette end into his coffee cup. Oh well, he pushed his chair away from the table, no use sitting here all day. He'd be much more comfortable in his own room. Quite worn him out, it had, all that thinking.

The head waiter was holding the dining-room door open for him. Dover acknowledged the service with an absentminded grunt.

'Goodnight, sir!' snarled the head waiter.

Dover yawned.

Twenty-four hours later he was still yawning, but his heart was no longer in it. There was a limit to the amount of sheer inactivity that even Dover could endure. He was moreover feeling lonely, even neglected. He missed having somebody to talk to. MacGregor, with a lack of consideration which was so typical of the younger generation, had completely abandoned him. The selfish young swine hadn't even been on hand at mealtimes. God knows what he was up to. He appeared from time to time, bright-eyed and excited, gabbled incoherently about being hot on the trail and then dashed off again before Dover could ask him any questions. The only consolation left to the Chief Inspector was an unshakable conviction that his sergeant was heading straight up a gum tree and doing no harm to anyone. Still, it would be nice to know exactly what the young fool was up to, even if it was only to pour cold water on his boyish enthusiasm. There is no doubt that if Dover had not sunk so far in black lethargy this is precisely what he would have done.

He sat glumly in the hotel lounge, an exile while they made his bed and dusted his room. The receptionist appeared.

'There's a telephone call for you, Mr Dover.'

'Who is it?' said Dover scowling. He had no intention of answering the phone if there was somebody like that potty Chief Constable puffing and blowing down the other end.

'Somebody called Veitch, I think,' said the receptionist who prided herself on her total indifference to everything and everybody connected with her work.

'Never heard of 'em,' grunted Dover, sinking back in his chair and closing his eyes.

'Oh, charming, I'm sure!' The receptionist tossed her head haughtily and minced away.

In a few moments she minced back again. 'He says he's Sergeant Veitch from the police station. He said to tell you he's the station sergeant.'

'I don't care if he's the Queen of Sheba,' retorted Dover. 'What does he want?'

'He didn't say, dearie.' The receptionist's tone sharpened. 'I expect he's waiting to tell you that himself.'

'Tell him I'm not in.'

'I'm afraid I can't do that. I've already told him you said you didn't know who he was.'

Dover regarded her sourly as she tripped off. 'Stupid cow!' he muttered and dragged himself resentfully to his feet.

At the reception desk in the entrance hall he picked up the telephone. 'Well?'

'It's Sergeant Veitch here, sir ... '

'I know that, you damned fool! Wadderyewant?'

There was a slight hesitation at the other end. 'Well, sir, I was wondering if you'd like to come round and have tea with us this afternoon?'

Dover regarded the telephone receiver with mixed surprise and suspicion. 'Who's us?' he demanded cautiously.

'The wife and me, sir.'

'Where do you live? I've damaged my foot pretty badly, you know, and I can't ... '

'Oh, I'd come and fetch you from the hotel in the car, sir. And bring you back afterwards.'

'What time?'

'Well, how about, say, a quarter to five, sir?'

Dover thought it over. It'd make a change if nothing else. But, tea? There was a funny thing for one copper to invite another to. Doubtless it was a tactful euphemism for something a sight stronger.

'All right,' said Dover. 'A quarter to five.' He put the phone down.

The receptionist shuddered. If there was one thing she did like to see in a man it was nice manners.

The station sergeant presented himself at a quarter to five on the dot, which was just as well as Dover was a great stickler for punctuality in others. With a depressing lack of graciousness the Chief Inspector allowed himself to be shepherded out to the waiting car. It was big and new and the heater was going full blast.

'Glad to see you can afford to run a car like this,' he remarked. 'It's more than I can on my pay.'

The station sergeant managed a smile and gave Dover a cigarette.

Unmollified, Dover slumped back in his seat and unburdened himself of a carping and endless commentary on the station sergeant's driving. The station sergeant was a good driver, which is probably why they reached his house all in one piece. A less controlled man would have headed the car straight for the nearest lamp-post out of sheer vexation.

'Well,' said Dover as they slid to a gentle halt before a neat-looking semi-detached, 'maybe I've been a bit too hard on the wife. She isn't the worst driver in the world after all.'

Chapter Eleven

By the time Dover was installed in the place of honour at the tea-table several things were becoming clearer. Judging by the tea-table itself, covered by a lace cloth and dripping with doilies, nothing stronger than tea was going to be offered. Indeed, if the pious pictures on the walls and the seven missionary collecting boxes on the mantlepiece were anything to go by, this was, regrettably, a strictly teetotal household.

The second point, which even Dover grasped, was in its way equally repugnant. He hadn't been in the house thirty seconds before he realized that Mrs Veitch was the one who wore the trousers. Not literally, of course. The mere idea of Mrs Veitch in slacks would have been enough to make strong men tremble. Another fifteen seconds passed and Dover was grimly forced to recognize that she was also the one, metaphorically speaking, wearing the police uniform. And a grisly old bogy she made, too.

Sergeant Veitch was hardly given time to get his coat off before he was directed into the kitchen to brew the tea and told to finish off laying the table.

'I can't abide sandwiches and bread-and-butter left out on plates and going all dry and curly at the edges,' said Mrs Veitch as she placed Dover at the top of the table nearest the fire. 'Can you?'

'No,' said Dover.

Sergeant Veitch scuttled in with the teapot.

'For goodness sake, Sydney,' his wife rebuked him sharply, 'why don't you put an apron on? If you get that suit marked again ... ' Out of deference, no doubt, to the presence of their visitor she left the threat unfinised.

The Veitchs kept a good table and were hospitable. Goodies of every description were piled liberally on Dover's plate. Each offering was accompanied by a short history of how its ingredients had been acquired, at what cost, and how they had been transformed to their present state by Mrs Veitch's own hands, usually according to a formula which had been handed down in her family for generations.

This domestic gloss was contributed exclusively by Mrs Veitch. In twenty-five years of connubial bliss Sergeant Veitch had learnt the hard way not to open his mouth in his wife's presence, except for the insertion of her culinary triumphs. When on occasion Mrs Veitch appealed to him to support her assertation that her home-made veal and ham pie, for example, was the best he had ever tasted, he contented himself with nodding his head enthusiastically.

Dover was amazed, remembering the sergeant's bullying manner at their first encounter in the police station. It was obviously the only chance the poor devil got to assert himself. Dover thought with, if not affection, at least satisfaction, of his own lady wife. She'd have got the back of his hand very smartly if she ever showed the faintest sign of developing into a second Mrs Veitch. By God, she would!

They had reached the trifle, completely non-alcoholic, when Mrs Veitch abruptly stopped talking about how good a cook she was and got down to the basic motive behind the invitation to Dover.

'How's your investigation going?'

Dover spluttered through a mouthful of soggy cake and cream, a fair proportion of which splattered all over Mrs Veitch's clean table cloth. It says a great deal for her single-mindedness that she refrained from comment.

'You don't seem to have been overworking yourself lately,' she remarked reprovingly.

Dover choked on a bit of purple stuff with which the trifle had been liberally decorated. 'My foot,' he explained.

Mrs Veitch sniffed.

Dover tried again. 'It's a very tricky case.'

'Remorse,' said Mrs Veitch.

'Eh?'

'Cochran committing suicide. Remorse for an ill-spent and dissolute life.'

'Oh,' said Dover. 'We thought there might be some tie-up with that Hamilton business,' he added casually.

'Did you? No, I think you're barking up the wrong tree there. Some raspberries and cream, Mr Dover?' Dover's eyes bulged but he nodded his head. 'They're our own raspberries, picked straight from the garden. We've got some very good bushes, haven't we, Sydney?' Sergeant Veitch offered his usual silent agreement. 'The best bushes we've ever had, the ones we've got now. The cream's fresh, too. I always buy it from Hutchinson's; that's a farm a couple of miles down the road. Of course, I can get it from the Dairy but I like Hutchinson's better. They've got Jersey cows, you see. Of course, the Dairy's handier but Sydney doesn't mind getting the car out and popping down to Hutchinson's, do you, Sydney?'

Sydney, musing gently about wife-murderers who had got away with it, missed his cue and nodded his head. His wife, ever sensitive to the possibility of worms turning, glared at him. Sergeant Veitch smiled weakly and obediently shook his head.

Dover accepted his dishful of raspberries and cream. 'The Hamilton affair's giving us a real headache,' he observed.

It wasn't giving Mrs Veitch any. 'That Country Club, that's where you ought to be looking. Disgusting place. I can't think why they don't close it down.' She stared accusingly at her husband.

Dover struggled on through the raspberries. 'Hamilton was all right when he left the Country Club. In fact, he reached his own front door quite safe and sound, as far as we can tell.'

Mrs Veitch frowned. 'You're not thinking of accusing his wife, I hope? Not but what she wouldn't have been justified in murdering that brute a dozen times over.'

Dover belched gently.

'Have some of this Madeira cake, Mr Dover. I can thoroughly recommend it, even if I do say it as shouldn't. I baked it myself and if there's one thing I do pride myself on it's my cakes. They're really very good, aren't they, Sydney?' She was already wielding the cake knife.

Dover's eyes glazed over. He was near bursting point but it went strictly against the grain of his nature to refuse. 'Just a small piece,' he gasped.

'No,' said Mrs Veitch, 'not Mrs Hamilton. Well, it wasn't a woman's crime in any case, was it? She's only a poor, thin mite of a thing. She couldn't possibly have coped with lugging that great lump around, never mind chop him up like that.'

'She's got a very hasty temper,' said Dover with feeling.

Mrs Veitch dismissed this. 'I expect you frightened her.'

Dover slowly forced another mouthful of cake down. Although appearances might belie it, he was really thinking quite hard. 'I've got a theory about Hamilton,' he began. Then he changed his mind. 'My sergeant has a theory about Hamilton.' He watched Mrs Veitch carefully. 'You see, young Arthur Armstrong, the taxi-driver, swears that he found Hamilton's house out of all those houses in that great long street on a dark night. Now, I expect you know Armstrong. He's as blind as a bat.'

'Huh!' said Mrs Veitch non-committally.

'Now my sergeant – Sergeant MacGregor, that is – he thinks he can explain how Armstrong found Hamilton's house so easily.'

Sergeant Veitch and his wife were all ears, much to Dover's gratification. He always expected to be the centre of attention and got very shirty when, as frequently happened, he wasn't. He paused to let the tension build up.

'All right,' snapped Mrs Veitch impatiently. 'How did he find it?'

'Dead easy,' smirked Dover. 'He didn't!'

'He didn't?'

'No, he just thought he did.'

'Clear as mud,' observed Mrs Veitch. 'Have one of these maids of honour. They're … '

Dover raised a heavy hand and broke the habits of a lifetime. 'No,' he said.

'Well, finish off those cream cheese sandwiches. I don't like having things left hanging around.'

Dover shook his head and returned the conversation to less painful channels. 'Sergeant MacGregor reckons that somebody in one of the other houses – and they all look the same, don't they? – he reckons that somebody put the number of Hamilton's house up nice and clear on another house.'

There was a moment's silence. 'And how did they do that?' asked Mrs Veitch quietly.

Dover shrugged his beefy shoulders. 'It wouldn't have been too difficult. You could cut out the number nice and big in a sheet of cardboard, for instance, and then stick it up on the fanlight over the front door. If you left the light on in the hall, the number'd stand out so clearly that even Armstrong would see it.'

'Well, swelp me!' said Sergeant Veitch with unflattering astonishment. 'That's clever.'

'Sydney!' His wife's voice brought him promptly to heel. 'You'd better start clearing the table.'

But Sydney had got the bit between his teeth now and, possibly thinking that Dover's presence provided him with at least temporary protection, ignored his wife's hint. 'Do you mean, Mr Dover, that Hamilton was lured into another house and cut about here?'

'That's Sergeant MacGregor's theory.'

'It's an idea. They'd just have to carry his body out when it was all over, and his clothes, and pop 'em over the garden wall. Yes,' – Sergeant Veitch nodded his head – 'it's an idea all right.'

'Rubbish!' Mrs Veitch rattled her tea cup in the saucer. 'What about those two men in that little green van that Doris Doughty saw? It's obvious that whatever happened to Hamilton happened a long way from Minton Parade.'

It came as no surprise to Dover to find that Mrs Veitch knew as much, if not more, about the Hamilton business than he did. 'Miss Doughty may have been mistaken,' he said mildly.

'What, Doris Doughty? Never on your life! I've known her for years. We've served on Ladies' League committees together since I don't know when.'

'My sergeant,' said Dover, watching Mrs Veitch from under eyelids which, weighed down by sandwiches and cake and trifle, were growing heavier every minute, 'my sergeant thinks there's something fishy about Miss Doughty's story.'

'Oh, does he, indeed? And I'd like to know what he knows about it when he's at home.'

'He's a very astute detective,' said Dover, choking slightly over the words.

'Oh, is he?' Mrs Veitch was scathing. 'Well, handsome is as handsome does, if you want to know my opinion. And what does this paragon of yours think is wrong with Doris Doughty's story?'

'He says,' said Dover slyly, 'that it sounds as though she'd learned it off by heart. Most witnesses, you know, tend to change bits and pieces every time they tell their story. They remember some details they've never mentioned before and they forget others. Now, your Miss Doughty, according to my sergeant, doesn't change a single word.'

For a split second Mrs Veitch looked disconcerted. Then she turned viciously on her husband. 'I thought you were going to start clearing this table, Sydney? We don't want to be sitting here surrounded by empty pots all night. Another cup of tea, Mr Dover?'

'I don't mind if I do,' said Dover, passing his cup.

'Sydney, go and brew a fresh pot!'

Reluctantly Sydney withdrew to the kitchen.

'You want,' Mrs Veitch said unpleasantly, 'to keep an eye on this sergeant of yours. I hear he was at that Country Club again last night.'

'Was he now?' murmured Dover in wide-eyed astonishment.

'Didn't you know?'

Slowly Dover shook his head. 'He doesn't have to tell me what he does in his free time.' He smiled suggestively. 'He's a big boy now, you know.'

'Well, I shouldn't have thought that Country Club was the place for any young policeman unless he was on duty. And not even then, come to think of it.'

'Oh, I think he took a bit of a fancy to one of the girls,' explained Dover indulgently. 'We were there the night before, you know. On duty, of course. I seem to remember he was getting very chummy with one of the, er, hostesses, I think they call them.'

'I know what I call them!' Mrs Veitch spat the words out. 'Dirty little trollops, that's what I call them! Dressed up as chickens, too – disgusting! We'll have to tackle the Council again. They must close that place down.'

'Oh, I don't know,' said Dover casually, 'it seemed harmless enough to me.'

'To the pure all things are pure,' was Mrs Veitch's somewhat inappropriate rejoinder. 'I must say, though, I'm surprised at your sergeant. Really surprised. He looks such a nice, decent, clean-living boy.'

'Who? MacGregor?' Dover began to laugh and then, since

the exercise was so unusual for him, to cough. 'Oh dear,' he spluttered, 'you should know him as well as I do! Talk about a girl in every port! He's a proper young devil, he is, where women are concerned. He'll come a cropper over it one day, you mark my words. Why, he's had maintenance orders made out against him from one end of the country to the other.'

Mrs Veitch's face froze. 'He ought to be thrown out of the police.'

'I agree, but you want to try getting it done. There's no law against leading a loose and immoral life, is there? Besides, he's dead clever. And, as I told you, he's a first-class detective and we don't want to lose him if we can help it. Chaps of his ability are few and far between these days.'

Mrs Veitch piled up a few plates to help her husband who was trotting patiently in and out of the kitchen, wearing his apron. 'Has he had any more bright ideas about this Cochran case?'

'Oh, he's full of 'em. He thinks it's tied up with the Hamilton business and then he's spotted one or two other points. Did you know you'd had a sort of epidemic of people here in Wallerton dropping out of circulation for about a week and then coming back different?'

Mrs Veitch was sitting very still. 'What do you mean?'

'Well, there's a man called Chauncey Davenport and there's Arthur Armstrong.'

'I don't call that an epidemic. Chauncey Davenport had amnesia and Arthur Armstrong went for psychiatric treatment. Everybody knows that.'

'Young Cochran spent a week in bed before he committed suicide.'

'I don't see what that's got to do with it.'

'Here!' Sergeant Veitch paused dramatically in the midst of his labours. 'You might be on to something there, Mr Dover. We've had more of these temporary disappearances. Nobody's taken much notice because the chap's always turned up again. In fact, usually I've just picked it up on the old grape vine. We haven't been told about it officially. Now, let me see, there's that fellow – what's his name? – works as a van-driver for Pilkingtons and has ten or eleven kids. Now he sheered off for a week just after Christmas. And then there was ... '

'Sydney, is that the hot water tap you've left running? I don't want all my good hot water going to waste.'

'No, dear,' said Sergeant Veitch, effectively deflated.

'You'd better just get this table cleared and then leave the washing-up. You can do it when you get back, but time's getting on and Mr Dover won't want to be late for his dinner.'

With some difficulty Dover extricated himself from behind the table and got to his feet. His stomach, usually loose and flabby, was blown up as tight as a football.

'Of course,' he remarked as he graciously permitted Mrs Veitch to help him on with his overcoat, 'I've just been telling you what my sergeant thinks. He gets these daft ideas from time to time.'

'Oh, so you don't share his views, Mr Dover?'

'Well, they sound pretty far-fetched, don't they? And what do they add up to? Damn all, if you ask me. No, I'm sure there's a much more straightforward solution somewhere. The trouble is' – he accepted his bowler hat from Mrs Veitch – 'young MacGregor's like a blooming terrier. Once he gets an idea he won't let it go, however crazy it seems. Of course, once in a blue moon, he comes up trumps.'

Sergeant Veitch drove slowly and carefully through the rain-lashed, deserted streets of Wallerton. It was several minutes before he spoke. 'Mr Dover,' he said in a low voice, 'you're up to something, aren't you?'

Dover, his stomach beginning to feel a trifle uneasy as his digestive juices fought it out with Mrs Veitch's high tea, was non-committal. 'What makes you think that?'

'Oh, I can tell. I wasn't born yesterday. You're up to something all right, though I'm blowed if I can see what it is.'

'Nothing for you to worry your head about,' said Dover smugly.

'Oh, it's like that, is it? You're one of these lone wolves. You keep it all to yourself and work it all out and then come up with a solution that's been staring the rest of us in the face all the time but we couldn't see it.'

'Something like that,' Dover admitted modestly. Sergeant Veitch had seen more detectives on the telly than he had in real life and was more than ready to believe that the scions of New Scotland Yard moved in a mysterious way.

'But what's it got to do with my wife?'

'Oh, nothing,' said Dover, over-heartily.

'Come off it! You can't kid me!'

'Just tell me one thing,' said Dover. 'Is your wife really a big bug in this Ladies' League?'

'Not half! She'll be a vice-president in four years if old Mrs McKenzie kicks the bucket this winter. One of the leading lights in the Ladies' League, my wife is. And has been ever since we were married. Makes life very difficult for me at times, I can tell you.'

'More fool you,' said Dover unsympathetically.

'Oh well,' – Sergeant Veitch's loyalty sounded a bit forced – 'she's not so bad, really. Very good-hearted woman underneath.'

'Humph,' said Dover.

'Is there anything I can do, Mr Dover?' asked Sergeant Veitch, not unmindful of the fact that a generous commendation from a senior Scotland Yard officer wouldn't do his career any harm.

'Yes, there is one thing. Young Cochran, just before he rode off on his bicycle to Cully Point that morning, what had he been doing in the nick?'

The sergeant, much to Dover's annoyance, removed one hand from the steering wheel and scratched his head. 'Well, he'd just been pottering about, really. Reading the force orders and glancing through the books and what not. Generally seeing what had been happening while he was on leave, and getting up to date with what was going on. You know the sort of thing.'

'Right,' said Dover, moving uncomfortably in his seat and wondering if perhaps it wouldn't be wiser to skip dinner. 'Now, first thing tomorrow morning, I want a copy – not just a list – a copy of everything Cochran looked at that morning. And not just the stuff in the files. I want all the stuff pinned up on the notice boards as well.'

Sergeant Veitch's face fell. 'But, it'll take hours and hours.'

'I don't give a twopenny damn if it takes years and years,' said Dover who got a real kick out of making life miserable for other people. 'I still want it first thing tomorrow morning.'

'What do you call first thing?' asked Sergeant Veitch dolefully. 'I don't go on duty till six.'

'Ten o'clock,' said Dover, naming the hour at which he considered the day to break.

'I still don't see how I'm going to do it,' grumbled Sergeant Veitch. He was already picturing his constable assistant sweating away over the task. He might even take one of the brighter lads off patrol for an hour or two to lend a hand. 'I mean, it'll be very difficult to sort out what was new and what wasn't, won't it? I suppose that's what you want; the stuff that had come in while he was away?'

Dover nodded.

'It's going to be some job,' Sergeant Veitch said again in an attempt, which he knew was hopeless, to soften Dover's heart.

'Well, that's your problem,' Dover pointed out comfortably. 'And do it yourself. I don't want every Tom, Dick and Harry in the place knowing what's going on and gabbling about it.' This was a good example of how Dover endeared himself to his subordinates. He didn't care two hoots whether every man, woman and child in Wallerton was conversant with the task he had off-loaded on to Veitch's cringing shoulders. He was well aware that Mrs Veitch would be informed in any case, especially if it looked as though the information was confidential. And what you told Mrs Veitch you told the world. Dover knew, too, how Sergeant Veitch's mind worked: lumber somebody else with it. It was, after all, the system on which Chief Inspector Dover himself relied. In insisting that the Sergeant performed the task single-handed, Dover was merely being thoroughly bloody-minded.

His spirits perked up considerably after this ignoble little triumph and he wished the sullen sergeant a cheery goodnight when the car dropped him at his hotel. Still buoyantly bouncing on the crest he strode into the dining-room and polished off a dinner that would probably have kept an Asian family for a week. His good humour sagged a little when he found that, once again, MacGregor was not in attendance. He repaired hesitantly to the bar after dinner to have a brandy to settle his stomach. It was the first time for many years that he had entered such a place unaccompanied. It made him feel naked. History was about to be made as he fumbled in his pocket for the exorbitant sum that the bar-tender, quite brazen-faced about it, appeared to be demanding. But fate, in the person of a dear old lady who'd been propping up the bar since opening time, intervened.

'Have it on me,' she said unexpectedly.

Dover's gratitude made him speechless. Gallantly, however, he moved along the counter so as to keep in touch with his new found benefactor and finished up by passing the remainder of the evening in her company. She was a motherly old soul, treating Dover like a son to such an extent that for the Chief Inspector to have offered to stand his round would have been insulting. She was clearly very wealthy and more than a little tipsy. What more could you ask? Dover was disconcerted to find, after an hour or so's rather incoherent conversation, that she was under the impression that he was a sanitary inspector, but he didn't hold it against her and, indeed, gave her some very detailed and quite unsound advice on her plumbing problems.

When the old lady became totally paralytic and was removed from the bar by the united effort of three of the hotel staff, Dover decided it was time for bed. MacGregor was still not in his room. Dover poked around amongst MacGregor's private possessions without finding anything he hadn't seen before and left a note instructing his assistant to contact him at the earliest opportunity. He propped the note up on the dressing table, and withdrew to his own room.

He was snoring like a pig when MacGregor poked him gingerly. Dover heaved over on to his other side.

MacGregor poked again, harder.

With a snort Dover opened his eyes and immediately closed them again. 'Warisit?' he mumbled.

'It's me, sir. Sergeant MacGregor.'

Dover screwed his mean little eyes up against the light.

'Watimeisit?'

'A quarter to four, sir.'

Dover moaned, and rolling over, buried his head in the pillow. 'You bloody fool! What do you want to go waking me up at this time for?'

MacGregor sighed, unobtrusively of course. He seemed to have spent his entire professional life carrying on exchanges of this nature. 'Your note, sir. You said you wanted to see me urgently.'

Dover lay flat on his back and pushed the bed clothes away. 'Trust you!' he said bitterly. 'Trust you!' He lapsed into thought for a moment. 'I shall have to go down the corridor now, you damned fool!'

Grunting and groaning he got out of bed and groped for his overcoat. 'If I catch my death,' he muttered accusingly, 'it'll be all your blasted fault. A quarter to four!'

He plodded resentfully out of the room, slamming the door behind him.

MacGregor sat on the edge of the bed and listened to the distant but unmistakable sounds of his master's progress. At last the Chief Inspector came thumping back. He looked more wide awake now but was as bad-tempered as ever.

'You still here?' he demanded sulkily as he dropped his overcoat on the floor and clambered back into bed.

'You did say you wanted to see me, sir,' protested MacGregor who was very tired.

'Not at a bloody quarter to four in the morning, I didn't,' snapped Dover, pulling the sheet up over his head. 'Wherevyebin?'

'The Country Club, sir.'

Dover uncovered one eye and glared. 'It's all right for some,' he observed sarcastically. 'Push off! And put that damned light out before you go.'

Chapter Twelve

MacGregor returned to Dover's bedroom at nine o'clock the following morning. The precise hour had been carefully selected. MacGregor combined his own refined instincts with the reports he received from the dining-room staff to the effect that that fat old bounder was having his breakfast in bed. MacGregor was also the unwilling recipient, via the manager, of complaints from a large number of the other residents about the noise Dover had been making throughout the night.

'I'm surprised you didn't hear him yourself,' said the manager peevishly. 'Bang, crash, wallop it was for hours.'

'I don't know what you expect me to do about it,' said MacGregor, although he did, only too well.

'I thought you might have a tactful word with him; ask him to show a bit of consideration. He wouldn't like it if it was somebody else, would he?'

'No, he certainly wouldn't,' agreed MacGregor. 'He'd be the first to complain. But,' he added stoutly, 'he'd do it himself and not expect somebody else to do it for him.'

'Oh well, if that's your attitude!' said the manager and walked off in a huff.

Despondently MacGregor mounted the stairs to his Chief Inspector's room. If the old fool had had a disturbed night he was likely to be even more obstreperous than usual. If his blasted stomach was as bad as he was always claiming it was, it was a pity they didn't invalid him out with it.

Dover, propped up in bed and brooding over the remains of his breakfast, certainly didn't look very bright. His eyes were bloodshot and his complexion even more pasty-coloured than usual.

'I had a nasty bilious attack last night,' he informed MacGregor pathetically. 'It was you waking me up that brought it on.'

'Perhaps it was something you ate, sir.'

'Awful, it was,' said Dover. 'I was up half the blooming night.'

'So I heard, sir.'

'I ought to see a doctor, really,' said Dover gloomily. 'Not that they seem to be able to do much for me.'

'Well, I could perhaps get the local police surgeon to call in, sir.'

Dover poked disconsolately around on his tray to see if there were any scraps of sustenance that had been overlooked. Suddenly his face cleared. 'That's a good idea, laddie! I could do with some expert advice. Yes, you tell him I'd like to have a word with him tomorrow morning. Round about ten o'clock'll suit me. Tell him it's urgent.'

'*Tomorrow* morning, sir?' MacGregor raised his elegantly shaped eyebrows.

'That's right.' Dover nodded. 'Tomorrow morning. You fix it. Now, what have you been up to lately, apart from just buggering around?'

'Well, sir,' – MacGregor drew up a chair – 'I really think I may be on to something. I got this lead at the ... '

'Yes,' said Dover, 'well, never mind that now. Here, take this tray! Ooh, that's better. I keep getting cramp in my legs. At least I hope it's cramp. It may be something worse. You never know. Now then, there's a few things I want you to do for me, if you can spare the time, of course.' Dover's irony was, as always, heavy-handed. 'Now, did you go to that Country Club place last night?'

'Oh yes, sir, that's what I was trying to tell you. You see ... '

'Good.' Dover went over MacGregor like a steamroller. 'Well, you're to go there again tonight. And tomorrow night and every night until I tell you to pack it in. Got it?'

'But, I'd arranged to go to Galeford tonight, sir. I'm going to meet a man who ... '

'I do wish, just once in a while, laddie,' said Dover injecting a note of world weariness in his voice, 'you'd do what you're told without arguing the toss every blasted inch of the way.'

'Very good, sir,' said MacGregor stiffly.

'Right! It's the Country Club every night for you until I tell you to stop. I want you to be the first in and the last out. Got it?'

'What, exactly, am I supposed to be doing, sir?'

'Enjoying yourself, laddie!' leered Dover. 'Just behave like the other customers. Have yourself a ball! Go gay! Start living a bit! But keep your expenses down because I'm damned if I'm going to countersign any great long claim just for you to go drinking yourself silly.'

'I'm afraid I don't exactly see ... '

'And the other thing,' said Dover, gazing blankly at the ceiling, 'is that animal doctor woman.'

'Miss ffiske, sir?' asked MacGregor frowning.

'That's right. Miss ffiske with two little f's. Well, I want you to go and call on Miss f-f-ffiske th-th-this m-m-morning.' He chuckled. He liked his little joke, Dover did.

MacGregor priggishly pretended not to have noticed. 'What for, sir?'

'Eh?' said Dover, still obsessed with his own wit. 'Oh, go and ask her about the night Hamilton k-k-kicked the b-b-bucket.'

MacGregor permitted himself a faintly patronizing smile. 'I really think that would be rather a waste of time, sir. Miss ffiske has already told us all she knows, which in any case didn't amount to much. I had several other things scheduled for this morning, sir, and I really do think ... '

Dover went to the trouble of heaving himself up in bed so as to bring the full force of his personality to bear on the unfortunate MacGregor. The boot-button eyes narrowed, the snub nose wrinkled menacingly, the unshaven jowls quivered. It was an arresting sight. Even the debonair MacGregor involuntarily drew back. Dover said nothing. This was chiefly due to the fact that he couldn't for the moment think of anything sufficiently intimidating to say, but it certainly heightened the impression he was trying to make.

'Very well, sir,' said MacGregor weakly.

Slowly Dover nodded his head. 'That's better, laddie. Now, you're to stop there precisely half an hour. Not a minute more, not a minute less. Savvy?'

'Half an hour, sir? With Miss ffiske? But why?'

Dover smiled in what he hoped was an enigmatic manner and solemnly tapped the side of his nose with his forefinger. 'That's my little secret, laddie. Now, I don't want you hanging around here all day wasting my time. Hop it!'

When MacGregor had retreated unhappily from the room Dover sat up in bed and rocked backwards and forwards in silent and malicious mirth. The look on MacGregor's face! Oh Lord, it was enough to make a cat laugh! That'd teach the toffee-nosed young pup! That'd show him there was still a bit of life in the old dog. Thought they knew everything, these young coppers did. They read a couple of flipping books and before you knew where you were they were trying to teach their grandmothers to suck eggs. Well, there was one grandmother here who'd sucked more eggs than Sergeant cleverboots MacGregor had had hot dinners. And bigger eggs and more complicated eggs than some he could name, too.

With a scowl Dover abandoned the imagery which was getting far too complicated and winced slightly as he suffered yet another of those small twinges of doubt. They had been assailing him ever since a possible solution of the Hamilton and Cochran affairs had first dawned on him. It had been a far-fetched, and really rather amusing, explanation of various things that seemed to have been happening and Dover had had, in his own ponderous fashion, a bit of a giggle over it. His good humour had faded rapidly, however, when almost in spite of himself he began to analyse the implications and found that he was hitting the jackpot every time. He began to get frightened. It was unnerving enough for a detective of his calibre to stumble, however fortuitously, upon the solution of a case, but to stumble on such a solution was hair-raising. His first instinct was to shift the burden on to younger and more capable shoulders – but MacGregor would die laughing. It would be the biggest joke that had echoed round the corridors of Scotland Yard since that old fool of a judge had congratulated Harry Tobias on resisting the offer of a bribe.

What was he to do then? He could, of course, just forget the whole thing. The Chief Constable's patience was bound to be exhausted before long and he would soon be only too glad to see the back of the Scotland Yard men. It was a way out but Dover, incredible as it may seem, was not entirely devoid of professional pride. He would like to emerge from this messy, neither-one-thing-nor-the-other case with flying colours. For one thing, it wouldn't do him any harm up at the Yard where his credit was currently at a very low ebb. Several nasty and unkind insinuations had recently been made in his hearing about the carrying of overweight passengers and Dover had had the idea that these remarks were directed towards him. Yes, a glittering success even in a mucky little backwater like Wallerton wouldn't come amiss. All right. He'd make the effort. He'd solve their flipping case for them and they could put that on their needles and knit it.

A spiteful little sparkle came into Dover's eye as he pondered over what method he would have to employ to achieve his ends. He didn't underestimate the difficulties with which he was going to be faced. He wasn't going to tie this case up with a couple of plaster casts and an old shoe lace, that was for sure. No, what he'd have to do was put the wind up 'em, force them to act again, and then nab 'em red-handed. Piece of cake, really. With Master Charles Edward MacGregor as the unwitting bait. Dover grinned to himself.

A clock somewhere outside struck ten. Sergeant Veitch, who had been waiting outside for several minutes, tapped gently on the bedroom door.

'You're late!' snapped Dover when he saw who it was.

'The church clock, sir ...'

'It's slow,' said Dover. 'Well, have you got what I wanted? Gimme!'

The station sergeant handed over a thick file of papers.

Dover flicked contemptuously through them. 'Aha!' he grunted triumphantly as he selected one small single sheet. He thrust it in front of Sergeant Veitch's face. 'Are you sure Cochran saw this before he took off?'

The sergeant focused his eyes as best he could on the paper which was now being waggled energetically up and down. 'Well, yes, sir.' He grabbed the paper to hold it steady. 'You see, sir, there's Cochran's initials down in the corner.'

Dover snatched the paper back. 'Where?'

'There, sir. Oh.' Sergeant Veitch got his glasses out and put them on. 'No, I'm sorry, sir. He doesn't seem to have initialled it. Well now, that's funny. I remember drawing his attention to it myself. He should have initialled it to show he'd read it because, of course, he's one of the chaps mentioned on it.'

'I can see that,' said Dover. 'I'm not blind. Could this have been the last thing he was looking at before he hopped it?'

'Well, it could, I suppose, sir,' said Sergeant Veitch uncertainly. 'That might explain why he hasn't ... But I don't get it, sir. Why should a bit of paper with the date of the annual medicals on it upset him? If that's what you're getting at.'

'Why, indeed?' said Dover, shovelling all the other papers back into the file. 'Here, you can get rid of this lot.'

The sergeant's jaw dropped. He shuddered to think how many hours he'd spent sorting all those blasted papers out. 'Don't you want them, sir?'

'No.' Dover tipped the file into the sergeant's lap. 'They're of no interest to me. I've got the one I want.'

'Oh. I see,' said the sergeant, rising to his feet with sullen resignation. 'Is there anything else you want, sir?'

Dover had already assumed a prone position with his face to the wall. 'Tell 'em to send my coffee up at eleven sharp. And I want it hot, too.'

'The Chief Constable, sir,' began Sergeant Veitch.

'I've no time to be bothered with the Chief Constable.' Dover's voice was muffled by the blankets which he had pulled up over his ears. 'You tell him I'll have some concrete news for him in a day or two. And I don't want bothering till then. Got it?'

'Er, yes, sir.' The sergeant stood for a moment as though unsure of what to do. 'Well, good morning then, sir.'

There was no reply.

It was half past two before Dover sallied forth from the hotel. The rain, for once, had stopped and it was quite sunny. People, residents and visitors alike, looked happier. In Wallerton you soon learnt to be grateful for small mercies. What matter that a cold sea breeze was cutting down the streets and blowing sand into everybody's face?

Dover, with the help of two or three passers-by, eventually found his way into the street in which Hamilton, alias Sunny Malone, had lived and died. He shuffled down it at a leisurely pace, pausing only to stick his tongue out at the front door from behind which Mrs Hamilton had struck him such a dastardly blow. At the next gateway he stood still and examined the house in front of him. It looked exactly the same as all the others except for the small brass plate on the door bearing Miss ffiske's name, qualifications and profession.

Dover ambled up the steps and rang the bell.

Miss Gourlay put up a gallant resistance. 'I'm very sorry, Chief Inspector, but it's quite impossible for Miss ffiske to see you now. She's just going out on her rounds. She's a very busy woman, you know, and these poor sick animals; they're absolutely dependent on her. If you like, I'll make an appointment for you to come back this evening.'

'I want to see Miss ffiske now. You just nip along and tell her.'

'No!' said Miss Gourlay in a sudden rush of bravery. 'I will not! She works far too hard as it is and I'm sick to death of people thinking she's at their beck and call.'

'Do you know, miss, what the penalty is for obstructing the police in the execution of their duty?'

'No!' Miss Gourlay retorted cheekily. 'Do you?'

As it happens, Dover didn't. Not specifically at any rate. 'Six years!' he blustered.

Miss Gourlay burst into a peal of girlish laughter. 'Rubbish!' she squeaked. Really, she was quite enjoying herself. Men weren't so awful after all, not if you stood up to them and treated them like human beings. She must tell Hazel about it afterwards.

Meanwhile Dover had had enough. It was undignified for a detective of his seniority and experience to be seen standing on doorsteps bandying words with stupid chits of girls. He'd tried the diplomatic approach. Now it was time for action.

'Oh, dear!' said Miss Gourlay as Dover began merely to walk forward over the threshold. She tried to stop him but she would have had more success against a tank. Dover triumphantly entered the hall to find himself confronted by an agitated Miss ffiske, hurrying to see what all the commotion was about. She was wearing a trilby hat of almost unbelievable ugliness and a good heavy overcoat.

'What on earth is it now?' she demanded.

'Just a few more questions about the night Mr Hamilton died,' said Dover blandly, pushing his bowler hat back on his head.

'I told him you were too busy to see him now, dear,' wailed Miss Gourlay, 'but he just wouldn't take any notice. I told him he couldn't see you without an appointment. I said ... '

'For God's sake, Janie, shut up!' Miss ffiske, arms akimbo, swung round to face Dover. 'Now, look here, you, I'm just getting a bit fed up with this. I told you all I know, which is precisely nothing, the first time you called. I told your dratted sergeant all I know, which is still precisely nothing, when he was here wasting my time this morning. I happen to have my living to earn and I don't propose ...'

'What?' Dover rolled his eyes and clutched at the hall stand for support. 'What did you say?'

Miss ffiske stared at him in some stupefaction, as well she might. Dover hamming it up was enough to make the blood run cold. 'Are you feeling all right?'

'What,' gasped Dover, his chest heaving spasmodically to signify surprise and horror, 'what did you say about my sergeant?' He rolled his eyes again for good measure.

Miss Gourlay skipped agilely past him and took shelter behind Miss ffiske.

'I just said that I told your sergeant for the second time ...'

'When?' howled Dover, his voice trembling with a sense of impending doom. 'Oh, when?'

'This morning,' Miss ffiske stammered, her self possession beginning to desert her in the face of this histrionic orgy.

Dover fell back against the wall and clutched his heart. 'This morning?' His voice rose to a hoarse shriek. The English stage lost nothing when he decided to become a policeman. 'Do you mean that Detective Sergeant MacGregor was here this morning' – a long dramatic pause – *'alone?'*

Miss ffiske looked anxiously at Miss Gourlay. 'Well, yes,' she said at last.

Dover, never one to underplay a scene, grabbed his head with both hands and sank quivering on to a convenient chair. 'Oh, my God!' he groaned.

'Is anything the matter?' asked Miss ffiske, backing a little way down the hall.

'You may well ask,' intoned Dover. 'You may well ask.' He managed to inject a sob into the phrase on the repetition.

'Should I telephone for the police, dear?' whispered Miss Gourlay.

'Don't be a damned fool, Janie, he *is* the police.'

Dover looked annoyed. He groaned to swing the attention

back to him. 'Sergeant MacGregor,' he said in a sepulchral voice, 'should not have come here by himself.'

'Oh,' said Miss ffiske, much relieved, 'is that all?'

'Sergeant MacGregor has been expressly forbidden to interview members of the opposite sex unless he is chaperoned by a senior police officer.'

'Good grief!' said Miss ffiske. 'Why?'

Dover dropped his voice a couple of octaves for the punch line. 'He is not to be trusted. There have been a number of unfortunate, er, incidents.'

Miss Gourlay clutched Miss ffiske.

Dover addressed Miss ffiske fearfully. 'I sincerely hope, madam, that he made no improper advances towards you?'

'I should like to see him try!' said Miss ffiske stoutly. 'He just came ... '

'Or to you, madam?'

Miss Gourlay, wide-eyed, cowered further behind her friend and shook her head.

'Thank God!' said Dover piously. 'Thank God!'

'Good grief,' said Miss ffiske, trying to bring the conversation back to a terrestrial level, 'you're going on as though the man's a sexual maniac.'

'But he is, madam, he is! You don't know how lucky you've been.'

'Well, in that case,' said Miss ffiske with a remarkable show of common sense, 'what's he doing in the police force?'

Dover scowled at her irritably. 'Because we can't catch him at it, that's why!' he snapped.

'Well, I must say, he looked a perfectly nice, respectable young man to me.'

'He would! That's part of his technique. You'd be surprised at how many innocent young girls he's lured to their doom that way.'

'Well, he didn't try to lure me.'

Be a brave man who did, thought Dover grumpily. 'I suggest, madam,' he said aloud, 'that if he comes hanging around you again you get in touch with me without delay.'

'I don't think that will be necessary, thank you very much!' was Miss ffiske's tart rejoinder. 'I can assure you that I am more than competent to deal with that sort of thing. And, should I have any complaints to make about Sergeant MacGregor's behaviour, I shall make them at a considerably higher level than yours.'

'Suit yourself!' mumbled Dover crossly. 'But just don't say I didn't warn you, that's all.'

'If I am raped by a detective sergeant from Scotland Yard under your command, you will have to face more than reproaches!' said Miss ffiske sourly. 'Now, Janie, I'm going out on my rounds. You'd better lock the door behind me and put the chain on. Just in case.'

Dover, not being left much choice, took his leave. He was not unsatisfied with his performance. In fact, he was rather pleased with it. He didn't get much opportunity of playing character parts so that, when he did, he flung himself in to it heart and soul. He congratulated himself unreservedly as he made his way back to the hotel. The seeds had been sown. The trap had been baited. The hook had been dangled. All that remained now was for the master mind to take things easy and let the insidious poison of suspicion do its work.

There are few people who can hold a candle to Chief Inspector Dover when it comes to taking things easy, though it must not be assumed that he did absolutely nothing to further his case in the ensuing twenty-four hours. On the very next morning he received the police surgeon in his hotel bedroom and was closeted with that bewildered gentleman for an hour and a half. Professional secrecy has thrown an impenetrable veil over the proceedings but it can be surmised that Dover's stomach, corns and sore toe were not the exclusive topics of discussion. Dover wanted information, and the police surgeon, unworthily wondering from time to time if he was dealing with a particularly nasty type of obsessional neurotic, provided what answers he could. He pointed out rather stiffly to the Chief Inspector that this was not a matter which cropped up frequently in a respectable practice, not even in one which also embraced the local police force.

When the doctor, sworn to secrecy, had gone Dover permitted himself a rich chuckle of congratulation. He was more firmly convinced than ever that he was on the right lines. As was his wont, once he had made up his mind very little, and certainly not contrary facts and contradictory evidence, could induce him to change it. MacGregor had frequently lamented this in the past. On this particular occasion, however, MacGregor was not going to be informed that Dover had all but solved the case. In the next few days whenever Dover saw his sergeant he listened attentively to that young man's elaborate reports of the trails he was following, and said nothing of his own astonishing deductions. MacGregor might have been forgiven for thinking, as he did, that Dover was indulging even more luxuriously than usual in his favourite pastime of putting his feet up. But MacGregor would have been wrong.

As the days passed and as the fancy took him Dover sallied forth from time to time into the highways and by-ways of Wallerton to add a finishing touch or two. These finishing touches were added with a certain ham-fistedness, but then delicacy was never one of Dover's strong points.

His usual technique was to roam the streets of Wallerton in search of ladies who were members of the Ladies' League. Dover's eyesight was not as good as it had been. The weather was nearly always inclement and plastic macs are not as transparent as all that. His habit of approaching close to middle-aged ladies and staring fixedly at their bosoms did not pass unnoticed. Some ladies, not sporting the blue ribbon for which he searched, were even more distressed when, having examined them in vain, the Chief Inspector uttered a disgusted ''Strewth!' and hurried away.

Not that things were much better when he did espy his prey. He was then faced with the problem of engaging them in conversation. The respectable matrons of Wallerton were horrified to find themselves accosted by a large, fat and uncouth lout who, perhaps standing beside a shop window display of lingerie would address them with some such remark as 'I'm surprised some of these young girls don't catch their death wearing flimsy things like that, aren't you? Ah, but that's the younger generation all over. I don't know what they're coming to these days, straight I don't. Take that young Sergeant MacGregor of mine, for instance. Got the morals of a randy bull, that lad ... '

Sometimes he rested his feet in a café. Pretty Polly's Parlour was a favourite place because everybody who was anybody went there for morning coffee. Dover would select his victim and, braving the black looks, would join her at her table. From there on he would play it by ear. The prey and her friends might well be admiring some near-by baby. Dover would leap in.

'I wonder who's paying the maintenance order for that one?' he would ask jovially. 'Oh, you needn't look surprised! There's more born out of wedlock these days than in it, if you ask me. I don't know what's got into the younger generation, straight I don't. Take that young Sergeant MacGregor of mine, for instance. Got the morals of a tom cat, that lad ... '

Mrs Cadogan (known in the trade as Pretty Polly) couldn't understand it – all these cups of coffee completely untouched or with only a mouthful taken out of them. Oh well, she thought philosophically, as she tipped the contents of the cups back into the urn, it helped to keep the overheads down.

Before the week was out MacGregor had acquired a reputation which Don Juan might have envied. (There was more than a soupçon of doubt about the Chief Inspector, too, but that's beside the point.) As usually happens, the subject of the gossip remained in blissful ignorance of the calumny which was beginning to besmirch his name. MacGregor's days were spent in dashing hither and thither round the countryside following lines of investigation which would, he was confident, lead him to the men who had mutilated the dead body of the late Mr Hamilton. His nights were spent, at Dover's insistence, in living it up at the Country Club. The strain was beginning to tell. Dover noted with great satisfaction the increasing signs of exhaustion which were starting to show in MacGregor's face. The lad was getting to look quite dissipated.

'I do wish I didn't have to keep going to that Country Club, sir,' complained MacGregor one day when he had been granted a brief audience. 'I really can't see what good it's doing. And it's as dull as ditchwater, too.'

Dover raised his eyebrows. 'I thought it was supposed to be a right old sink of iniquity.'

'I dare say it is, sir, usually. But not when I'm there. They all sit around playing stud poker for matches. All I'm doing is ruining their trade. Why, last night Joey the Jock even offered me fifty quid to stay away from the place. He said I'd bankrupt him if I kept coming much longer.'

'Fifty quid!' said Dover with an envious whistle. 'You lucky devil!'

'Naturally I didn't accept it, sir.'

'Oh, naturally!' sniffed Dover. 'You wouldn't! Still, if the offer's open tomorrow night, I should take it.'

'You're not suggesting I should accept a bribe, are you, sir?'

'It's not a bribe,' objected Dover. 'As long as you take care he doesn't hand it over in front of witnesses or give you marked notes or anything, you're as safe as houses. I wish somebody'd offer me fifty quid on a plate like that!'

'Does this mean that you don't want me to go to the Country Club after tomorrow night, sir?'

'Yes, just tonight and tomorrow and then you're through. Wallerton's grape vine's dead efficient, and quick. A day and a half, say; that should be bags of time.'

'I'm afraid I don't understand, sir.'

Dover scowled at him. 'Hard luck, laddie,' he said. 'Still, never mind, you'll understand all right in good time. Now, what's today? Wednesday? Right, so you'll go to that Country Club tonight, see? But on Thursday night you stop in here, in the hotel. Now, my guess is that somebody'll try and contact you, during the evening probably. They may telephone or they may come round, I dunno. But, whatever they do, you fall in with it, see? They'll probably want you to leave the hotel so don't make any bones about it, you just go. Do whatever they want you to.'

MacGregor eyed Dover with a suspicion that was entirely justified. 'But, where will you be, sir?'

'Ah,' said Dover with a happy grin, 'that's a good question, laddie. I'll be around, never you fear.'

'Is this going to involve me in any, er, danger, sir?' asked MacGregor dubiously.

'Don't be daft!' said Dover. 'Would I do a thing like that to you?'

Chapter Thirteen

MacGregor showed a marked reluctance to leave after this urbane piece of reassurance. He tried, without success, to find out precisely what Dover was up to. His appeals for clarification fell on wilfully deaf ears. It wasn't often that Dover went to the trouble to work out an elaborate scheme like this and he wasn't, as he himself put it, going to have it all buggered up at the last minute.

'But, sir,' said MacGregor who was getting extraordinarily uneasy about the whole thing, 'I could play my part much better if I knew what it was all about.'

'No!' Dover's bottom lip jutted out obstinately. 'I want you to behave naturally.'

'Look here, sir,' said MacGregor taking his courage in both hands, 'I'm not a bit happy about all this. I can't imagine what good it's going to do. Now, my own private investigations really are getting somewhere. There's no doubt about it, Hamilton had been getting mixed up with some very dicey characters, and some that wouldn't stop at violence, either. Not local layabouts but real full-time villains from all over the place. He'd been backing some pretty nasty, highly organized professional gangs. Now, if he double-crossed them, or they even thought he had, they'd fix him good and proper. And they'd fix Cochran, too. It's my theory that one of these gangs, and I've a jolly good idea which one, got the idea that Hamilton had shopped them over their job. He'd financed them, you see, to the tune of a couple of thousand quid if my information is correct, and of course he knew all the details. Well, the job was a complete flop. The police were waiting for them. Most of the big boys got away, but four or five of the small fry got themselves nabbed. There's no doubt about it, somebody tipped the police off. It may or may not have been Hamilton. I think the gang thought it was. And they probably thought he'd told Cochran. Well, they gave Hamilton a real going over in the course of which he dies on them. Now, just look at Cochran's position. He knows who it was who did for Hamilton. He knows they'll be after him. They've got to save their own necks. He knows he'll get no mercy from a vicious bunch like that so he hides in his lodgings for a week to keep out of their way. But on the Monday morning he's got to go back to work. He can't hide any longer. He's got to put that uniform on and get back on the beat. He suddenly realizes that he's just a sitting target. The gang can get him any time and he appreciates only too well what's going to happen to him when they do. So, out of sheer desperation and terror, he cycles up to Cully Point.'

Dover opened his eyes. He stretched himself and yawned. 'Oh?' he said, blinking. 'Are you still here, laddie?'

'I'm just going, sir,' replied MacGregor coldly.

'Well, don't forget what I told you. Tomorrow evening you stop in the hotel and wait for the summons. And don't worry, laddie! I've got it all planned out. You'll be as safe as houses.'

When MacGregor had gone Dover bestirred himself with a most unusual display of energy. He rummaged around in his suitcase until he found the pile of headed writing paper that he had already pinched from the hotel lounge. He selected the grubbiest sheet and then began to search for a pen. He eventually unearthed a rather nasty ball-point bound together with sticking plaster. Lamenting, not for the first time, that finders can't be choosers, he sat himself down on the edge of his bed and began laboriously to compose a letter to the Chief Constable.

It took him a long time as he was rather out of practice when it came to putting pen to paper. Nowadays he shoved all that sort of menial drudgery on to MacGregor. However, he got to the end at last and read the epistle through. Clear as daylight. Any fool could understand what he was getting at. He crossed out the odd word here and there, which didn't improve the general appearance. With some regret he addressed one of his envelopes. He'd only been able to collect ten of them and it seemed a pity to use one. Still, the letter was highly confidential and the sacrifice must be made. He licked the sticky stuff and stuck the flap down, leaving a perfect thumb print on the back as he did so.

With a considerable sense of martyrdom Dover trudged off to make arrangements for the delivery of his letter. On the way he saw a little notice pointing to the railway station. He looked at it thoughtfully. He supposed he might as well go there first. He turned in the indicated direction and found himself thirty seconds later at a complicated road juncture and completely lost. Being a great believer in using his head to save his legs, he grabbed the nearest passer-by and, detaining him by brute force, demanded to be told where the bloody station was.

Six passers-by later Wallerton's Central Station was actually in sight. Dover was glad. He was getting worn out manoeuvring the conversations he had forced upon perfect strangers from a simple request to be put on the right way to an elaborate account of how he and MacGregor were going to shake the dust of Wallerton off their heels in a couple of days' time. Some of the perfect strangers had been resigned and listened to all this rigmarole with kindly indulgence. Other perfect strangers got highly obstreperous and objected strongly to being detained in the cold and the pouring rain. Dover had had quite a job with some of them, being obliged to clutch them firmly by the collar or by the arm. However, the Chief Inspector stuck to his self-appointed task, priding himself quite erroneously that, having put his shoulder to the wheel, he was not the man to turn back.

He staggered into the booking hall at the railway station and flopped down on the nearest bench. While he recovered his strength he stared sullenly at posters of semi-naked lads and lassies romping on sunlit beaches. The edges were already peeling in the damp. There were very few people about and those that were looked as though they were sheltering from the rain.

Dover pulled himself to his feet and went across to the ticket office. He bent down and peered through the glass partition which is placed there to prevent travellers breathing germs on the booking staff.

There was nobody there.

Dover waited a full fifteen seconds before his patience gave out. He hammered on the glass and bellowed through the little slit at the top.

Eventually a young man appeared. He had long flowing locks which he was combing tenderly with a pink pocket comb held in his left hand. In his right hand he clutched a partially eaten bar of chocolate.

He looked at Dover. 'Hello, darling!' he said cheerfully, 'where do you want to go? Or don't it matter, eh? I 'spect you're like me, eh? It don't matter as long as it's far far away from Squaresville here. And to think I come for the surfing! I shoulda gone to the North Pole. Well, now, Daddy-o, we've got some real pretty tickets for Sudley Burbiton and all points east. You pays your money and you takes your choice.'

'I don't want to buy a ticket,' snarled Dover.

'Oh, just come for a chat, have you, darling? Well, I'd like to oblige but I'm already spoken for. We could never be nothing more than good friends, see?'

Dover took a grip on himself. 'I want to make inquiries about trains to London.'

'Ah, well,' said the young man triumphantly, 'you've come to the wrong hole, haven't you, darling? The inquiry office is over there, see?'

'Is it open?' demanded Dover suspiciously.

'Oh, you're a clever puss, aren't you, darling? It's not exactly what you'd call open and it's not exactly what you call closed. I'm supposed to be in there but the fire's gone kaputt, see? So I come in here where it's warmer. What can I do for you, darling – in the way of transport, natch?'

'Is there a train to London a Thursday evening?' said Dover, determined to get this over as soon as possible.

'There is indeed, darling,' agreed the young man. 'Thirty five minutes past six of the clockio, change at Sudley Burbiton.'

'Sudley Burbiton? Where in God's name is Sudley Burbiton?'

'You might well ask, darling! Well, it ain't the centre of the universe, that I can tell you. It's a dopey little burg about an hour away from here by the courtesy of British Rail.'

'An hour? Does the train stop anywhere else between here and this Sudley Burbiton?'

'It stops everywhere, darling, and three times in between,' said the young man, finishing off his chocolate and swopping his comb for a nail file.

'What's the first stop?'

'The first stop, darling? Let's see ... ' He tapped the nail file thoughtfully against his front teeth. 'Well now, the mighty iron horse that breathes smoke and fire will grind to a shattering halt at Abbots Brook.'

'Right,' said Dover, making up his mind in a rush because the thought of shelling out his own money was painful. 'Give me a single to Abbots Brook.'

'Second class, of course, darling?' The young man disappeared out of sight. A second or two later he was back again. 'Look, darling, it's taking the food out of my mouth but I've taken a fancy to you, see? You don't want to go to Abbots Brook by *train*. Not from here. The station's miles away from the village. You want to go by bus. Everybody goes to Abbots Brook by bus.'

Damn and blast it! fumed Dover to himself. It'll be all round the blooming town now that I'm going to Abbots Brook! He searched miserably through his pockets. If this part of his plan was going to work he'd have to make the supreme sacrifice.

'Give me a single to London,' he said hoarsely.

The young man shrugged his shoulders. 'I wish you'd make up your mind, darling,' he said crossly. 'If they was all like you I'd be kipping here. Three pounds seventeen and fourpence.'

Dover went white. 'Three pounds seventeen and fourpence?' he yelped. 'It's highway robbery!'

'I couldn't agree more, darling. I always go by scooter myself.'

Shattered, Dover handed four crumpled pound notes over and left the railway station, a sadder but wiser man. After years of never lifting a finger for himself – he maintained a wife and a sergeant for that sort of thing – he was just beginning to discover how the other half lived. And it was grim. The money it was costing him! For a moment the thought of chucking the whole thing up crossed his mind. But then he remembered MacGregor and the prospect of putting the wind up that young gentleman good and proper was too attractive to resist. No, the show must go on! He could always get a refund for the ticket.

At the police station he caught Sergeant Veitch taking things easy and refreshing himself with a mug of tea.

'What on earth are you doing here, sir?' asked the sergeant, quickly slipping a book confiscated from a local newsagent under the pile of Police Gazettes. 'The Chief Constable's just this minute gone round to your hotel. I made sure you'd be there at this time in the morning.'

'Well, I'm not,' said Dover, lifting up the flap of the counter and heading for the nearest chair. 'What does he want, anyhow?'

'Well, he wanted to see you, sir. He seemed a bit upset that he hadn't had any progress reports from you.'

'Old fool!' said Dover.

'I'll ring up the hotel and see if I can catch him, shall I, sir?'

'Wafor?'

'To tell him you're here, sir.'

'I can see why you never got beyond sergeant,' Dover observed pleasantly. 'Now, how about nipping up to the canteen and getting me a cup that cheers but does not inebriate?'

'Eh?'

'Oh, for God's sake!' snapped Dover. 'A cup of tea, you fool!'

'Oh, I'm sorry, sir. I'll send Jimmy here.'

'You won't send "Jimmy here", you'll go yourself! The exercise'll do you good. I want to have a word with "Jimmy here" myself – private. So I don't want to see your ugly mug for another ten minutes. Now, push off! And four lumps of sugar in mine!' he bawled as the station sergeant unhappily moved off in the direction of the canteen. 'Right, laddie!' Dover eyed the bright young police cadet who instantly snapped, quivering, to attention. 'So you're "Jimmy here", are you?'

'Yessir!'

'Well, take the weight off your feet and pin your ears back because, if you slip up, laddie, you'll have me to answer to.' Dover scowled horribly.

'Yessir!'

'Now, can you keep your trap shut? Because you're not to breathe a word to a living soul about what I'm going to ask you to do. Now then, Thursday night – that's tomorrow night – at 6.35 p.m. on the dot, not a second earlier and not a second later, you're to take this letter to the Chief Constable and give it to him personally. Got it?'

'Yessir!' The cadet's eyes sparkled with excitement as he took the dog-eared letter which Dover held out to him. 'Matter of life and death, is it, sir?'

'It may come to that, laddie,' said Dover solemnly. 'And it'll be on your head if anything goes wrong, so just watch it. Make sure you know exactly where the Chief Constable's going to be on Thursday night.'

'Yessir! I'd already thought of that, sir.'

'Oh, had you? And there's another thing. Just before you leave here, tip off whoever's on duty to get every man he can lay his hands on standing by. It's up to the Chief Constable, of course, but I reckon he'll be grateful.'

'Going to be a punch-up is there, sir?'

'Wouldn't surprise me if they issued firearms,' said Dover smugly.

The police cadet whistled. 'Will you be leading us, sir?'

Dover looked at him sharply to see if the cheeky young pup was taking the mickey. Surprisingly enough, he wasn't. 'No, laddie,' said Dover, 'unfortunately I have to go up to London that night. There's nothing confidential about that, by the way. In fact, you can spread it around as much as you like. And you might mention that Sergeant MacGregor is resuming his holiday on the Continent the following morning.'

'Ooh! I get you, sir.' The police cadet was a bright lad. 'That's to put 'em off the scent, is it, sir?'

Dover nodded wisely.

'Will you be wanting railway warrants, sir?'

Dover's face didn't so much fall as collapse. Railway warrants! And there'd he been lashing out his hard earned lolly on bloody well buying a ticket! 'You can make one out for me, laddie. First class, of course. Never mind about Sergeant MacGregor's for the moment. I don't know where he's going to anyhow. And now, sonnie, here's a chance for you to show your initiative,' Dover beamed at the likely lad. 'Nip back to the railway station and get me my money back on this ticket.'

'Yessir!' The police cadet thundered smartly to his feet. He put the envelope for the Chief Constable in his pocket, reached for his cap and took the railway ticket, all in one motion. It made Dover ache to watch him. 'I expect there'll be a small deduction, sir.'

'Deduction?' howled Dover. 'There'd better damned well not be! Three pounds seventeen and fourpence I paid for that ticket and three pounds seventeen and fourpence I bloody well want back again.'

'But they always deduct something, sir. It's the regulations.'

'Look, laddie, if you haven't learnt how to bend regulations at your age, you'd better hand that uniform in and go back on the farm. Get tough! Lean on 'em! Push 'em around a bit! I don't give a damn what you do as long as I get my three pounds seventeen and fourpence back. Now, get moving!'

The station sergeant appeared diffidently on the scene, a cup of tea in his hand. 'Is it all right ... Here, where's that kid going?'

'Just running a little errand for me.'

'What am I supposed to tell the Chief Constable, sir? He'll play merry hell if he finds out you've been here and I didn't let him know.'

'Don't tell him.'

'You'll have to see him some time, sir. You can't go on playing box and cox with him for ever.'

'Don't have to,' announced Dover smugly. 'Thursday night, I'm going back to London.'

'This Thursday, sir?'

'And MacGregor'll be clearing off on Friday morning.'

'Are you going for good, sir?'

Dover nodded. 'It's not my habit to go on flogging a dead horse,' he said righteously. We're getting nowhere fast on this blooming business.'

'But what about Sergeant MacGregor, sir? I thought from what you were saying that he was on to something?'

'Ah,' said Dover, looking sly, 'I can't answer for what MacGregor's going to do. He's young and keen. He only *says* he's going off on Friday morning. It's not like him to leave a case in mid-air but he says he's going off on holiday and who are we to say him nay, eh?'

'You mean he might be staying on in Wallerton under cover like?'

Dover shrugged his shoulders and didn't answer.

'The Chief Constable's going to blow his top when he hears,' said Sergeant Veitch gloomily. 'He'll do his nut, I'm telling you. 'Specially if he hears it second-hand. He likes to think people trust him, you know, and that they aren't afraid to tell him things. Load of old tripe, of course, because he's the most bad-tempered bastard I've ever clapped eyes on. You *are* going to see him before you go, aren't you, sir?'

'No,' said Dover.

'Phone him up, perhaps?'

'Yes,' said Dover, getting bored with all this. 'I'll phone him up. Don't you worry about it.' It was a blatant lie but it seemed to satisfy Sergeant Veitch who didn't relish the prospect of explaining to the Chief Constable that the birds from Scotland Yard had flown without even saying goodbye.

'Here,' said Dover suddenly, 'he's not likely to come back again, is he?'

'Oh my God, I hope not!' Sergeant Veitch paled. 'No, I remember now, he said he'd got to get back for some committee meeting or other.'

'Fine,' said Dover. 'In that case you can treat me to lunch in the canteen.'

For the remainder of his time in Wallerton Dover, when he wasn't eating or sleeping or packing, resumed his peregrinations round the town. By the time he sat down to his high tea on the Thursday evening there can't have been many people in Wallerton who didn't know that the Chief Inspector was leaving on the 6.35 and his sergeant some time on the following morning. It had been an exhausting job but Dover felt it had been worth the trouble.

He had even bestirred himself to the extent of calling, yet again, on Miss ffiske and assuring her that she had nothing to fear now that the lascivious MacGregor was about to leave town. Miss ffiske gave Dover a very odd look. Dover thought this extremely significant. He also trotted round to Mrs Jolliott, the late Constable Cochran's landlady. He excused the obvious inconvenience of his call – Mrs Jolliott was washing her front steps and wouldn't haave stopped for the Duke of Edinburgh himself – by saying that he had come to say goodbye. Mrs Jolliott, scrubbing brush suspended in mid scrub, also gave him a very peculiar look. Dover was in a seventh heaven of delight. The master plan was swinging into action. The mice were sniffing at the cheese. Soon they would nibble and then ...

wham! The trap would snap! Congratulations, applause, a place in the annals of Scotland Yard. What more could a detective ask? Dover rubbed his hands in joyous anticipation. He'd show 'em all, by God he would! They'd be green with envy when this little lot was over.

At six o'clock he was ready and waiting for his taxi. MacGregor brought his suitcase downstairs and helped the Chief Inspector on with his overcoat.

'Are you sure you don't want me to go to the station with you, sir?'

'You stop here,' said Dover. 'You've had your instructions. And God help you if you muck 'em up!'

'But are you sure you can manage, sir?'

'Of course I can manage!' exploded Dover. 'What do you think I am? A congenital idiot? I was catching trains when you were still in wet nappies.'

'I'm still not terribly clear about what you've got in mind, sir. I mean, are you going away for good, or what? And what am I supposed to be doing?'

'It's all taken care of, laddie,' said Dover impatiently. 'Where's that flaming taxi?' He looked at MacGregor in alarm, 'It won't be that Armstrong chap driving it, will it?'

'Oh, no, sir! I made a point of ringing up the other firm. Oh, that reminds me, sir, the Chief Constable ... '

'Here it is!' Dover fastened up his overcoat. 'Bring the bag, laddie. There's no time to waste.'

The Chief Inspector arrived safely at the station with no more than twenty minutes to wait. He settled himself in a first-class compartment and scowled furiously at any other passenger who dared to approach within twenty yards He pulled a particularly revolting face if the possible intruder was a woman. He didn't want any of them watching his every move, thank you very much! Just as long as they'd spotted him obviously departing from Wallerton, that was all he wanted.

Doors slammed, whistles blew. The train jerked off. Dover sat on the edge of his seat, his suitcase on the floor beside him, and grinned.

Chapter Fourteen

THE train didn't stop at Abbots Brook. It didn't stop at Abbots Corner, Abbots Gate or Sarah's Bottom. The tiny deserted stations rushed past Dover's horrified eyes. After ten minutes of nervously telling himself it would be all right, he was forced to admit that it probably wasn't. He began to get worried. With a curse he picked up his suitcase and struggled out into the corridor. It took him another ten minutes to track down the guard. He found him at last in an empty compartment at the very end of the train.

Dover, scarlet in the face from his exertions, dragged back the sliding door.

The guard looked up, automatically brushing a few crumbs off his tunic. He had a large packet of sandwiches on his lap and his feet were propped up on the opposite seat.

'Why,' demanded Dover in a strangled voice, 'didn't this bloody train stop at Abbots Brook?'

The guard examined him casually from head to toe and then, obviously unimpressed, opened up a sandwich and inspected the contents. 'Never does,' he said, taking a large bite. 'Cheese and pickle! And very nice, too.'

'They told me in Wallerton that it stopped at Abbots Brook.'

The guard shook his head. 'They was wrong then, weren't they? The 5.35 does. The 7.35 does, but not the 6.35. Don't ask me why. Been like that ever since I come on this route.'

'But that bloody young fool ...'

'Ah.' The guard took another bite. 'That'd be Percy. He's a right casual young burk. You don't never want to take no notice of what young Percy says. Why, if I had a quid for every passenger he's dropped in the dirt, I'd be a rich man.'

Dover heaved his suitcase into the compartment ahead of him and flopped down on the seat opposite the guard. He pulled out his handkerchief and mopped his face. 'I've got to get off this train,' he said.

The guard was unsympathetic. 'Well, there's the door, mate. If you want to wait till the train stops, though, you'll have to stick it out to Gibberford.' He lugged out a heavy silver pocket watch. 'That'll be another twenty minutes.'

'It's a matter of life and death,' said Dover.

The guard had heard this one before, several times in fact. 'Well, unfortunately, I'm not God Almighty, mate, or I might be able to help you.'

'You can stop the train, can't you?'

'I can,' agreed the guard comfortably, but I'm not going to. I live in Sudley Burbiton and the wife'll have my supper ready for me. You don't want always to go thinking of yourself, you know. There's others on the train besides you.'

'I'm from Scotland Yard,' said Dover, hunting through his pockets. 'I've got a warrant card here somewhere ... '

The guard shook his head. 'I shouldn't bother, mate. It won't make no difference. The answer's still no.' He unwrapped a small meat pie.

Dover scowled helplessly. 'It's a very serious offence,' he began.

'So's stopping trains,' retorted the guard. 'More than my blooming job's worth.'

'I've got to get off this train!' yelped Dover.

The guard nodded his head at the door. 'Try jumping, mate. They say you don't hurt yourself if you roll over and over when you land.'

'You'll live to regret this!' threatened Dover.

'Oh, yes?' said the guard, wiping his hands fastidiously on his waistcoat.

'I'll fix you!' blustered Dover, jowls wobbling. 'I'll have you harried from pillar to post! I'll make you rue the day you were born! I'll ... '

'Why don't you just belt up?' asked the guard equably. 'You'll be doing yourself an injury, working yourself up like that at your age.'

Dover clenched his fists in a paroxysm of fustrated fury and, then raising his eyes to heaven, he saw his salvation. The communication cord!

'Save your energy,' said the guard. 'It's disconnected – Tom up front living in Sudley Burbiton too and this being his last run for the night.'

'Oh God!' moaned Dover and buried his head in his hands.

But the guard wasn't made of stone. Dover pathetic was more effective than Dover rampant. 'Here,' he offered kindly, 'have a sandwich. You'll feel better with something inside you.'

And Dover did. By the time he'd finished off all the remaining sandwiches and got through a couple of crumbly jam tarts, he felt much better. He was able to regard his predicament with a certain amount of detachment. It was damned hard luck on MacGregor, of course, but even for him you could hardly call it the end of the world, could you? He'd learn to live with it in time. Lots of other people had. Dover sniggered to himself. Why, it might even turn out to be a blessing in disguise. The lad'd be able to concentrate on his job without dissipating his energies on a lot of external distractions. Dover chuckled.

The guard looked at him curiously. Gawd, you didn't half meet 'em on his job. One minute they were blubbering all over you, sobbing out some blooming hard-luck story, and the next minute they were laughing their flipping heads off.

'Feeling better, are you, mate?'

Dover wiped his eyes. 'Eh? Oh yes!' He swayed backwards and forwards as he tried to control his mirth. 'No good crying over spilt milk, is it? Like I say, there must be hundreds of people in the same boat, if you did but know it. I don't suppose it even shows ...'

The guard stopped ruminating on the imponderabilia of human nature and pricked up his ears as he caught a change in the rhythm of the train.

'Craig's Crossing!' he shouted excitedly. 'Come on, mate, you're in luck! Look lively, now, you'll only have a couple of seconds.'

Before Dover could say him nay, the guard had seized the suitcase and pulled it over to the door.

'Here – what the blazes?' squeaked Dover, scrambling to his feet and endeavouring to get his suitcase back again. He finished up in an untidy heap on the opposite seat as the train's brakes slammed on. When, having floundered around like a stranded whale, he got himself into an upright position, he found that the guard had already got the carriage door open.

'No!' shrieked Dover.

He was ignored. As the train juddered to a halt the suitcase was tossed out regardless on to the line.

'You bloody fool!' screamed Dover, plunging clumsily towards the door in a futile effort to recover his property.

'Come on!' roared the guard, rejoicing that he was able to help his fellow man at no cost to himself.

'No!' howled Dover again, seeing what was inevitably coming.

It was no good. The guard, who did early morning exercises to keep himself fit, caught the Chief Inspector off-balance. Dover was already moving in the direction of the door. His effort to switch into reverse was thwarted by the guard's grasp on his collar. Dover made the mistake of trying to strike the Good Samaritan in the stomach instead of grabbing hold of some immovable portion of the carriage. The guard laughingly side-stepped the foul blow and, with a cunning thrust, got Dover nicely poised in the open doorway. Then, still holding securely on to the collar of Dover's overcoat, he applied his knee to the small of Dover's back, and pushed. The bulk of Dover's body was propelled through the doorway but the restraining grasp on his collar prevented him from being flung forwards on his face. He found himself on the track in a more or less upright position, having scraped his back nastily on the protruding step as he descended.

There was an ominous clanking from the front end of the train. Dover instinctively leapt clear. Before he had time to turn round and express his heart-felt opinion on the recent happenings, the train was already moving. The guard slammed his door shut and stood waving cheerily from the open window.

'Your lucky day!' he called.

Dover made some suitable reply. Then he stood impotently waving his fist at the departing train. When at last it disappeared from view, he turned to contemplate his surroundings.

''Strewth!' muttered Dover. He looked round him again. 'Population explosion!' he grumbled. 'Standing room only by 2010! Bloody well looks like it, doesn't it?' Some cows in an adjoining field stared moodily at him. He was just on the point of picking up a handy sized lump of stone and chucking it at them when a tiny fragment of civilization caught his eye. A cottage! It lay away in the distance across no less than three fields but, unless Dover's eyes betrayed him, it was a cottage. Cursing profusely Dover picked up his suitcase and made his way gingerly across the railway line. By God, somebody was going to pay for this!

William Dibden and his sister, Wilhelmina, made a point of never opening their door to anyone after six o'clock at night. They'd heard too many stories of old-age pensioners being murdered in their beds to be caught napping themselves.

Wilhelmina clutched her tea-cup and huddled closer to the kitchen range. 'You'll have to do something,' she said. 'They'll kick that door down before long. You'll have to do something.'

William wasn't having any. He winced as the hammering on the door grew louder and more insistent. 'There's only one of 'em,' he muttered. 'I told you that before. A great hulking brute. Looked a right ruffian.'

'You'll have to do something,' said Wilhelmina. She was a great believer in constant dripping. 'They'll have that door down before long.'

'I don't know what you expect me to do about it.'

'I thought you were supposed to be a boxer?'

William snorted. 'That was over forty years ago, and I was a bantam.'

'You knocked Tom Pritchard out, didn't you?'

'He slipped and hit his head on a post,' said William grimly.

'Oh? First I've heard of that. I always thought knocking Tom Pritchard out was your main claim to fame.'

William sighed. He should have kept his mouth shut. She'd never let it drop now.

'You'll have to do something,' said Wilhelmina yet again. 'We'll never be able to hear the telly with this row going on.'

'Don't be daft.'

'David and Goliath,' said his sister.

'You haven't seen him. He's like the side of a house.'

'You'll have to do something.'

'Why don't you go out and have a chat with him. Likely he wouldn't hit you, you being a woman.'

Hoarse, unintelligible cries were now supplementing the kicking.

Wilhelmina had a better idea. 'Suppose you stand behind the door with the poker and then I'll let him in and you hit him?'

'He's twice my height,' objected William.

'You could stand on a chair. You'll have to do something. He'll have that door down before long and then where'll we be?'

William looked reluctantly at the poker. 'All right,' he agreed, 'but don't blame me if I kill him.'

It took some time to get one of the kitchen chairs placed strategically behind the door and even longer to hoist William up on to it. Then it was found that he'd forgotten the poker. Mumbling something about it being just like a man Wilhelmina shuffled back across the room to get it.

'Are you ready now?'

William grasped his poker irresolutely and nodded.

Wilhelmina pulled back the bolts, turned the key in the lock and opened the door a couple of inches.

'And about ruddy well time!' roared Dover, pushing the door back and striding in. There was a shriek from William who found himself knocked off his chair and flattened up against the side wall.

'William!' cried his sister, hurrying as fast as she could to the rescue.

'Never mind him!' said Dover callously. 'Where's your telephone?'

'He's dead!' Wilhelmina screamed. 'He's dead! I know he's dead.'

'Of course he's not dead!' snapped Dover impatiently. He reached down and seizing William by the coat collar tugged him to his feet and shook him. 'He's as right as rain. Now, where's your telephone?'

'We haven't got a telephone,' said Wilhelmina, escorting her dazed brother back to his seat by the fire. 'And if it's money or valuables you're looking for you've come to the wrong house. We ... '

'Where's the nearest telephone then?'

'The nearest telephone? Oh, well now, the nearest telephone? That's asking something, that is.'

'Hey, you!' Dover lowered his face to William's and bellowed. 'Where's the nearest telephone?'

William, now trembling like a leaf, cowered further back in his chair. His mouth opened but no words came. Dover, getting exasperated, shook him again.

'The nearest telephone, you old rag-bag!'

Wilhelmina shrieked. William groaned. Dover let fly a string of oaths. Just his luck to pick on a pair of animated fossils. And look at the time!

Eventually William found his voice. It turned out that the nearest telephone was a mile and a half away as the crow flies and three miles round by the road. Prompted further by the Chief Inspector, William admitted that in this context the crow flew over two wheat fields, a swollen brook and the meadow with Harrison's bull in it.

Dover flopped down into Wilhelmina's chair. 'Give us a cup of that tea, missus! Now, how do I get there by the road?'

It was a complicated journey and neither William nor Wilhelmina possessed the gift of clear and concise explanation. Neither seemed a hundred per cent sure of the difference between right and left and both bickered fiendishly about whether it was quicker to go round by Quidgery Lane or not. Dover's meaty paws itched to knock their heads together.

'Is there anybody round here with a car or a motor-bike? Well, a bloody bicycle, then?'

The grey heads shook regretfully.

'There's my tricycle,' said William suddenly.

Wilhelmina roused on the instant. 'Our tricycle!' she corrected him. 'Don't you go telling this gentleman it's your tricycle.'

'I bought it,' said William sulkily.

'I lent you the money.'

'Only half of it.'

'Which you've never paid me back, never to this day.'

'That doesn't make the tricycle yours.'

'I didn't say it was mine!' crowed Wilhelmina triumphantly. 'I said it was *partly* mine.'

'Oh well, if that's the way you feel about it, just you let me have your account and I'll settle it when I get my pension tomorrow.'

It says something for the pathetic state to which Dover had been reduced that he let this conversation go on so long. The last few hours had taken their toll. Dover tried to organize his life so that as little exertion as possible was involved, but the amount of physical energy he had been forced to expend since he left Wallerton was practically his entire ration for a normal year.

Wearily he separated William and Wilhelmina who were on the point of coming to blows. 'Where's this blooming tricycle?'

William got excitedly to his feet and shouldered Wilhelmina out of the way. This was a man's conversation. 'In the shed outside. Come on, I'll show you.'

'Don't you go out in the yard in those slippers!' said Wilhelmina in a last attempt to muscle in.

'Oh, belt up!' chirped William.

A few minutes later he proudly wheeled his tricycle out for Dover's inspection. 'Good as new, it is, mister. Clean as a new pin and oiled regular as clockwork.'

Dover wrinkled his nose. He looked at the tricycle and then he looked at William and then he looked at the tricycle again. 'Do you mean you actually *ride* that bundle of scrap iron?'

'Once a week when I go into the village to get the pensions and do the shopping. You'll find it goes a real treat. You can't fall off it, you see, not like a bike.'

Dover pondered. He weighed the pros and cons. The cons won. 'You ride it,' he said, 'and I'll stand on this bar thing at the back. Hang on a minute while I fetch my suitcase.'

'Eh?' said William, aghast.

'I can't just ride off with it,' Dover pointed out reasonably. 'How'm I going to get it back to you? Why, you don't know me from Adam. I might steal it.'

William gulped. 'I'll trust you,' he said hoarsely.

'Oh no, you won't!' Wilhelmina, wearing a war-surplus greatcoat, joined them in the yard. 'That tricycle belongs to me as well, and don't you forget it. You're not letting a complete stranger walk off with it just for the asking.'

With such an ally Dover couldn't lose. Protesting feebly the old man was hoisted up into the saddle and Dover's suitcase roped securely across the handlebars in front of him. Wilhelmina tied a thin khaki scarf round his neck and Dover, one foot on the back cross-bar and one on the ground, gave him a good initial shove-off.

The journey to the telephone kiosk was eventful and took almost as much out of Dover as it did out of William. The trouble was that William just wouldn't knuckle down to it. At first he complained about his heart and then his legs and tried to cap everything by saying he was coming over all dizzy.

'Stop talking so much!' Dover bellowed heartlessly in his ear. 'Save your breath for pedalling!'

A major contretemps occurred when they came to the hill. Dover was disgusted, and said so. Half a mile long it might be, but the gradient was so gentle as to be almost non-existent. No, he had no intention of getting off. William was to stop this endless whining and get a move on. He, Dover, would assist from time to time by a scootering action with his right leg should William falter.

'Oh no! Not that, for God's sake!' wheezed William. 'You damned near ruptured me last time! It makes these pedals fair fly round.'

Dover snorted, and scootered regardless whenever William's speed began to drop. In between times he urged on his driver by frequent cries of exhortation and encouraging thumps in the back. Luckily for both of them the last five hundred yards was downhill William's feet were whirled round at a rate of knots while Dover, grim-faced and terrified, hung round his neck with the tenacity of a giant octopus.

Their speed increased. The telephone box rushed nearer.

'The brakes!' howled Dover. 'Put the bloody brakes on!'

William's teeth were chattering too violently to tell Dover that the brakes didn't work. They were passing the telephone box. Dover abandoned William to his fate and baled out. The tricycle shot completely out of control across the road and landed up in the ditch. William, flung clear just in time, lay coughing and panting on the grass verge. Even Dover could see that there was no sense to be got out of him at the moment. Without saying a word he strode across to the old man and turned him over on his back. In the third pocket he tried he found William's purse. Feeling very honest he extracted only the fourpence he needed and put the rest back.

Chapter Fifteen

THE police car made it from Wallerton in fifteen minutes. William had got his tricycle back on the road though he still wasn't up to facing the return journey.

'Perhaps we could give him a lift, sir?' said the driver as he put Dover's suitcase in the boot.

'We've no time to waste on him!' snorted Dover, getting into the car. 'We've got a job to do!'

'I'm glad to hear it,' the Chief Constable said caustically as he slid across the seat before Dover sat on him.

'Oh, it's you,' said Dover foolishly.

'Who were you expecting? Snow White and the seven dwarfs?'

Dover refrained from verbal comment.

'Now, look here, Dover.' The Chief Constable's voice was unfriendly. 'Before we go any further with this charade, I want a full explanation and I want it now. Thanks to your letter, I've got the police station in Wallerton cram-jam packed with policemen of assorted sizes. They don't know what for, I don't know what for, and I have a horrible suspicion that you don't know what for either. God help you if I'm right!'

Dover assumed his most aggrieved expression. It was wasted because the Chief Constable couldn't bear to look at him. 'There's nothing to worry about,' he said in an offended tone. 'I've got the situation under complete control.'

There was a sceptical grunt from his travelling companion.

'By the way,' said Dover, 'where are we going?'

'Straight up the creek, as far as I can see.'

'I think we ought to get back to my hotel as soon as possible. I'm getting a bit bothered about Sergeant MacGregor.'

'You hear that, Taylor?' the Chief Constable barked at his driver. 'Biggest bloody ears in the force, that fellow,' he muttered. 'What's all this about MacGregor?'

'Well, he's a sort of decoy you see, sir,' said Dover ingratiatingly. He didn't make a habit of calling senior officers 'sir'.

'Go on!'

'Well, you see, sir, things have started going a bit cockeyed with that train not stopping. I meant to be back in Wallerton by a quarter to seven at the latest. Then I'd have contacted you and we'd have kept a watch on MacGregor and then when they grabbed him we'd have walked in at full strength and caught 'em red-handed.'

'Who's them?'

'Why, the Ladies' League, sir.'

You could practically see the steam coming out of the Chief Constable's ears. 'The Ladies' League!' he exploded. 'What the purple blazes has the Ladies' League got to do with it?'

'Oh, they're at the back of the whole caboodle, sir,' explained Dover.

'You're mad!' said the Chief Constable slowly. 'You're stark, staring mad! You need treatment, you do. It's overwork, I expect. Turned your brain, that's what it's done. You great, fat, blithering slob, do you realize my wife belongs to the Ladies' League?'

'That's why I had to move so carefully, sir. Everybody's wife belongs to the Ladies' League, and if I'd told you all about the plan to use MacGregor and everything, it'd have been all round the place in five minutes flat. Those women have got an organization that would put the Gestapo to shame. You just think about it, sir – every other woman in the whole of Wallerton a potential spy. The mind boggles!'

'Mine certainly does.'

'It's quite simple, really,' said Dover with an easy assurance that was perfectly genuine, 'once you get the hang of it.'

'Well, I should be grateful to be let in on the secret. What is it that the Ladies' League are supposed to have done?'

'We'll start with the Hamilton affair, sir,' announced Dover firmly. He had no intention of letting off his nuclear device without a suitable build-up. The Chief Constable had a very florid complexion and Dover didn't want a heart attack on his hands on top of everything else. 'You remember Hamilton? A dog's dinner in his own front garden? All right, now we know Hamilton was mixed up with quite a few crooks, financing their various jobs.'

'No!' roared the Chief Constable in blank amazement. 'I

didn't know anything of the kind. Why wasn't I told about all this?'

'Oh well, never mind about it now,' said Dover hurriedly. 'It doesn't really matter. Hamilton dealt with professional villains, not homicidal maniacs. No professional would have wasted his time and his energy chopping up a dead man. No, the motive behind the attack on Hamilton was something quite different.'

'But the Ladies' League were nevertheless responsible?' asked the Chief Constable with withering sarcasm.

Dover nodded. 'What happened was something like this. Hamilton went off to the Country Club as he frequently did. He had a drop too much to drink and came home by taxi. All perfectly normal. He'd done it before. Now, the taxi-driver was called Armstrong. He's as blind as a bat but he's quite sure that he found Hamilton's house without any difficulty. But the houses in Minton Parade are as alike as two peas in a pod and the house numbers are practically invisible even in broad daylight. So, how did Armstrong find Hamilton's house with no trouble at all?'

'Go on,' said the Chief Constable, 'surprise me!'

'The answer's simple,' said Dover, 'he didn't. Oh, he pulled up at a house numbered 25 all right, but it wasn't Hamilton's house. It was a nearby house where somebody had stuck huge and unmistakable figures on the fan light over the door – at least, I reckon that's how they did it. Armstrong sees these figures, stops, Hamilton gets out of the taxi and goes unheedingly into a house which looks just like his. Any little discrepancies he's too sozzled to notice. Inside this house they're waiting for him. As soon as he's got one foot over the threshold they nab him.'

'The Ladies' League?' asked the Chief Constable, not quite so bumptious now.

'Of course. The house next door belongs to Miss ffiske, the veterinary surgeon. She's a leading light in the Ladies' League.'

'You're not accusing her?' gasped the Chief Constable.

'I certainly am. Mind you, she'd got accomplices, but she was the king pin. She had to be, of course, because of the operation.'

'What operation?'

'The operation they were going to perform on Hamilton, of course. Why else do you think they grabbed him?'

'I've no idea,' the Chief Constable shook his head in bewilderment.

'Well, I'm guessing now, of course, but the main outline's clear enough. They whipped Hamilton into the operating theatre. Did you know that your precious Miss ffiske has a proper operating theatre in her house? Well, she has. She uses it for animals in the normal way but it's an operating theatre all the same. Well, the operation had only just got started when Hamilton mucks the whole scheme up by dying on them. I'll bet that fair put the cat amongst the pigeons! Now, they'd got a flipping corpse on their hands, and a corpse with the tell-tale marks of the operation on it. Panic all round, with nobs on! All they can think of doing is mutilating poor old Hamilton still further in an effort, successful as it turned out, to cover up the signs of the operation. Then they took Hamilton's body and all his clothes and dumped them over the wall into his own front garden. It'd be the early hours of the morning by then so, of course, nobody saw them.'

There was a pregnant silence while both the Chief Constable and his driver up in front digested what they had heard.

'I have in my time,' said the Chief Constable thoughtfully, 'been forced to listen to a considerable amount of sheer, undiluted poppycock. I have, however, no hesitation, in stating that this unspeakable rigmarole of yours takes the cake – to put it crudely.'

'It holds water,' said Dover sulkily. 'You just try picking holes in it.'

'All right! Hamilton usually came back from the Country Club in his own car, didn't he? Well, how did anybody know that on this particular night he was going to return in a taxi driven by a near-blind taxi-driver?'

'Somebody must have tipped them off.'

'Who?'

'Oh, heck,' I don't know,' said Dover crossly. 'Somebody. Anyhow, what does it matter? That's just a minor detail.'

'And what about the evidence of that actress woman, Doris Doughty?'

'Ah, but she's a member of the Ladies' League, too! Her

evidence isn't worth the paper it's written on. She was primed with what she'd got to say and every time she was asked about it she reeled it all off like a bloody old poll parrot. There was no green van and no two men. That was all made up just to put us off the scent.'

'Now, look here, Dover,' said the Chief Constable, trying a kindly, man-to-man approach, 'this is getting ridiculous. Why on earth should Miss ffiske, a highly respectable and respected woman, kidnap a man like Hamilton and operate on him? What was she doing, for God's sake? Taking his appendix out?'

'She was castrating him,' said Dover calmly.

'She was doing what?' The Chief Constable's blood pressure went up like a lift in a Manhattan skyscraper.

'I know it sounds a bit queer, sir, but you can take it from me that that's exactly what she and her friends were doing. You must know Hamilton's reputation, sir. He was an absolute devil where women were concerned. And you know what the Ladies' League is like. All right – they clashed! The Ladies' League disapproved strongly of Hamilton's way of life and, being a practical body of women, they put their heads together and cooked up a way of putting an end to his fun and games.'

'I don't believe it!' wailed the Chief Constable.

'They did the same thing to your nephew, young Cochran.'

'Oh, *no*!'

'Oh, yes!' said Dover without mercy. 'The details varied a bit, I grant you. Obviously, in his case, that landlady of his, Mrs Jolliott or whatever she's called, was the prime mover, assisted by her retired district nurse lodger. I reckon they were waiting for him when he got back that Sunday night. Miss ffiske'd do the operation in the house. Then Mrs Jolliott gives it out that he's cancelled his leave and keeps everybody away from him while he's recovering. How else do you explain him spending a week in bed? He was convalescing, see. Mrs Jolliott and her lodger looked after him. I checked with your police surgeon. He says that the type of operation they'd probably do on your nephew would take about a week to recover from. Oh, it all fits. Mrs Jolliott and her nurse friend are members of the Ladies' League. What more do you want?'

'A hell of a lot,' growled the Chief Constable. 'Why did Peter commit suicide, for one thing?'

'That's a good question.' Dover nodded approvingly. 'Why have they all kept their traps shut about what's happened to them? Well, put yourself in their shoes, sir. Would you go shouting it from the housetops? I wouldn't! And I don't pride myself on being a flipping Casanova, though I don't mind admitting in my younger days ... '

'Peter killed himself! I'm still waiting for you to explain that.'

'Annual medical,' said Dover. 'When he got back to duty on the Monday morning, he found his annual medical was due. You ask your station sergeant, he'll confirm it. Well, your nephew knew only too well that once he got a proper going over by a doctor the cat'd be well and truly out of the bag. And doctors are only human, aren't they? Your nephew just couldn't face it if it got out. He'd be the laughing stock of the entire town. People sniggering behind his back and making jokes to his face. And he was another one, you see, always chasing after the girls and making out what a fine fellow-me-lad he was. I reckon the poor devil just couldn't face it, and I can't say I blame him. That only left Cully Point, didn't it? Oh, and that wasn't an accidental choice, either. He didn't want his body found, you see. Poison or gassing or shooting himself – there'd be a post mortem, wouldn't there? Well, they wouldn't be likely to overlook something like castration, would they?'

'But this is quite incredible! My wife is a member of the Ladies' League and she thought the world of Peter. How could she be a party to castrating the boy? It just doesn't make sense.'

'Oh, I don't suppose she knew anything about it. After all, she doesn't live in Wallerton, does she? This business'll be confined to a handful of ringleaders; the militant elite, as you might say.'

'But they're all such highly respectable women. If this comes out there'll be the most terrible scandal.'

'Well,' said Dover, leaning back and blowing out his cheeks, 'it's going to come out now, all right. You can't sweep this under the carpet. And the Ladies' League won't be the only ones to suffer. What about all the other poor devils who've had their wings clipped by Miss ffiske and company? They're going to feel pretty sick about it.'

'You don't mean that there are others, besides my nephew and Hamilton?'

'Dozens, I shouldn't wonder,' sighed Dover. 'It all depends how many men there are in Wallerton who've been paying more attention to the fair sex than your precious Ladies' League thinks right and proper. I know of three other cases myself.'

'Oh, my God!' groaned the Chief Constable.

'There's that fool of a taxi-driver, Armstrong, for a start. He cleared off for a week's psychiatric treatment kindly arranged for him by a member of the Ladies' League. Psychiatric treatment, my eye! You'll remember what Armstrong's favourite pastime was? Well, they cured him all right! And then there's that fellow, Chauncey Davenport.'

'Chauncey Davenport? Why, I know him quite well. We've met several times. You don't mean to tell me he's been ... Well, well!' The Chief Constable's eyes glinted maliciously. 'Of course! There was that queer business of him losing his memory or some such cock and bull story. Missing from home. I remember. Well, that was a fishy business and I said so at the time. Admittedly, I was thinking more of a week in Brighton with a barmaid, knowing Chauncey. And now you come to mention it, he has been keeping rather quiet lately. I thought his wife had been reading the riot act to him – it's her money, you know – but you think ... ?'

'I *know*,' said Dover. 'He started a fight the other day when one of his pals jokingly suggested that he was, er, acquiring female characteristics. Chauncey Davenport didn't think it was funny.'

'You don't mean to say that that's what happens?' The Chief Constable was highly interested.

'Can do, so it seems,' Dover said. 'And Chauncey Davenport shot off like a bullet out of a gun when your station sergeant suggested that the doc should have a look at him. Same pattern, you see. And then there's a chap Sergeant Veitch mentioned. His wife's had a dozen kids or so. The Ladies' League must have thought she'd had enough. He disappeared for a day or two but I should think they only sterilized him. There is a difference, you know.'

'Is there?' asked the Chief Constable, almost smacking his lips.

'Castration puts the kibosh on *everything*,' explained Dover solemnly. 'Sterilization only means that you can't father kids.'

'Go on!'

'Well, I don't know all the details,' said Dover with becoming modesty. 'I just got a broad outline from your police surgeon. It's not a subject I've paid much attention to in the past.'

'But, you've no proof, have you?' objected the Chief Constable, coming down to earth with a bump. 'I can't see people like Chauncey Davenport stepping into the witness box and admitting that he's let a bunch of crazy women geld him, can you? Have you got anything else?'

Dover shook his head. 'No, nor ever likely to get it, either. These Ladies' League women, you know, they aren't fools. Unless one of 'em decides to spill the beans, which isn't likely, we haven't a thing we could even apply for a warrant on, never mind convince a judge and jury. That's why I set up this MacGregor thing.'

'You don't mean you've let MacGregor ... '

Dover nodded. 'What else could I do? I reckoned we'd just let 'em get it all set up and then walk in and nab the lot of 'em. I went to a lot of trouble to prepare the ground, too,' he added resentfully. 'Wore myself out, I did, slogging round telling everybody that MacGregor was the gayest spark since last Guy Fawkes night. Trying to build him up as some sort of sex tomcat.' Dover frowned. That didn't sound quite right. 'I've been on the go for days. Oh well, I suppose I shouldn't complain. God only knows, I ought to be used to it by now. They give you assistants but, if you want a job doing properly, you've still got to do it yourself.'

'So you've tried to build MacGregor up as a threat to Wallerton's fair maidens,' mused the Chief Constable, thus displaying a greater ability to grasp the situation than Dover would have given him credit for, 'in the hope that they'd try to deal with him as, according to you, they've dealt with others of the same ilk. What, if anything, makes you think the Ladies' League is going to play?'

Dover scowled. They were always the same, these perishing Chief Constables, niggle, niggle, niggle. 'Of course they'll play,' he blustered. 'They won't be able to resist it. I'm telling you, MacGregor's reputation stinks to high heaven. I've had him hanging around that Country Club night after night. And then I let the word drop in the right quarters that it was MacGregor who was on to the Ladies' League. I made it out that he was beginning to connect 'em with the Hamilton business, see? They'll have to fix him to save their own fat necks.'

'I don't quite follow that,' said the Chief Constable. 'If by fixing him you mean – *fixing* him, that's no safeguard for them, is it? He'll still be able to talk, won't he? Are you sure they won't just try to kill him?'

'Good grief, sir!' 'They're not murderers! Besides, MacGregor wouldn't talk. None of the others have done. That's the Ladies' League's strong point. Their victims won't make a cheep to anybody.'

The Chief Constable shivered. 'This MacGregor fellow of yours must be a brave man. Fancy volunteering to run a risk like that! Rather him than me.'

Dover tried to look nonchalant. 'Well, actually, he doesn't know.'

'Doesn't know?'

'I thought it better not to tell him. What the eye doesn't see and all that. I just told him I was going back to London and more or less left it at that.'

'He must have thought your behaviour was very odd.'

Dover looked annoyed. 'I don't see why the devil he should. I've been very subtle about the whole thing. I passed the word around that I was leaving Wallerton for good tonight and that MacGregor was going off on leave first thing tomorrow morning. That was to force their hand and make them act tonight, you see. This way they'll be able to keep MacGregor out of circulation for a week or so after the operation without anybody asking any awkward questions. Nobody'll even know he's missing. And if there are any questions later, he'll be the first one to cover up what actually happened.'

The Chief Constable looked at his watch. 'It's gone nine o'clock.'

Dover wriggled uncomfortably. 'Well, I expect we'll be there in plenty of time. They probably won't make a move till much later on.'

'You hope.'

'It wasn't my fault the damned train didn't stop where they said it would,' objected Dover, seeing only too clearly that, once again, he was going to be left holding the can if anything went wrong.

'We're there,' said the Chief Constable as the police car drew up outside the hotel. 'What do we do now?'

Dover peered morosely out of the window. 'I suppose we'd better find out if MacGregor's still there. Just in case.' The driver switched off the engine. 'I can't go,' said Dover. 'That'd give the whole game away.'

'We'll send Taylor then,' said the Chief Constable.

'I don't know that that's a good idea,' objected Dover. 'He's in uniform. They may be keeping MacGregor under observation before they snatch him. It'll blow the whole works if they see a copper walking in.'

'Well, what do you propose?' asked the Chief Constable impatiently.

'Perhaps you could just nip in, sir?'

'I am not in the habit of nipping in anywhere and I am, I flatter myself, a rather well-known figure in this town and in the whole county. Suppose you lend Taylor your hat and coat so that he can cover his uniform up?'

'I'd sooner borrow yours, sir,' said the driver quickly.

'The Chief Inspector's more your size,' the Chief Constable said firmly. 'Now, come on! We don't want to mess about here all night.'

In the confined space in the back of the car Dover divested himself with considerable difficulty of his bowler hat and dusty overcoat. Taylor reluctantly donned the garments which were pushed across the back of the seat to him. Dover and the Chief Constable watched him cross the pavement and go into the hotel. The bowler hat had sunk down over his eyes and the skirts of the overcoat all but brushed the ground.

'With a bit of luck,' said the Chief Constable grimly, 'he'll get a sixpenny hand-out and a cup of tea by the dustbins. Otherwise I should think they'll just take one look at him and dial 999.'

'That's a good overcoat,' said Dover, bridling.

'I'm sure,' agreed the Chief Constable dryly. 'Oh well, at least he's got a move on. He's coming out already.'

Taylor, looking like something out of an early Chaplin movie, scurried furtively across the pavement and thankfully concealed himself in the car.

'Well?' demanded the Chief Constable.

'He's not there, sir,' said Taylor in a hushed voice. 'He left about half an hour ago. They've no idea where he's gone but he left after taking a telephone call. It was a woman's voice, the receptionist said.'

Chapter Sixteen

'THE one thing we mustn't do,' said Dover, snatching his bowler hat back and examining it for unfair wear and tear, 'is panic.'

'On the other hand,' the Chief Constable pointed out as Dover settled back comfortably in his corner and closed his eyes, 'we don't want to take it too casually, do we? After all, MacGregor is in considerable danger.'

Dover opened his eyes reluctantly. 'Not really, sir,' he said. 'The doctor told me it's a pretty simple operation. It must be, mustn't it, seeing as how this vet woman tackles it without a qualm?'

'That's hardly the point, is it?'

'No,' said Dover with a grunt, 'I suppose it isn't.' He pulled himself into a more upright position. 'Well, I suppose we'd better put our thinking caps on Er, you haven't got a cigarette on you by any chance, have you, sir? I seem to have mislaid mine somewhere.'

'I don't smoke,' snapped the Chief Constable, thus putting himself finally and irrevocably beyond Dover's pale.

'I've got some, sir,' volunteered the driver who had at last got himself extricated from the sticky embrace of Dover's overcoat.

'Oh, thank you, laddie. Well, now.' He puffed smoke in the Chief Constable's face. 'What's our next move, eh? That's the problem, isn't it?' The Chief Constable wound his window down. 'Well, it's my considered opinion that our next port of call should be the house of Miss ffiske.'

'You think that's where they've taken him?'

'Without a shadow of doubt,' said Dover confidently. 'That's where the operating table is and she's the one with the know-how. They'll have taken him there for sure.'

'And what do you propose doing about it?'

Dover gazed glumly out of the window. As usual, everything was being shoved off on to his shoulders. What a life! 'Well, we shall have to go and rescue him, shan't we, sir?'

'How?'

'Well, I suppose you got all your men waiting at the police station, have you?'

'Forty men, four girls, two vans, three police cars and a dog,' said the Chief Constable heavily. 'And all of them ringing up the overtime at a rate of knots.'

'We'll have the lot of 'em surrounding Miss ffiske's house. Back and front, covering all exits. When they're in position, we'll go in.'

'Go in? We can't do that. We haven't got a warrant.'

Dover sighed. One of these stick-to-the-rules, go-by-the-book nits, on top of everything else! 'Once they see we're there in force they'll realize the game's up,' he said. 'We'll get in all right.'

None too happily the Chief Constable got on the radio and gave the necessary instructions. Dover yawned. His stomach rumbled. 'Here,' he snorted, 'I haven't had any dinner! I'm starving.'

'Perhaps you would like me to postpone the whole operation until you've had something to eat?'

The irony rolled off Dover like water off a duck's back. 'Oh, I don't think we should do that, sir. Not with poor MacGregor in the fix he's in.'

A couple of minutes later the car arrived in Minton Parade and parked unobtrusively a hundred yards or so from Miss ffiske's house.

A figure moved silently out of a patch of darkness and came across to the car. It was Wallerton's own police Inspector. He saluted the Chief Constable.

'We are all in position, sir,' he reported in a low voice. 'I've kept the dog and her handler by me, in case you need them, sir.'

'Anything happening?'

'Quiet as the grave so far, sir.'

'Any lights on in the house?'

'No, sir.'

The Chief Constable turned to look inquiringly at Dover.

Dover dutifully assumed an air of quiet confidence. 'That's what you'd expect, isn't it? They're not going to hang a neon sign up outside the front door advertising what they're up to.'

'No,' agreed the Chief Constable doubtfully. 'You're sure they're here?'

'Where else?' demanded Dover.

'Well, what's your next step?' asked the Chief Constable, consulting his watch. 'Time's gtting on.'

Dover sighed. 'Your next step.' Talk about co-operation! 'When you've checked that all your men are in position and all the exits blocked, I'll go and knock on the front door. Soon as they open up we'll go in.'

'We?'

'I'll want half a dozen of your stoutest lads to back me up,' said Dover hastily. 'Your authority on the front door step would be a help, too.'

The Chief Constable chewed his lip unhappily. 'I still don't like it. It's all highly irregular. Miss ffiske is a very influential member of the community.'

'Suit yourself,' said Dover sinking back in his corner, folding his arms and closing his eyes. 'I reckon MacGregor'll understand.'

'Oh dear!' said the Chief Constable. 'Well, I suppose we've got no choice. I just hope to goodness they really are castrating MacGregor in there, otherwise we shall all have some very tricky questions to answer.' He opened the car door. 'Well, aren't you coming?'

'No point in us all getting wet,' Dover pointed out reasonably. 'I'll wait here while you check your men. Be sure to tell 'em they're to stop anybody leaving that house, whoever they are.'

Rather irately the Chief Constable got out of the car and strode off into the darkness and rain. Dover settled back to wait, wondering idly if perhaps they weren't already too late. He took it philosophically. A chap couldn't do more than his best, could he?

'Excuse me, sir.' Dover reluctantly opened his eyes. 'I wonder if you'd mind if Sukey waited in the car with you? She can't stand the wet.'

Before Dover could utter a word an enormous, vicious-looking and extremely damp Alsatian dog climbed on to the seat beside him.

'What the blazes!' exploded Dover. 'Here, get it out of here!'

'Don't push her, sir! She can't stand being ... Well, I did warn you, sir.'

Sukey, Wallerton's one and only police dog, was almost as fat and lazy as Dover himself, and even more bad-tempered. Even in her prime she had seen her role as more ornamental than useful. Now that she was approaching retirement it was as much as her handler could do to get her to pose for the photographers before retreating to her warm kennel and leaving the master race to get on with the work.

When Dover tried to push her out of the car, she resented it. Dover found himself pinned in his corner with Sukey breathing in his face. Her hard brown eyes squinted malevolently and she bared her yellowing teeth.

It took them seven and a half minutes to extricate Dover from Sukey's damp and smelly clutches. Her handler exhausted his entire vocabulary of canine commands to no avail. It could have been Greek for all Sukey knew or cared.

Eventually it was the Chief Constable, as befitted his superior rank, who found the solution and cut the Gordian knot. Since Sukey wouldn't move, Dover would have to. Gingerly the Chief Inspector edged himself out of the car. Sukey was mildly gratified to find that she was now in full possession of the entire back seat.

'Bloody animal ought to be shot!' snarled Dover, brushing disconsolately at the muddy paw marks on his coat. 'If she comes near me again she'll get the toe of my boot in her guts! I don't know what people want these damned great dogs for anyhow. I've never heard of one of 'em doing anything to earn its keep. We could all get a rise if they didn't waste their money on those over-fed, pampered brutes.'

'Chief Inspector Dover!' The Chief Constable cut ruthlessly into what looked like being a lengthy tirade. 'May I remind you that Detective Sergeant MacGregor may at this very moment be in great personal danger? And also that a large number of the members of my force have been hanging round in the pouring rain for hours? Some of them are not as young as they used to be and a little consideration on your part for the inconvenience of others would not be out of place.'

Dover scowled, muttered some inaudible vulgarity under his breath and stumped off resolutely up the nearest flight of steps. It was unfortunate that, once again, it was the wrong house.

When he was at last confronted by the right front door he knocked loudly on it. He rang the bell. He thumped the door. He kicked it.

'There's nobody at home,' said the Chief Constable, manfully restricting himself to this simple observation.

'They're just not answering,' retorted Dover. 'We'll have to break in. Anybody got an axe?'

The Chief Constable groaned. If this ever got into the papers! 'There's a window open at the back. I'll send somebody in that way.'

Constable Perkins, an eager and innocent young man, agreed to place his future career in jeopardy and volunteered for the job.

'I won't forget you, Perkins!' said the Chief Constable, clapping the lad encouragingly on the shoulders and rapidly planning how to leave the young nit holding the baby should there be any unfortunate repercussions.

Constable Perkins methodically searched the house from attic to cellar. There was a general air of gloom as he made his report. Everybody looked expectantly at Dover.

Dover blew his nose, turned up his coat collar and resettled his bowler hat.

'Well?' demanded the Chief Constable.

'They must have taken him somewhere else,' said Dover.

'Where?'

Dover scratched his head. 'God knows,' he admitted. 'What time is it?' Fourteen assorted policemen consulted their watches and produced fourteen versions of the hour. Dover shrugged his shoulders. 'If you ask me it's too late anyhow. We might just as well pack it in now for all the good we'll do. MacGragor'll turn up in due course and maybe we can persuade him to prefer charges. After all, he won't be able to keep what's happened a secret, not with all us knowing. He might just as well go the whole hog and then we can nab 'em.'

The Chief Constable could hardly believe his ears. 'Are you seriously suggesting that we just abandon Sergeant MacGregor to his fate and go home to bed?' he howled.

Dover had the grace to look slightly uncomfortable. 'Well,' he said grudgingly, 'I suppose we could go on looking if you feel like that about it, but I thought you were worried about your men and the overtime they were knocking up.'

'Where,' the Chief Constable said grimly, 'a man's, er, health is concerned, I don't allow trivial considerations of that sort to influence me.'

Dover scratched his head again. He wasn't much of a one for flogging lost causes but he sensed that the general consensus of opinion was against him. 'We could try Mrs Jolliott's,' he suggested without enthusiasm. 'They might possibly have taken him there.'

The Chief Constable burst into frenzied activity. Orders were barked out, men rounded up, cars and vans marshalled once more into action. In a remarkably short space of time the whole cavalcade was roaring off to Mrs Jolliott's house. Sukey still reigned supreme on the back seat of the Chief Constable's car and, since neither the Chief Constable nor Dover felt up to arguing with her, they crowded into the front with the driver.

Mrs Jolliott's house was as dark and deserted as Miss ffiske's had been. The rank and file were looking bewildered and fed up. Most of them hadn't the remotest idea of what was going on and, very sensibly, stolidly discounted the ridiculous story that Sergeant MacGregor had been kidnapped. In Wallerton? Don't be daft!

Dover himself was desperately anxious to concede defeat but the Chief Constable, glancing at his watch every two minutes, meanly refused to let him off the hook. 'Think, man, think! You started all this. Where else could they have taken him to?'

'How the hell do I know?' grumbled Dover.

'We must do *something*!'

'Maybe you could grill that taxi-driver, Armstrong? They must have taken him somewhere. If you thumped him around a bit it might make him remember.'

'We haven't *time*!' wailed the Chief Constable.

Yet another sodden uniformed figure approached the car. This time it was Sergeant Veitch. He touched the peak of his cap perfunctorily with one finger and sneezed. 'Will you be wanting us much longer, sir? The men are ... '

The Chief Constable ignored him. 'You must have some idea,' he said to Dover. 'We can't just leave it like this.'

'It's not my fault,' protested Dover. 'We've tried Miss ffiske's and we've tried Mrs Jolliott's. You can't blame me if they're not there.'

'Was you wanting Miss ffiske or Mrs Jolliott then, sir?' asked Sergeant Veitch, sneezing again.

The Chief Constable clutched at him like a drowning man reaching for the lifebelt. 'Do you know where they are, Sergeant?'

'Well, of course, sir. It's the monthly meeting of the Ladies' League. They'll be in the Civic Hall, same as usual.'

'Monthly meeting?' gasped the Chief Constable. 'In the Civic Hall?' The colour drained from his face.

'That's right, sir,' said Sergeant Veitch. 'They usually take the Beatrice Bencher Memorial Room, seeing as how there's getting on for a hundred of 'em attend regular, even on a stinking night like this.'

'A hundred of 'em? Oh, my God!' The Chief Constable turned an ashen face to Dover. He cleared his throat. 'You don't think they're going to make a sort of ceremony out of it, do you?'

''Strewth!' said Dover, feeling distinctly queasy.

'A sort of horrible orgy?' breathed the Chief Constable in a shaky voice. 'One hundred self-righteous, middle-aged, middle-class harpies, all gloating while your poor sergeant's lying there bound and helpless ...'

'Here,' said Dover, 'steady on!'

'What else can it be?' the Chief Constable demanded, his eyes popping. 'Sergeant MacGregor's missing, you've uncovered what these she-devils have been doing to every man with a spark of life in him in the town, and now we know that they're all gathered together in some unholy conclave in the Civic Hall – and in the Beatrice Bencher Memorial Room at that. My God! I remember that boot-faced old battle axe, and her husband, too, poor swine. I should think he'd have volunteered for castration if he'd been given the chance. I know I would in his shoes.' He shivered. 'Well, don't just sit there like a great lump, Dover! We've got to get cracking!'

'Now, don't let's be too hasty, sir,' said Dover, jibbing, not unnaturally, at the thought of tackling the flower of Wallerton's womanhood en masse and on the rampage.

'Hasty?' snorted the Chief Constable, his face now red with excitement. 'We haven't a moment to lose! Sergeant!'

Once again the orders flew in all directions. The Chief Constable prided himself on being a man of action and he welcomed every opportunity to live up to his reputation. Disgruntled constables moved unwillingly out of the doorways where they had been sheltering from the rain. Unkind remarks were made about silly old buggers who changed their minds every five minutes and who ought to get out of that bloody car and see what it's like hanging round all bloody night in a cloud-burst. In spite of confused and contradictory instructions and a widespread lack of enthusiasm, the Chief Constable managed at last to get his troops on the move.

The sound of the car roaring into life roused Dover. He regarded his surroundings miserably. It hadn't been a nightmare, after all. This was for real. Sukey was snarling to herself on the back seat and the Chief Constable was bouncing about like a cat on hot bricks on the front. By now Dover had got round to blaming the whole business on MacGregor. Serve him damned well right if he got what was coming to him!

'Faster!' roared the Chief Constable, setting the siren wailing.

Much to Dover's relief the journey was a short one. He got out of the car and wrapped his overcoat round him. In a few seconds the rest of the party assembled and were placed strategically round the Civic Hall, a gaunt building decorated with two strings of coloured lights and standing exposed to all the elements in the centre of the promenade.

'Right!' said the Chief Constable, squaring his shoulders. 'Forward!'

Dover shambled after him as the Chief Constable strode up the wide ceremonial steps, his chin jutting out and a little swagger-stick tucked militantly under his arm. Sergeant Veitch and half a dozen dripping policemen fell in behind. Sukey and her handler marched proudly in the rear. The Alsatian had an unerring instinct for the limelight and had insisted on being let out of the car. Even now, ears pricked and eyes alert, she was looking around for the gentlemen of the press.

They all tramped into the entrance hall. Posters advertising jumble sales and classes in flower arrangement flapped frantically in the gale which blew through the open door. A man in shirt-sleeves and a peaked cap emerged from a cubicle. The Chief Constable charged across to him with a yelp of delight.

'The Ladies' League, my man! Are they still here?'

Sullenly the caretaker nodded.

The Chief Constable slapped his swagger-stick on the side of his leg. It hurt him but he stiffened his upper lip and took it like a man. 'Lead us to them!'

The caretaker shook his head. 'Can't. Got me orders. Nobody's to be allowed in.'

'This is a police matter.'

'They'd scalp me.'

'I take full responsibility.'

'You can take a dose of salts, mate, it makes no odds to me.'

The Chief Constable bristled and drew himself up even straighter. 'I am the Chief Constable of this county.'

'And I am the Custodian of the Civic Hall and I've got my orders.' The caretaker had but recently retired after twenty-five years service as a private soldier in the army and was inclined to avail himself of every opportunity to get his own back.

The Chief Constable's eyes narrowed and he prepared to launch himself into a modified and intimidating version of the Riot Act when Sergeant Veitch tugged gently at his sleeve.

'This way, sir,' said Sergeant Veitch.

They all trooped off. The caretaker returned to his cubicle. 'Think they're the flipping Lords of Creation,' he remarked sourly to the young lady who had ducked discreetly out of sight when the posse had burst in. 'Here, what you put your clothes on for? You're not going, are you?'

'With five hundred coppers thumping around the place, I'm certainly not staying,' retorted the young lady and flounced off into the night, her honour by an inexplicable quirk of fate still intact.

Meanwhile the hue and cry was wending its way along empty, dimly-lit and seemingly endless corridors. Dover and Sukey were both showing a marked tendency to lag behind. Dover was beginning to develop some very profound doubts about the advisability of the forthcoming activities, and Sukey's paws were hurting her. As they scurried round yet another corner Dover saw salvation loom in sight: a dimly-lit sign with the word 'Gentlemen' written invitingly on it.

'I shan't be a minute,' said Dover to the nearest constable. 'Just tell the Chief Constable to carry on without me. I'll be along in a couple of shakes of a lamb's tail.'

So saying he pushed open the door of the Gents and disappeared inside. Sukey, for reasons best known to herself, followed him. Together they remained in these somewhat insalubrious surroundings for five minutes, after the elapse of which Dover judged it safe to emerge.

His luck was out. The Beatrice Bencher Memorial Room was less than a stone's throw away and, to Dover's great disgust, the whole damned shoot of them were still huddled outside the door.

'Where the hell have you been?' hissed the Chief Constable, who might also have begun to have second thoughts.

'You shouldn't have waited,' said Dover.

The Chief Constable snorted and consulted his watch. 'My chaps should be in position now. You can go ahead.'

Dover surveyed his companions sullenly and picked the one least likely to start answering back. 'You open the door,' he said with what was meant to be a fatherly smile.

The bright-eyed young policeman nodded smartly and stepped forward. The door was locked.

'What else did you expect?' snapped the Chief Constable. 'Come on, you lads! Get your shoulders to it!'

The local constabulary may not have been noted for their brains but nobody could question their brawn. Six stalwart men charged the door. It burst asunder with remarkable and unexpected ease, hinges and locks giving way at the same moment. The six stalwart men tumbled into the Beatrice Bencher Memorial Room in a scrabbling confusion of boots and caps.

With a courteous gesture and a touching deference to superior rank Dover motioned the Chief Constable to precede him over the prostrate bodies.

Chapter Seventeen

AFTER the collapse of the door there had been a moment of comparative and, in retrospect, blessed quiet while nigh on a hundred members of the Ladies' League recovered from the shock. Then it started.

There were screams and shouts and yells. Some ladies fainted, others collapsed into hysterics. Those made of sterner stuff bawled orders and instructions and demanded at the tops of their stentorian voices to know what was happening. Chairs and tables were overturned and a minor stampede developed towards the fire exit at the far end of the room. Even the Chief Constable's resolute advance faltered.

The room was in darkness, lit only by an odd flickering patch of brightness on one of the walls.

Dover, peering vaguely about him, fastidiously repelled a covey of ladies who were fluttering, like moths, towards the light which streamed through the demolished doorway.

'Lights!' roared the Chief Constable. 'Somebody switch the bloody lights on!'

Much to his surprise, somebody did. In the harsh glare of the fluorescent strips the two sides gawped in astonishment at each other.

The Chief Constable's eyes swept the scene before him. With a sinking heart Dover looked round, too.

'Well?' demanded the Chief Constable, clearly preparing to bite the hand which had led him thus far by the nose.

Dover looked again. He would have given a great deal to see an anaesthetized MacGregor laid out on an operating table with a fiendish veterinary surgeon, scalpel in hand, bent over him. Nothing so gratifying met his eyes. The body of the hall was still filled with milling, clutching, squealing, swooning females while, at the far end, was a low platform holding only a long table and a dozen or so empty chairs. On the wall over the table was a large screen on which a film was still being projected.

'Cor!' rasped one of the policeman throatily, and forgot himself so far as to dig Dover companionably in the ribs. 'Get a load of that, mate!'

Dover did. The picture on the screen was faint but unmistakable. A young lady of improbably dimensions and no clothes was saucily cavorting with a gentleman in a similar state of undress on an enormous double bed.

'Cor!' breathed the policeman again and wiped the back of his hand across his brow. 'They're not going to ... ? By God, they are! Cor!'

But, much to his and Dover's disappointment, one lady at least had kept her head when all around were losing theirs. With a final gobbling whine of seductive music and a loud click, the screen went blank.

'Hubert! What, may I ask, is the meaning of this disgraceful intrusion into a strictly private meeting?'

The ladies were rallying, led by the Chief Constable's own formidable spouse. The unfortunate man cringed as, supported by some very militant-looking members of the sorority, she bore down on him.

His miserable and confused explanations were quite unacceptable. More and more ladies pulled themselves together, switched on the offensive and crowded round demanding enlightenment. It looked as though a very nasty situation was about to develop. One Amazon, who bore a marked resemblance to the winner of the 1962 Grand National, picked up a chair leg which had got broken off in the initial panic and weighed it thoughtfully in her hand. Unobtrusively, the male constables began to retreat from the room. Only the few policewomen moved amongst the members of the Ladies League, soothing and explaining, and they looked as though they would need very little inducement to change sides.

A hand grasped Dover's coat collar and shook him. It belonged to an enraged Miss ffiske. She was shouting something at him. Dover turned away to find Mrs Jolliott, arms akimbo, on the other side of him. Out in the middle of the hall Doris Doughty had been hoisted up on to a chair and was already launching fervently into Henry the Fifth's battle speech before Agincourt. As several well-permed heads turned to listen to her rousing declamation, Dover managed to catch the Chief Constable's bloodshot eye.

'Come on!' gasped Dover, struggling to free himself from the clutching hands. 'Weve got to get out of here!'

'Where to?' demanded the Chief Constable, fighting his way ruthlessly to Dover's side.

'There's only one place we'll be safe. Follow me!'

They made it to the gentlemen's cloakroom by the skin of their teeth. The Ladies' League, excited and intent on vengeance as they were, remembered that they were ladies and hesitated. Even the most dauntless was forced to think twice before she breeched this last bulwark of masculine privacy.

Inside the cloakroom Sukey was cowering in a corner. She snarled automatically but, seeing the expression on Dover's face, wisely lowered her gums over her teeth and accepted the intrusion. Dover leaned his forehead against the cool white tiles.

'That was a bloody near squeak!' he groaned shakily. 'What's got in to 'em, for God's sake? Another couple of seconds and they'd have lynched us.' He dragged himself over to one of the two available seats and sat down, exhausted.

'It was those films,' explained the Chief Constable, whose better half had managed to insert a few explanatory facts into the torrent of abuse she had let fly at him. 'I say, do you really think they'll not dare to follow us in here? I wish we could lock that door.'

With an effort Dover hoisted himself to his feet. 'Maybe we ought to take up action stations,' he sighed. 'Just in case.'

He faced the appropriate wall. It took a moment for the penny to drop. Then the Chief Constable got the idea and with a sigh of his own took up his position beside Dover.

'What about the films?' asked Dover wearily.

Wild shouts could be heard from the corridors outside. Shrill voices were calling for tar and feathers.

The Chief Constable glanced nervously over his shoulder. 'God, listen to 'em! The films? Oh, it was a batch they'd got hold of from some scruffy agency in London. You know, the sort they show in the more disreputable strip clubs, and worse. The Ladies' League were sort of going to review them and then write up to members of Parliament and what have you complaining about the degradation of womanhood.'

'If that bit I saw was anything to go by, they must have had quite a night of it.'

'Not half,' agreed the Chief Constable. 'They've been watching 'em for hours. Of course, that was what all the secrecy was about. No wonder they kept the doors locked. Naturally they didn't want people to know what they were doing. Well, you can understand it, can't you? The Ladies' League having an evening of dirty films? They'd never live it down. You can't blame 'em for going berserk when we broke in, can you?' He looked anxiously at Dover. 'Do you reckon they'll calm down, given time?'

'We could swear a solemn oath never to reveal what we saw to a living soul,' suggested Dover gloomily. 'Maybe that'd satisfy 'em.'

'And maybe it wouldn't,' the Chief Constable rejoined miserably. 'Damn it, Dover, this is all your bloody fault! If it hadn't been for you and your crack-brained theory about 'em castrating MacGregor, we wouldn't be in this mess!'

'It wasn't a crack-brained theory!' snapped Dover crossly. 'My God, you've seen what they're like. They're capable of anything! We'll be damned lucky if they don't castrate us before we get out of here.'

'Rubbish,' said the Chief Constable, blenching.

'And where's MacGregor, eh?' Dover pressed home his defence. 'You tell me that! Lured away by one of those old bags and kidnapped, that's where he is. Poor devil, they'll have cooked his goose for him good and proper by now. I don't envy you having to face him when he turns up again. You won't be able to look him in the eye after what you've let them do to him.'

'Me?' squeaked the Chief Constable. 'It wasn't my fault! You were the one who buggered everything up. If you'd told me properly what your plans were I'd have ... '

'Told your wife!' said Dover nastily. 'That's why I'd got to keep it all under my hat. I couldn't trust any of you! I ... '

'Now, look here, you!'

The argument waxed loud and furious. Even Sukey opened her eyes as the two poliecmen shouted and raged at each other.

They were just on the point of resorting to an exchange of physical violence when the cloakroom door opened. Two hearts stopped beating as one.

'It's only me, sir,' said MacGregor with a most inappropriate smile.

Dover sagged with relief and then stiffened with fury. 'Where the hell have you been?'

The Chief Constable was a kindlier man. 'Are you all right, sergeant? I mean, are you ... ? Have they ... ? You are all right, aren't you?'

MacGregor stared at him in some amazement. Such concern for his welfare on the part of a senior officer was unexpected. 'Yes, I'm fine, thank you, sir. Er, how are you?'

'Where've you been all evening?' snarled Dover.

MacGregor turned to him eagerly. 'That's what I wanted to tell you, sir. I've got a real lead at last. You see, just after you'd gone, this girl rang me up ... '

'What girl?'

'Sibyl, sir. You remember, one of the Chicks at the Country Club. We've got quite pally what with me being there every night and I think, in her own way, she's taken quite a fancy to me.'

There was a sceptical snort from Dover.

'Well, sir, tonight she phoned me up and said she'd got some information about the Hamilton set up and how much was it worth. Well, I still don't know how you knew she was going to ring me, sir, but I remembered what you said and so naturally I arranged to meet her. We went off to some pub or other out in the country to talk things over. We had a bit of an argey-bargey about the money side of things but in the end we settled on a mutually acceptable figure and then she started talking.' MacGregor's eyes glistened with excitement. 'She told me, sir, the name of the man who's taken over Hamilton's racket – subbing any likely villains with a big job on hand. You'll never guess who it is, sir! You could have knocked me down with a feather, sir, when I heard. It's ... '

'Now, just hold your horses a minute, sergeant!' The Chief Constable's voice and face were grim. 'Are you standing there and calmly telling us that you've just been out with a girl all evening?'

'Well, not just out with a girl, sir,' protested MacGregor, disappointed at the lukewarmness with which his wonderful news was being received. 'I know the identity of the man who's taken over where Hamilton left off. Well, you can see what that means, can't you, sir? He must be the man who fixed Hamilton, mustn't ... '

The Chief Constable wasn't listening. 'Do you mean you haven't been kidnapped? That nobody's even *tried* to castrate you? That you've got all your faculties intact?'

Macgregor drew back slightly. He glanced at Dover for enlightenment, but the Chief Inspector had retreated back into his cubicle to rest his feet. 'Er, yes, sir.'

'Yes, what, you damned fool?' roared the Chief Constable.

'Yes, I'm perfectly all right, sir. And no, nobody's tried to, er, castrate me.' MacGregor smiled cheerfully and tried not to look as though he thought the Chief Constable had gone stark staring bonkers.

The Chief Constable clutched his head. 'Ruined!' he yelled. 'I'm ruined, that's what I am! Of all the blasted gibbering idiots it's ever been my misfortune to meet! What am I going to tell my Standing Joint Committee? What am I going to tell my wife? What am I going to say to that screaming horde of women outside? What am I ... '

'I'm afraid I don't quite understand what's going on, sir. I called in at the police station and they said ... '

'Oh, shut up!' snarled the Chief Constable. 'Where's the blundering fool who started all this?'

'He's in there, sir.' MacGregor nodded at Dover's cubicle, the door of which had now been quietly closed.

'Well, get him out! I want to have the pleasure of tearing him limb from limb with my own bare hands.'

It was some time before Dover could be induced to emerge from a refuge which, if not savoury, was at least comparatively safe.

The Chief Constable had gone well past the stage at which he would listen to reason. Such arguments and explanations as Dover still had the strength and interest to put forward were brushed aside or shouted down. The Chief Constable had now only one aim in life: to rid his county of this stupid fat slob at the earliest possible moment.

'You, too!' he bellowed at MacGregor. 'I want the pair of you out of here, double quick. And God help you if you ever set foot in Wallerton again!' His voice dropped menacingly. 'And if you ever so much as breathe one word about what's been going on here tonight I'll personally make you sorry you were ever born – both of you. Just forget it, see? Hamilton, my nephew, maniac lady vets, sinister conspiracies, the lot! Not one word, if you value your lives!' He controlled himself with an effort. 'Now you, sergeant, get outside and see if those women are still hanging around. It sounds as though the coast might be clear now and, if it is, you're to get my car stationed outside the main door with the engine running. Understand? Tell my driver that once you and this great oaf are inside he's to drive precisely one hundred miles due north and dump you there – wherever it is. By my calculations that should land you in the middle of Sabat Moors and how you get back to civilization from there is your business. It won't break my heart if you never make it.'

'But, sir,' protested MacGregor.

'Don't argue!' stormed the Chief Constable. 'Move!'

MacGregor moved. In a remarkably short space of time he was back again. The ladies had withdrawn, retreat was possible, the car was waiting.

There were no prolonged farewells. The Chief Constable contented himself with breathing heavily down his nose. Only Sukey felt called upon to make some gesture. As Dover was leaving she waddled over to him and offered a paw. It was an unexpected token of sympathy from one idle lay-about to another.

It was nearly a month later when the Chief Constable suddenly disappeared. He was missing for nearly a week. Amnesia, they said, brought on by overwork. He resumed his duties after a short rest as though nothing had happened but, somehow, he never seemed quite the same again.

Now Back in Print

Margot Arnold

The first four adventures of Margot Arnold's beloved pair of peripatetic sleuths, Penny Spring and Sir Toby Glendower:

The Cape Cod Caper	*192 pages*	*$ 4.95*
Death of A Voodoo Doll	*220 pages*	*$ 4.95*
Death on the Dragon's Tongue	*224 pages*	*$ 4.95*
Exit Actors, Dying	*176 pages*	*$ 4.95*
Lament for A Lady Laird	*221 pages*	*$ 4.95*
The Menehune Murders (cloth)	*240 pages*	*$17.95*
Toby's Folly (cloth)	*256 pages*	*$18.95*
Zadock's Treasure	*192 pages*	*$ 4.95*

"The British archaeologist and American anthropologist are cut in the classic mold of Christie's Poirot...."

– *Sunday Cape Cod Times*

"A new Margot Arnold mystery is always a pleasure...She should be better known, particularly since her mysteries are often compared to those of the late Ngaio March."

– *Chicago Sun Times*

Joyce Porter

American readers, having faced several lean years deprived of the company of Chief Inspector Wilfred Dover, will rejoice (so to speak) in the reappearance of "the most idle and avaricious policeman in the United Kingdom (and, possibly, the world)." Here is the series that introduced the bane of Scotland Yard and his hapless assistant, Sgt. MacGregor, to international acclaim.

Dover One	*192 pages*	*$ 4.95*
Dover Two	*222 pages*	*$ 4.95*
Dover Three	*192 pages*	*$ 4.95*
Dover and the Unkindest Cut of All	*188 pages*	*$ 4.95*
Dover Goes to Pott	*192 pages*	*$ 4.95*

"Meet Detective Chief Inspector Wilfred Dover. He's fat, lazy, a scrounger and the worst detective at Scotland Yard. But you will love him."

– *Manchester Evening News*

Available from bookshops, or by mail from the publisher: The Countryman Press, Box 175, Woodstock, Vermont 05091-0175. Please include $2.50 for shipping your order. Visa or Mastercard orders (10.00 minimum), call 802-457-1049, 9-5 EST, Monday – Friday.

Prices and availability subject to change.